Chris couldn't discern any pain or fear on his father's face to show that his heart was bothering him again.

He was flushed, but it only seemed to be with excitement, so Chris reluctantly allowed his attention to be drawn elsewhere.

It landed on the woman standing just in front of his father. She was beautiful. She was familiar. She was *achingly* familiar.

He caught her chin, tilted her face upward and got lost in the ocean of her blue eyes. "Adelaide."

A fleeting smile touched her lips. "Hello, Chris."

"What are you doing here?"

Olan slapped Chris's back just hard enough to knock some sense into him. "Son, is that any way to greet your fiancée?"

Time slowed. Chris knew exactly what was going to happen. The truth was going to come out. He could almost see the disbelief, the shock, the disappointment on his father's face. His imagination went even further until he saw Olan's face whiten, his hand covering his heart as he sank to his knees in pain. Chris couldn't let that happen. Instinctively, he caught Adelaide by the arms, then stifled whatever she'd been ~~planning~~ to say with a quick,

Noelle Marchand is a native Houstonian living out her childhood dream of being a writer. She graduated summa cum laude from Houston Baptist University in 2012, earning a bachelor's degree in mass communications and speech communications. She loves exploring new books and new cities. When she's not scribbling out her latest manuscript, you may find her pursuing one of her other passions—music, dance, history and classic movies.

Books by Noelle Marchand

Love Inspired Historical

Bachelor List Matches

The Texan's Inherited Family
The Texan's Courtship Lessons
The Texan's Engagement Agreement

Unlawfully Wedded Bride
The Runaway Bride
A Texas-Made Match

Visit the Author Profile page at Harlequin.com.

NOELLE MARCHAND

The Texan's Engagement Agreement

HARLEQUIN® LOVE INSPIRED® HISTORICAL

Recycling programs
for this product may
not exist in your area.

 ™ LOVE INSPIRED BOOKS

ISBN-13: 978-0-373-28347-7

The Texan's Engagement Agreement

Copyright © 2016 by Noelle Marchand

Printed in U.S.A.

Therefore, seeing we also are compassed about by so great a cloud of witnesses, let us lay aside every weight, and the sin which doth so easily beset us, and let us run with patience the race that is set before us, looking unto Jesus, the author and finisher of our faith, who for the joy that was set before Him endured the cross, despising the shame, and is set down at the right hand of the throne of God.

—*Hebrews* 12:1–2

Dedicated to you.

Chapter One

March 1889
Peppin, Texas

Chris Johansen was running out of time. Worse yet, he was running out of women.

He had to find a bride before his parents figured out his long-distance engagement to the sweetheart of his youth had ended years ago. If they did, they'd send for a mail-order bride from their old country of Norway faster than he could say "Goodbye freedom." Or, "Hello, stranger."

He'd tried to find himself a wife among the women of Peppin, but all he had to show for his efforts was a bruised ego. Every single one of the women he'd expressed an interest in had turned him down flat. They'd also turned right around and married other men within months or even weeks of his failed proposal. Isabelle Bradley was no exception. He'd proposed to her only a few weeks ago. Now, in a matter of minutes, she was going to marry the town blacksmith and become Mrs. Rhett Granger. Chris had been asked to play his fiddle at the reception. First, he was supposed to collect his twenty-year-old sister, Sophia, from their parents' house.

The rich strains of Mendelssohn's "Wedding March" grew louder as he approached the front door. He followed the music to the parlor where his father, Olan, served as conductor for his siblings. Fifteen-year-old Viktor avoided Chris's gaze, concentrating on his cello. Hans, the brother whose birth had come as a surprise to their parents eight years ago, sacrificed a few warbling notes of the flute to offer a gap-toothed grin. August, at eighteen the brother closest in age to Chris, caught his eye and offered a sympathetic look.

As the tension built, Chris waited until his father's decisive, swirling hand motion brought the music to a halt before saying, "Please, tell me the only inspiration for this music is the wedding ceremony for Rhett and Isabelle."

August lowered his viola and shook his head. "Pa found a bride for you."

"Congratulations," Viktor mumbled in an apologetic tone.

Chris glanced to his father for confirmation. Olan nodded. Chris swallowed hard. "Pa, we need to talk."

Chris didn't wait for Olan's response. He just turned on his heel and walked out onto the front porch, where his father joined him.

"I know what you're thinking," Olan said, "but please just hear me out."

Chris gave a single nod before sitting beside Olan on the porch swing. "Son, how long has it been since you've seen Adelaide?"

"About five years, I reckon."

His father shook his head. "And she's still holding you to a promise you made five years ago."

Not exactly. Chris glanced away, resisting the urge to loosen his shoestring tie. The stranglehold he felt had nothing to do with his tie and everything to do with guilt. When his parents had sat him down right after graduation to talk about his future, he'd told the truth by admitting his unannounced engagement to Adelaide Harper. At the time, he'd believed that she would follow through on her promise to return to Peppin one day and become his wife. However, Adelaide had broken off their engagement four years ago.

Chris had neglected to mention that small fact to his parents. Only Sophia knew, because she happened to be with him when he'd received Adelaide's last letter. Thankfully, she hadn't breathed a word about it to anyone.

"Adelaide ought to have sense enough to marry you. Or, at least, break things off so that you can marry a good Norwegian girl like Britta Solberg."

Chris narrowed his eyes. "Just a minute. Who is Britta Solberg?"

"Your aunt Karen's friend's cousin. By all reports, she is a steady, sensible girl."

"Who is looking for passage to America?"

His father looked downright insulted. "And what's wrong with that? It was only twelve years ago that we arrived in America ourselves. Don't forget that, or that not everyone back home is able to arrange a passage over here. It's our duty to help our family and friends. There isn't enough land to go around for farmers in the country. The factories in the cities barely pay enough for the workers to live on."

"I know, Pa."

"Then, please, be reasonable." Olan stood and placed a hand on Chris's shoulder. "I understand that your heart is attached to Adelaide, but is it possible that hers is not as attached to you?"

Knowing the answer to that, Chris couldn't hold his father's dark blue gaze.

"You are my oldest son and the epitome of everything that goes with that mantle—sensible, responsible, intelligent and a good example to your younger siblings. You deserve a woman who can match you. If you think that woman is Adelaide, then do something to fight for her. Otherwise, give Britta a chance."

It was on the tip of his tongue to tell the truth about everything. Yet, how could he? If his father was pressuring him this hard while under the impression that Chris was practically engaged to someone else, how much worse would it be if the truth came out?

Everything else in his life seemed planned for him, was it so horrible that he wanted to pick the woman he'd spend the rest of his life with? He knew exactly the kind he wanted, too. She would be someone who evoked only the safe, companionable kind of love. He'd had more than enough of the all-consuming variety and the heartbreak that went with it.

Olan squeezed Chris's shoulder before releasing it. "Think about what I said, but don't take too long to do so. I want to see at least one of my children married and, perhaps if the Lord is especially generous, hold my first grandchild."

Chris knew his father's words didn't stem from impatience but fear. Doc said that Olan's time on Earth was limited. How limited, it was impossible to guess.

One thing was for certain, stress made Olan's heart flutters and pains come stronger and more often. Chris, along with his mother, sister and three younger brothers did their best to keep the atmosphere at home and the store light, comfortable and peaceful. However, they all feared a day might be coming when their efforts wouldn't be enough.

Sophia interrupted his somber ruminations by stepping onto the porch. "Chris, I'm ready. We'd better go. I don't want to be late."

Chris barely managed to wait until they were out of their father's earshot before saying, "Tell me everything you know about this Bridget Saltzberg person."

"Well, I know her name is *Britta Solberg*, but that's pretty much it. No, wait. I do know one more thing." She pinned him with her ice-blue eyes. "You sure as shooting better not marry this woman because that will set a precedent, and there is no way I'm marrying some man I've never met from a country I hardly remember. Just tell our parents you won't do it."

"Have you forgotten that you're the only one who gets away with the saying no to our parents?" He released a long-suffering sigh. "They've spoiled you rotten, princess."

She gave an offended little laugh. "Surely, I deserve a little of it after growing up with four brothers and no sisters."

"Hmm. That's debatable."

She rolled her eyes, then joined arms with him and nudged him with her shoulder. "Don't give up on finding someone, Chris. You can't."

He covered her hand with his and gave it a gentle squeeze. Her encouragement was sweet even if it wasn't entirely altruistic. They didn't have time to discuss it any further for they arrived at Bradley's Boardinghouse where the wedding was set to take place. As they walked up the sidewalk laid out on the boardinghouse's immaculate lawn, Chris couldn't help shaking his head, "I can't believe the Bradleys are selling this place."

Sophia stopped in her tracks. "They are? How do you always know these things before I do?"

"You didn't know?" He grinned when she shook her head. "You've got to do a better job of keeping your ear to the ground. I guess you also don't know that Isabelle's father is going to take over running the hotel, which is why they are going to have the reception there. Or, that Isabelle and Rhett bought a new house to live in after they return from visiting his family. Meanwhile, her family will be moving to a house just down the street from theirs—"

"Thank you, town crier, but I'd like to see the bride walk down the aisle if you don't mind."

She was right to urge him onward, for they ended up being the last guests to take their seats. The bride was radiant. The groom looked more confident than Chris had ever seen him, which was saying something since Rhett had always been awkward around women. There was no stammering or hesitating from the bride or groom as they said their vows.

A few minutes, later Chris kissed the bride's cheek and offered his congratulations to the groom. Rather than releasing his hand after the handshake, Rhett caught his arm and hauled him into the empty kitchen. Chris managed to pull away from Rhett's grasp and frowned at him. "Hey, what's all this about?"

"Sorry for the manhandling. I need to get back to my guests and my bride so this has to be quick. Since Isabelle didn't accept your proposal, am I right to assume that you're still looking for a wife?"

Chris grimaced. "Yes, but I'd rather keep that news quiet if I can."

"You do realize you've tried to court nearly every woman in town, right?"

"Yes, but I assumed they'd all be good enough to keep it to themselves, or at the very least to each other. As it is, my parents don't know I'm looking for a wife and that's the way I want to keep it."

"They won't hear it from me. The reason I pulled you over here was to give you something that should help." Rhett glanced surreptitiously at the kitchen door before pulling a folded piece of paper out of his suit-coat pocket and holding it between them. "Wherever this thing goes, love seems to follow."

"Is that…"

Rhett nodded. "The Bachelor List."

"Really?" Chris almost didn't recognize the hushed, eager, nearly awed tone of his own voice. "Do you have any idea how much I pestered Ellie for a look at that?"

Their friend Ellie Williams was the most successful matchmaker in town. Her list of all the eligible men in Peppin—lined up with who she saw as their matches—had sparked a bit of a frenzy among the bachelors last fall. It had also helped her find her own match with her childhood-friend-turned-husband Lawson. However, she seemed to resent the attention it had brought her, and refused to answer any questions about who any man's match might be.

Chris wasn't sure how Rhett had ended up with it. At the moment, he didn't care. This list would point him in the direction of the woman who was meant for him. The love stuff he could figure out later.

He reached for the first real hope of success he'd had in months, only to see it disappear behind Rhett's back. Rhett gave him a tempering look. "Not so fast. This is a very powerful list—or, rather, God's been using it in very powerful ways. Quinn Tucker was able to convince Helen to marry him simply by showing her this…and because she loved the nieces and nephews in his custody who needed a mother. This list helped me recognize that I was in love with Isabelle and set me on the quest to win her heart. I know God will use it for good in your life, too, or else I wouldn't have felt prompted to give it to you. However, like anything with power, it comes with rules."

"What kind of rules?"

"You have to keep it safe and keep it secret. Don't change anything on it. If Ellie finds out you have it, she'll ask for it. Don't give it back to her. Instead, pass it along to another bachelor—as the Lord directs you, of course. Do you agree to all that?"

"I agree. Now may I have it?"

Rhett handed over the list, patted Chris on the shoulder and then left, presumably to return to his bride. Alone in the kitchen, Chris wasted no time in unfolding the list. He scanned the column of names for his own. Finding it, his gaze also landed on the name of the woman with whom he'd been matched. His jaw clenched.

Adelaide Harper.

This made no sense. Why would Ellie match him

with a woman who no longer even lived in Peppin? Actually, it wasn't that hard to guess. Ellie had been part of their childhood crowd. She must have seen them together and thought exactly what Chris had—that they were meant for each. That, somehow, someway, Adelaide would return to him and they would be together.

They'd all been wrong. He and Adelaide weren't together. And there was absolutely no chance that she would ever return to Peppin.

"There is absolutely no chance I'm getting off this train in Peppin." Leaning back in the chair of the small desk provided in their private Pullman car, Adelaide Harper crossed her arms and lifted her chin.

Her stepfather, Everett Holden, allowed only a hint of a humor to show in his eyes. "This is the last station that will allow us to transfer onto a train to Houston, so you'll forgive me if I get off here. Be so good as to send your mother and me a telegram when you get to Louisiana so that we know you've gotten that far safely. I hope you enjoy the rest of your trip."

Adelaide watched as he grabbed his suitcase, reporter's notebook and Kodak camera, then exited the private train car. With a satisfied nod, she turned her attention back to the manuscript spread out on the sloped writing surface of her portable desk box. If he thought he'd scare her into joining him with the prospect of an extended trip on a train, he had another thing coming. She'd like nothing better than to continue on alone. She did her best writing while traveling, which was why she always begged to go along with him on his rare but necessary business trips. They always used separate private cars which meant she could close the door and block out everything while the clack of the train wheels lulled her into the imaginary worlds she created on paper.

She also treasured the short breaks these trips gave her from her mother's constant attempts at matchmaking. Adelaide was almost certain that with a little more hard work she could become an independent woman who wouldn't have to settle for romance or marriage. Rose might realize that, if she ever acknowledged that Adelaide was a published and increasingly successful author.

They'd become a part of Houston's high society through her mother's marriage to Everett. His family name was one of the most respected in the city. Her mother expected Adelaide to be a proper society lady, and society ladies didn't stay spinsters or write dime novels. They got married, had children and dedicated their time to charity or musical accomplishments.

Adelaide had never fit into that world. She'd never truly fit anywhere, despite or perhaps because of the fact that she'd lived in so many places growing up. That's why she enjoyed writing. It gave her the chance to create a place that belonged to her even if she couldn't truly live there.

A knock sounded on the half-open door. Expecting to see her stepfather, she was surprised to find it was the porter, instead. "Miss, the gentleman said you needed help with a suitcase."

With a resigned sigh, she tucked her pencil and papers into a compartment of the portable desk before folding it into its box form. She did her best to ignore the mix of panic and dread filling her stomach as she nodded toward the suitcase. "Yes, please. It's on the bed."

She put on her hat, bending the brim to a daring angle that dipped low over her face. She had no illusions that it would keep her identity a secret for long in this town. Folks here were too observant and too friendly not to notice one of their own had returned. She wouldn't mind seeing some of the friends she had kept in touch with over the years. She just didn't relish the idea of word getting back to Chris that she was in town. Not that he'd care or want to see her. After all, she was the one who'd ended their engagement. She'd done it for a good reason, too—one far more important than she'd cited in her final letter.

Five years had passed since then. She was quite certain her heart was in no danger from him. Unfortunately, that didn't stop it from racing as she followed the porter down the corridor to the railcar's exit. Nor did it keep her hand from trembling slightly as the conductor took it to guide her across the gap between the tracks and the platform. Her gaze cautiously swept the busy depot as she went to stand beside her stepfather. "Pa, when is the next train out of here?"

"Ah, Adelaide, what a surprise! It's so nice of you to join me." Concern wrinkled his forehead slightly when she didn't so much as offer a smile. "One hour and fifteen minutes. That gives us just enough time to grab some dinner and check out the lead I have on the story I'm investigating."

"We are not eating dinner here." Her stomach growled in disagreement. Perhaps Everett could fetch some food and she'd eat it at the station—behind a stack of luggage where no one would find her. Suddenly, her eyes narrowed upon her stepfather. "Wait a minute. What lead? I thought we were only here because we needed to transfer trains."

"This *is* the only place for us to transfer, but one of the charities I'm investigating also happens to be based here."

"In Peppin? Really? You think someone here set up a fake charity to steal people's money?"

"No, I think someone in Houston is doing the stealing. I haven't discovered who that might be despite the threatening letters I've received."

Concern filled her. "Threatening letters?"

He waved his hand dismissively. "Nothing serious or out of the ordinary for an investigative journalist, I assure you. It only makes me more eager to break the story. I've a hunch whoever it is set up a fake charity in one of these out-of-the-way towns we've been visiting. The three we've been to so far have all seemed legitimate. I wasn't planning to visit a fourth on this trip, but we may as well check it out since we have to stop here anyway." He flipped through a few pages in his notebook. "Any chance you're familiar with this address?"

She leaned closer and was relieved to see that it was on Main Street but in the opposite direction from Johansen's Mercantile. "That has to be in the newer section of town. They were just starting to build in that area when Mother and I moved away. If you'd given me the address, I could have had one of my friends look into it for you."

He shook his head. "A good reporter finds out the facts for himself. Besides, if something is amiss I'll need some sort of proof. Think you can lead the way?"

"I'm sure I could." They checked their luggage with the stationmaster before heading off to investigate. Adelaide kept her head down as much as possible, but the glimpses she caught of the town proved it had gone through a surprising number of changes within the five years she'd been gone. There were so many more businesses, and everyone looked more fashionable and up-to-date than she recalled.

It only took a few minutes for them to find the building. It looked like any other business, except that it boasted no sign to indicate what type of business might be conducted inside, and all of its cobalt-blue shutters were closed tight. Knocking on the door yielded no answer.

Her stepfather set up his camera and took a few pictures as proof of the building's existence. "I think I'll talk to a few townsfolk while we're here to find out if they know anything about this place. The stationmaster told me there's a popular café on the other end of Main Street. Let's head over there and see what we can discover."

Adelaide bit her lip as alarm lifted her brows. Yet, for some reason, she couldn't find it within herself to protest as she followed Everett's purposeful step in the exact direction she'd wanted to avoid. They'd nearly reached the café when she heard a delighted gasp. "Adelaide Harper, as I live and breathe! That *is* you. I knew it."

Adelaide turned just in time to receive a hug from her former classmate. "Ellie O'Brien. No, it's Ellie *Williams* now. Isn't it?"

"It most certainly is." The blonde grinned and then transferred her smile to the man who came to stand beside her. "You remember my husband, Lawson, don't you?"

"Of course." She offered her hand to Lawson who had graduated a couple of years before her.

He gave it a friendly squeeze. "It's wonderful to see you again."

Adelaide responded in kind before introducing her stepfather to the couple. They soon realized that they'd all been heading to Maddie's Café and decided to share a table. As they ate, Ellie asked, "So, Adelaide, what brings you back to Peppin after all these years?"

Adelaide refused to follow the speculative glance Ellie sent out the nearby window, since she knew it would land directly across the street…on Johansen's Mercantile. Feeling a hint of warmth spread across her cheeks, Adelaide allowed her stepfather to explain the nature of their visit. He didn't go into detail, but what he said was enough to put a frown of pure confusion on Lawson's face. "There is no orphanage in Peppin. I ought to know. If there had been, I would have been put there when I first arrived in town ten years ago."

Ellie shook her head. "Lawson Clive Williams, you know that isn't true. My sister and brother-in-law never would have allowed it. Neither would the Williamses."

"You're right, honey. I just meant that I would know if there had been an orphanage in town."

Adelaide shrugged. "Well, the building is one of the newer ones. Perhaps it's in the process of being set up."

Both Ellie and Lawson seemed doubtful.

Everett hummed thoughtfully. "In that case, I'd like to find out just how long it's taking them to get started. Where's the local land office?"

"If you don't mind me tagging along," Lawson offered, "I'll take you there myself."

Ellie waved the men on saying, "We'll meet y'all at the mercantile."

As the men left, Adelaide's gaze snapped to Ellie's sparkling green eyes. "Ellie, I couldn't. Things didn't end well between Chris and me. He wouldn't want to see me."

Ellie tilted her head as her gaze slid between Adelaide and the mercantile several times. Finally the woman shrugged. "It seems to me, the question isn't would he want to see you, but…" Ellie placed her elbows on the table and leaned forward before lowering her voice. "Do you want to see him?"

Adelaide wavered. "Well, maybe…just a glimpse. A *glimpse*—simply out of curiosity…"

It only took a few moments for them to formulate their plan. Ellie would go into the mercantile and lure Chris over to the display window. Adelaide would catch a glimpse of him as she oh-so-casually and undetectably walked past. Afterwards, she'd just keep on walking right to the train station where Ellie would tell Everett to find her.

There was hardly any risk involved. There was nothing to be nervous about. There was no reason to examine why seeing Chris had become so important to her.

Adelaide waited until she saw a flicker of movement in the display window. Heart pounding in her chest, she strolled toward it. She stole a quick glance, only to accidentally catch the unmistakably kind gaze of Olan Johansen. Chris's father froze. Recognition flared in his eyes. He leaned forward and knocked on the glass as if he didn't already have her attention.

She realized she'd stopped in her tracks. Panicking, she started to turn one way then the other before realizing it would be incredibly rude not to acknowledge the man. She did so with a smile and a minuscule wave. He grinned, then beckoned her inside.

Her eyes widened. She shook her head. Still smiling, she began to back away muttering, "Oh, no. Oh, no. No. No. *No.* I am not going in there."

The man left the window an instant before he stepped onto the sidewalk. He was saying something, but all she could do was stare at the mercantile door, which somehow got ever closer. She was speaking now, responding automatically to whatever he'd said. "Yes, it's wonderful to see you, too. I'm surprised myself. I wasn't planning to be here. Oh, doesn't the store look wonderful? You've rearranged things, haven't you?"

"Chris!" She winced as Mr. Johansen's bellow echoed through the large store. "Chris, come here. Chris!"

Adelaide backed up a step as everyone but Chris gathered around to see what the commotion was about. Finally, Chris eased through the crowd with Ellie at his heels. He was just as tall as she remembered, but he'd filled out in muscle—a man now, instead of the boy she remembered. He moved with a sense of purpose and confidence that a less sensible woman might find downright intoxicating. His hair had grown out a little but it still reminded her of spun gold. His fingers raked it away from the worry that wrinkled his brow as his blue gaze landed on his father with a mixture of confusion and concern. "What is it, Pa? Are you all right? What's happened?"

"I'm better than all right. Look who's finally here." Olan caught her hand and lifted it, pulling her a step forward. Adelaide barely held back a groan. All she'd wanted was a glimpse of Chris. Instead, she was getting a whole lot of trouble.

Chapter Two

Chris's gaze continued to search his father's for any indication that he was in pain or short of breath. Olan hated the worry his heart condition added to the family. This wouldn't be the first time he'd tried to downplay one his heart episodes with a distraction. Olan was flushed, but it only seemed to be with excitement, so Chris reluctantly allowed his attention to be drawn elsewhere.

It landed on the woman standing just in front of his father. A hat dipped low over her right eye. Yet it did little to hide the perfection of her slightly turned-up nose, the rosy blush racing across her high cheekbones or the sweet curves of her bow-shaped lips. She was beautiful. She was familiar. She was *achingly* familiar.

He caught her chin, tilted her face upward and got lost in her light green eyes. "Adelaide."

A fleeting smile touched her lips. "Hello, Chris."

Silence filled the air. He released her. His words came out as more of a growl than a greeting. "What are you doing here?"

Olan slapped Chris's back just hard enough to

knock some sense into him. "Son, is that any way to greet your fiancée?"

Time slowed. Chris saw Adelaide turn toward his father. He knew exactly what was going to happen. The truth was going to come out. He could almost see the disbelief, the shock, the disappointment on his father's face. His imagination went even further until he saw Olan's face whiten, his hand covering his heart as he sank to his knees in pain. Chris couldn't let that happen. Instinctively, Chris reached for Adelaide. He caught her by the arms, tugged her toward his chest, then stifled whatever she'd been planning to say with a quick, ardent kiss.

All it took was one slow blink of her long lashes for the dazed look in her eyes to change to pure fire. She opened her mouth to say something rude and incriminating so he kissed her again—gently this time. For a second he feared she'd pull away. Instead, she responded hesitantly by lifting her chin. Her fingers tentatively touched the nape of his neck, then slid into his hair. Suddenly, he was the one who was distracted. It wasn't just by her kiss, either. It was the wisp of a dream that came with it, the vision of what could have been if she hadn't rejected him.

But she had—soundly and irrevocably with little explanation and no warning. He'd do well to remember that.

His father clamped a hand on Chris's shoulder, no doubt to remind him that they had a store filled with gaping customers. "Why don't you two take a walk and sort some things out?"

By "some things" Chris was certain Olan meant a wedding date. In response, Chris gave a quick wave and a nod on the way to the front door. He didn't have time to do anything else because Adelaide wasn't going to stay quiet for long. He barely managed to tug her outside, then into the nearby alley beside the mercantile, before she whirled and punched him in the shoulder. "Have you lost your ever-loving mind?"

He winced more at her yelling than the blow. Realizing they needed a bit more distance from the street for privacy's sake, he grabbed her hand and dragged her around to the back of the building. Placing his hands on the wall beside her waist, he caged her in and waited for the lambasting to stop. She'd lost her hat and a few tendrils of her auburn hair had tumbled loose to gleam in the sunlight. She distracted him from the temptation to smooth them back into place by pushing at his chest. It didn't move him an inch. Her eyes flashed in frustration. "What were you thinking?"

Realizing she'd finally taken a breath, he tilted his head and lifted a brow. "You know, all of this indignation would be a lot more convincing if you hadn't kissed me back."

She froze. A blush suffused her cheeks. Her eyes met his, then narrowed. Her gaze drifted to his mouth. From the look on her face, he wasn't sure if she was going to kiss him again or slap him. He figured a distraction was in order. "Adelaide, *what* are you doing here?"

To his relief, she calmed down enough to lean against the building though she continued to glare. "My stepfather had business in town."

"How long are you staying?" He forced the words out, not wanting to acknowledge that a small part of him had hoped she'd come back intending to fulfill her promise to marry him. Not that he would have agreed to anything that ludicrous. Trusting her with his heart would be akin to trusting Billy the Kid to look after the Johansen's cash drawer.

"We're leaving on the next train." Her gaze turned searching yet guarded. "Why did you kiss me?"

"I couldn't let you tell my pa that you weren't my fiancée anymore. He still thinks... Well, my whole family, except for Sophia, still believes that you and I are planning to get married eventually. I never told them we—*you* broke off our engagement."

"Then this is the perfect opportunity to do so." She tried to dislodge his hand from the wall but he refused to move, allowing the desperation he felt to show in his eyes. She gave a reluctant sigh. "All right, Chris. What is going on? Why don't they know?"

"It all started out innocently enough. On my eighteenth birthday, which was only a few months after you left, my parents sat me down 'to talk about my future.' They told me that when the time came for me to take a wife they wanted me to marry a girl from Norway."

"What girl from Norway?"

He shrugged. "Any girl, really. Of course, at the time, that didn't matter because I was engaged to you. I told them as much and showed them your letters. They were pretty shocked to hear I'd kept that from them, but they respected my commitment to you. They also agreed not to announce anything about it until your mother approved. But as much as they liked you, they never gave up the hope I'd change my mind and let them send for a mail-order bride."

"So even after I ended our engagement, you just let them keep on thinking you were engaged to me because that meant you had a safeguard of sorts against their meddling."

"Exactly." He grimaced. "I guess that was a pretty self-serving thing to do."

She bit her lip. "Don't say that."

"Why not?"

"Because it sounds like the kind of thing I would do."

He laughed. "Really?"

"Honestly. The stories I could tell you about my mother and her matchmaking attempts..." She rolled her eyes. "Actually, I'd rather not think about them. My point is, I understand why you did what you did. I just don't see how you got away with it for this long. It's been four years."

"It helped when I moved out of the house. That kept them from knowing your letters had stopped coming. They knew the fact that I didn't have your mother's approval was a sore point for me, so they didn't bring the engagement up often. If they did, I changed the subject."

"What about other girls? I know we never announced that we were engaged, but your parents and siblings knew. Didn't they notice you courting women who weren't me?"

Chris rubbed his jaw, wondering at the edge in her voice that made him feel lower than pond scum, as if he'd been unfaithful to her. *She'd* been the one who'd broken their engagement. Not him. If she hadn't wanted to him to court other women, she shouldn't have given up her claim on him. Still, it was a good question that begged an answer. "My parents didn't know I courted anyone else. It wasn't too hard for me to hide. After all, I've always had a lot of friends who were girls. We all spent time together in groups, so any courting I wanted to do was done then. Sophia would cover for me if things got sticky. It also helped that I'm one of five children. My parents can't always keep track of us that well. Besides, it's only been in the last year that my father really started to pressure me to settle down."

"Why the last year?"

"That's when…that's when his heart started acting up. Or, at least that's when he couldn't hide it anymore. That's part of the reason he's so anxious for me to get married. He wants to see at least one of his grandchildren before he—"

"Oh, Chris." Concern filled her voice as she placed a hand on his arm. "Isn't there something that can be done?"

He swallowed hard. "Doc Williams wants Pa to see a specialist for some more tests. Pa says there hasn't been time to go. I don't think that time is the problem. I think he's…"

"Afraid," she offered softly.

Chris nodded. "He knows he may not have much time left, but I guess he doesn't want to know how bad it really is."

"But what if there's something a specialist could do to help?"

"I hope there is. That's why I want him to see one. Until then, we may not know what—if anything— could make him better, but we know that stress can make it worse." He ran his fingers through his hair.

"This whole debacle with my supposed engagement has spiraled out of control. It's bound to upset him if I tell him I've deceived him all this time."

"I know, but he needs to know the truth."

Chris knew she was right. He couldn't keep this going. Especially not now with Adelaide's return. There was only one thing left to do. "I'll go back to the store. I'll take my pa aside and explain everything as gently as possible, like I should have done long ago."

"Wait." She caught his arm to keep him from turning away. "You don't have to go in there alone."

Chris recognized her offer for what it was—an olive branch bridging past the disaster of their engagement back to the friendship they'd once shared. He'd missed their friendship. He'd missed *her*. Unfortunately, going back to the way things had been before was impossible. Even now, the hurts from the past that should have been healed flared with old pain.

He took her hand, removed it from his arm and gave it a small squeeze before letting it go. "Actually, Adelaide, I'd prefer it."

Stunned by Chris's gentle but unmistakable dismissal, Adelaide stared at him as he turned on his heel and walked away.

She charted his progress down the alley as he neared the front of the store. His steps were determined but slow. His head was down. She recognized that posture. It meant he was thinking hard about something—no doubt trying to summon the words he'd need to break the news to his father.

Or some other way to twist the truth? Surely he wouldn't. Perhaps she ought to make sure.

She pushed away from the wall, grabbed her hat from where it had fallen in the dust and followed him inside the mercantile. She found that the number of customers hadn't dwindled in the least, which meant that folks were sticking around to see what would happen next. They might as well have gone home. All of the excitement was over. There was nothing more to see here.

She caught sight of Everett leaning against the store's gleaming oak counter with his arms crossed in front of him. He lifted one brow, then pinned her with his brown gaze. She swallowed and found herself easing closer to Chris's side. "Oh! Hello, Pa."

"Is there something you'd like to tell me?"

"Um, I—" Her panicked gaze refused to meet his. Instead, it flitted to where a wide-eyed Ellie stood by a shelf of books. Lawson stood beside her looking decidedly confused. Finally, she saw Mr. Johansen watching from his spot in front of the register. A smile tipped his lips, and he offered her an encouraging nod. Chris's words concerning his father's health filled her mind. She hadn't noticed it before, but there was a strain around Olan's eyes and tiredness to his bearing that hadn't been there five years ago.

She hated the mere possibility of anything bad happening to him. He was such a kind soul. Even when she and her mother had missed a payment or two toward their store credit, he'd always welcomed them into the mercantile and his home. He was a fixture in the Peppin community. He served on the school board, was a deacon at church and was always the first to support a charitable cause. He didn't deserve the embarrassment that would come his way if she answered her stepfather's question, in front of all these people, with complete honesty.

That being the case, she said the one thing that would make her sound guilty without being an outright lie. "I can explain."

"Well, you'd better. And, while you're at it, I'd like to know why this is the first I've heard of your engagement."

Chris turned to level her with his gaze. Surprise and bewilderment flashed across his face. To an outsider, his reaction might have seemed to be prompted by the news that she hadn't mentioned their engagement to her stepfather. However, she knew it was because she hadn't immediately spilled the truth. His jaw flexed. Indecision warred in his eyes before he gave in with a minuscule nod.

She swallowed, unable to drag her gaze from his even as she addressed Everett. She didn't want to lie— but there were some evasions she could make while still being honest. "Mother didn't want me to mention it."

Chris glanced away, freeing her to meet her stepfather's eyes. Everett frowned. "Your mother knew?"

"Well…let's just say she preferred to ignore it." That was also true.

"That does sounds like her." He ran a hand over his beard, weighing her words and searching her eyes. He gave up trying to figure her out with a little shake of his head. "Aren't you going to introduce me to your fiancé?"

"Of course. Pa, this is Chris Johansen. Chris, this is my stepfather, Everett Holden." She smiled as she watched the two them exchange a handshake. Everything would be all right. Rather than air all of the Johansen's family business before their customers, she'd given Chris a reprieve. He could tell his father the truth in private later. If he didn't... Well, as much as she hoped he would, that wasn't her concern. She was leaving on the next train out of Peppin.

Olan stepped around the counter. "You must come and have supper with my family this evening."

Everett nodded. "Yes, I think we'd better."

Panic filled her. "Oh, but our train—"

"It's all right. We'll stay at the hotel tonight and catch the train that leaves in the morning."

She bit her lip to keep from protesting again as Chris offered to see them to the hotel. Mr. Johansen waved his customers toward the register and it went back to business as usual inside the mercantile. Adelaide said goodbye to Ellie and Lawson before hurrying toward the door where Chris and Everett waited. They were already deep in conversation as her journalist of a stepfather plied Chris with question after question. By the time they made it to the hotel, Everett had learned Chris's entire life story, from his humble beginning in Norway to his future plan of running the mercantile for his family.

While Everett spoke to a hotel clerk about renting rooms for the night, Chris caught her hand and tugged her into a quiet corner of the lobby. "I know you're just trying to help. At least, I assume that was the motivation behind this. I would just like to point out that you're making things more complicated."

"I'm not sure that's possible. Look, I thought this through. Where's the harm in keeping up the act for one more night? I'll play along until it's time to leave, then we'll pretend to fight and you'll say we ended the engagement."

He shook his head while exasperation filled his voice. "Adelaide, we both know that your plans never work out. They always do the opposite of what you intended for them to do."

"Pardon me. It's been five years. You don't know the first thing about me or what I've accomplished anymore, so I'll thank you to keep your opinions to yourself." At his disbelieving look, she rolled her eyes. "Fine. Maybe you're a little bit right, but you have to admit my idea is much better than letting your father be humiliated in front of all of his customers. This plan will work."

He ran his fingers through his hair. "Well, it doesn't really matter because there's no going back now, is there?"

"Nope."

He sighed. "I'm going to go let my mother know we'll be having company for supper. I'll meet you and your stepfather here at six and we'll walk over to my parents' house together. All right?"

She nodded. He offered her a rather poor excuse for a smile before he hurried away. She rejoined her stepfather just as he handed a bellboy the check for the luggage they'd left at the station. After they were shown to their suite, Everett caught her arm and directed her to the settee in the parlor that connected their rooms. He sat beside her and looked her in the eye. "Explain to me again how you're engaged to that man."

Just like that, the truth came tumbling out. Everett listened without asking a single question until she finished. He stroked his graying beard. "That's quite a story."

"I shouldn't have misled Mr. Johansen."

"Maybe not. I understand why you did, though. Really, this is a matter that needs to be discussed between Olan and Chris—privately. There was no need to air their family business in front of all those customers. It would have caused unnecessary embarrassment."

She nodded. "That's what I thought."

He patted her hand. "You got caught in the middle of a messy situation and did the best you could."

"I did." She bit her lip. "What if Chris is right? What if I make everything worse?"

"Well, we can't back out on the dinner. That would be rude."

Her sigh turned into a groan. "I never should have walked past that store in the first place. I knew better. I just…"

"You wanted to see him, huh?"

"Yes. Don't ask me why." Twisting her lips to the side, she stared at her ink-stained fingers. Chris had looked good—too good…the kind of good that could only mean trouble for the woman who loved him. Those classic features of his were so handsome they ought to be carved in marble and placed in a museum. Not that she'd been swayed by them. Or by the way the sun set his wheat-gold hair glimmering. She'd just observed, that's all. That was different. She lifted her gaze back to Everett. "Why can't all men be like you? Honorable and kind and—"

"Plain?" He chuckled. "Don't look so shocked. I consider myself blessed to be not-quite handsome. It took me a year to convince your ma to marry me with this face. I can't imagine how long it would have taken if I looked as good as your young man. I know how you and your mother think. Y'all are outright snobs when it comes to the handsome men in this world. That's unfair of you, but I know there's a reason for it so I won't push you. I will say this. Chris Johansen might be worth a second chance if he's half the man his father seems to think he is. Of course, if Olan doesn't know the truth about the engagement, it makes me wonder what else he might not know about his son."

"Plenty, I'm sure."

As for giving Chris a second chance at breaking her heart...she wasn't that crazy.

Chapter Three

❧

I can't believe I'm doing this.

Chris stared at the front door of his parents' house, unwilling to pull the doorbell and begin this evening's charade. It was one thing to pretend the woman he'd asked to marry him had never ended their engagement. It was another thing entirely to parade a lie before his parents' faces. He wanted to turn around, go back to his apartment above the mercantile and forget any of this had ever happened.

"Steady." The low whisper from Adelaide's step-father meant the man understood Chris's struggle. Adelaide must have told him the truth. Now the only people in the dark were Chris's parents and younger brothers. He rolled his shoulders as though that might free him from the ever-growing burden of guilt resting there. It didn't.

He pulled in a deep breath, then rang the door-bell. A few moments later, Chris's mother opened the door and immediately enveloped Adelaide into a hug. "You've finally come, *and* you're staying for supper. What a wonderful surprise! You're so grown-up and even more lovely than before. Wouldn't you agree, Chris?"

His gaze skimmed from the fancy chignon of her auburn hair to her lacy cream blouse and dark blue skirt before he managed to catch himself. "She's always been beautiful."

Adelaide's lashes lowered demurely as a hint of a blush appeared on her cheek. "Thank you, both. It's lovely to see you, too. Marta Johansen, I'd like you to meet my stepfather, Everett Holden."

After their parents exchanged pleasantries, Chris glanced down the main hall in search of his siblings. Usually the boys came rushing to greet him as soon as he stepped inside the door. "Where is everyone, Ma?"

"They're waiting in the parlor."

He headed toward the double doors across the hall. "Why are the doors closed?"

"Just a moment." His mother rushed around him to stand in front of the doors. "Adelaide, would you come and stand beside Chris? Thank you. Now, Mr. Holden, I'll need help with the other door. Slide it to the left on the count of three."

Chris frowned. "Ma—"

"One."

"What is—"

"Two."

"—going on?"

"Three!"

The doors slid away. The rich, unmistakable strains of "The Wedding March" crashed over them. His mouth fell open at the sight before him. The parlor had been decked out with all manner of decorations. The largest and most prominent was the banner above the fireplace that read "Congratulations!" in Hans's big, slightly uneven letters. The little boy's grin was so big that he kept missing the notes on his flute. Next to him, Viktor played his cello while offering them a much shyer smile. August winked at Chris as he dramatically swayed in time with the mellow tones of his viola. Sophia caught his eye as she ran her fingers across the string of her harp while mouthing two words. "I'm sorry."

As usual, his father served as conductor for the quartet and soon brought the music to an end. Everyone looked at Chris with such pride and expectation. He had no idea how to respond. Adelaide saved him from having to figure it out by clapping for the ensemble. "That was absolutely beautiful! What a wonderful welcome. I can't believe how much all of y'all have grown."

His brothers rushed forward to greet her. Viktor and August remembered her well. Hans was eager to meet her again. Sophia's greeting was a bit less enthusiastic. She alone knew just how much Chris had been hurt by Adelaide's rejection. As their brothers continued to monopolize Adelaide's attention, Sophia sidled over to Chris. She gave him a congratulatory hug that was really just an excuse for her to whisper, "I've been praying for you since I heard. I would have come over to see you, but Ma kept me busy preparing all of this."

"It's all right. I—" The doorbell interrupted him. Marta rushed to answer it. Chris turned to his father for explanation. "Is someone else joining us for dinner?"

"Yes, indeed."

The satisfaction in Olan's tone put Chris on alert. "Pa, you know I don't like surprises."

His father simply clasped him on the shoulder without saying a word. Chris stiffened as their guest walked in. Pastor Brightly took one look at the parlor and grinned. Tucking the book he carried beneath his arm, the man rubbed his palms together. "All right, then. Who's ready for a wedding?"

His brothers cheered. Chris shook his head to clear it. Surely—*surely* this was a nightmare he would awaken from at any second. Adelaide's gaze connected with his from across the room and the panic in her eyes was undeniably real. They'd been ambushed. There was no way out but the truth.

Adelaide didn't quite seem to understand that. She sounded genuinely troubled as she said, "Oh, but I couldn't possibly get married without my mother present."

"I agree," Mr. Holden said, looking decidedly unamused by the turn of events.

Sophia took Hans's hand and shooed the other boys toward the kitchen. "Let's all go check on the cake, boys. Perhaps it's cool enough to frost."

Once Chris's siblings left, Pastor Brightly searched the faces of everyone left in the room. "Is there a problem?"

"Yes, there is a problem." Finally finding his voice, Chris crossed the room to stand beside Adelaide, then addressed his parents. "Y'all cannot possibly expect us to agree to a wedding with absolutely no warning."

Olan gave a tired sigh. "One would think that a five-year engagement is warning enough."

Marta went to place a comforting hand on her husband's back. "Adelaide and Mr. Holden, I understand your objections to having the wedding without Rose present, but you can always have another ceremony later. You also must remember that Rose has not approved of Chris for the past five years. I see little reason to hope that she will change her mind about my son unless she has the opportunity to get to know him as her son-in-law."

"I agree with my wife. I would also like to point out that if a young lady truly loved my son no one would be able to persuade her not to marry him."

If Chris hadn't already been watching Adelaide, he would have missed the hurt that flared in her eyes before her lashes lowered to cover them. Her voice trembled slightly, betraying her high emotions. "And you, Pa? What do you have to say about all of this?"

"Adelaide, you are old enough to know your own mind. It's your decision to make—yours and Chris's."

That was not the response that Chris had expected from the man. Yet, Chris realized, it was the only one he could have given that would truly allow Adelaide the freedom to choose. If Everett had outright forbidden Adelaide to marry Chris and she'd capitulated, she would have appeared weak. This, at least, would allow her some strength and dignity in her inevitable refusal.

Chris also realized that she would leave as soon as she articulated that refusal. He'd have no reason to see her again. She'd been ripped from him before without a goodbye. For some reason, he couldn't let that happen again. He touched her arm. "Come on, Adelaide. Let's talk about this outside."

A fierce March wind met them at the door. Not wanting to take a chance at being overheard, he kept walking until he reached the gate, then turned to face her. "I'm so sorry, Adelaide. If I'd had any idea that my parents would spring this on us, I would have done everything I could to prevent it."

The wind teased at her hair and skirt as she wrapped her arms around herself. "I know."

"You don't have to go back in there. I'll break the news myself."

She nodded. "I'd appreciate that. Please tell your siblings I said goodbye. It was nice to see them again."

She couldn't seem to look at him. He wasn't sure how or why, but what his father had said must have struck a nerve with her. Chris didn't know how he felt. Anger had deserted him—at least for the moment. The only emotion he was left with was one he couldn't seem to name. Whatever it was, it begged him to pull her into his arms. He shook the errant thought from his head. "Goodbye, Adelaide. Thank you for trying to help me."

"Goodbye, Chris."

He left her at the gate, announced to his family that there would be no wedding, now or ever, and said goodbye to Everett. Pastor Brightly left soon after. Chris removed himself to one of the chairs on the porch, feeling tired and bruised.

The sound of the front door opening interrupted his swirling, unmanageable thoughts. He glanced up as his father took the chair beside him. Jaw clenching, Chris shook his head. "You hurt her feelings."

"I did?" His father frowned and cast a concerned glance down the street in the direction Adelaide and Everett had walked. "That wasn't my intention. To be honest, I didn't think you'd let it go this far."

A beat of silence passed. Chris looked at his father. Olan's mouth slowly curved upward on one side. Chris straightened in his chair. "You knew."

Olan lifted an eyebrow and gave a single nod.

Chris's mouth fell open. "How long have you known?"

"Chris, you are my son. Do you really think I didn't see your hurt and anger the past few years? There's also the matter of you flirting with your sister's friends. The man I raised would never do that while betrothed to someone else."

"Why didn't you say something?"

"At first, I wanted to give you time to heal. Then I wanted you to come to me. Finally I just got sick of it and made you as uncomfortable as I possibly could to see when you'd finally break down and tell me."

Chris hiked his thumb toward the house. "The wedding. That's what that was about. You actually set me up with a fake wedding, and you say *I'm* the one who took it too far?"

"It wouldn't have been a fake if you'd gone through with it."

"You knew we wouldn't."

"Actually, I wasn't sure. Adelaide's always had a hold on you. She still does." Olan waved off Chris's protests. "I saw the way you kissed her."

"That was just to keep her quiet."

"Was it? Because, I'm pretty sure that by the time I slapped you on the back you'd forgotten not only where you were but why you were kissing her in the first place."

Heat crawled up Chris's neck. He stood and walked over to the porch rail. "Pa, what are you getting at?

Are you trying to make me admit that I care for her?
Why? What does it matter now?"

"We men don't like to talk much about our feelings. I understand that. However, the way I look at it,
feelings are a lot like seeds. You can bury them all
you want. They'll just keep growing. The only way
to conquer them is to dig them up, bring them to the
light and deal with them with God's help. You've kept
quiet about what you think and feel for Adelaide for
so long. That isn't a healthy way to live. I want you to
talk to me. For the first time in five years, be honest
with me and tell me what you're feeling."

"I feel…angry. Not just at her, but at myself." He
turned to face his father and forced himself to speak
the truth. "I could have fought for her. I thought about
it so many times. How hard would it have been to get
on a train to Houston and have an honest conversation with her? But I couldn't bring myself to do it. Not
after how she threw me away—threw away the future
I wanted us to have together. I thought we were in love.
I must have been wrong, if she was able to turn away
from it so easily. Since then, I've just been numb. I
tried to find a girl who would be content with that.
No one ever was. But maybe now that it's truly over,
I can finally put it all to rest."

His father was quiet for a long moment. Right when
Chris was beginning to feel uncomfortable for revealing all of that, Olan spoke. "What's stopping you from
fighting for her now?"

Chris gave a short laugh. "Oh, I don't know. San-
ity, probably."

"Hey." Olan leaned forward, brow furrowed. "I'm
serious. You might say you're ready to put it to rest,

but I can see you still have strong feelings for her. You need those settled before you can move on. *If* you can move on. Maybe all of this is God's way of showing you that you gave up too soon."

"Why would you, of all people, want me to go after her?"

"Does it matter?"

"It *really* does."

"I'd hate to see you start your marriage to another girl with this hanging over your head."

Suddenly realizing he no longer had a buffer to protect him from his father's attempts at an arranged marriage, Chris tensed. "Is this about Bridget Saltzberg?"

Exasperation painted Olan's features. "The girl's name is Britta Solberg. And, no. This is about you and the fact that being in love with someone else is a horrible way to start a marriage."

"Listen, I never said I was still in love with Adelaide. I'm not. If that's the only reason you think I should fight for her, then it's not good enough."

"I think it is. Marriage is challenging enough without that type of strain. Now, I have an idea and I think you're going to like it." At Chris's doubtful look, Olan shrugged. "Well, you'll like at least half of it. I'll agree to see a heart specialist in Houston if you'll agree to figure out your true feelings for Adelaide while we're there."

Chris stared at his father. "That, sir, is blackmail."

"Let's just call it…motivation."

"Unbelievable." Chris sank into the chair across from his father and shook his head in amazement. "You know there is no way I can turn that down. I can't even try to stall you because the sooner you see a doctor, the better. I almost can't even be upset at you for doing it because it's such a brilliant move."

Olan patted him on the knee, then stood. "I've got to take care of a few things before we leave, but there should be a train coming through about noon tomorrow. Be ready to get on it. And come inside. Your ma has a plate for you."

He'd been outmaneuvered, outthought, outplanned and there was nothing he could do about it. Not that he felt particularly interested in digging through his feelings for Adelaide. What did his feelings matter when she'd made her own stance perfectly clear? Still, for honor's sake, he ought to at least be in the woman's general vicinity once or twice if possible. He'd just have to keep his guard up, because there was no way he was going to get his heart tangled up with that woman again.

If a young lady truly loved my son, no one would be able to persuade her not to marry him.

Mr. Johansen's words reverberated in her head all the way back to Houston. They hurt, not because they had been cruelly meant, but because they were true. They meant her mother must have been right all along. Adelaide hadn't loved Chris. What they'd felt had been nothing more than a childish fleeting fancy.

It had been odd, though, to stand in the Johansen's parlor and catch a glimpse of what her life might have been. If she'd loved Chris, perhaps she would have flouted her mother's wishes. She might have run back to Peppin when she was eighteen to marry him in a ceremony very much like the ones his parents had planned yesterday. She might have lost her mother's approval but she would have gained his family's love and support. She'd be much closer to her old friends in Peppin—people who were warm, friendly, and accepting, unlike the society mavens Rose was trying so hard to impress.

It sounded rather idyllic until she remembered that Chris hadn't loved her, either. He never would have sought out the company of another woman if he had. Adelaide needed to remember that she hadn't ended their engagement only because she'd doubted the depth of her feelings, but also because she'd feared the life she could see folding out before her the moment she'd read Amy's letter. It was a life very much like Rose's had been up to that point—married young to a handsome salesman with a wandering heart. Adelaide could never abide that.

She'd locked away her thoughts of a future in Peppin with Chris and focused on finding some means of supporting herself so that she'd never have to rely on a husband. Thankfully, with Everett's help, she'd honed her talent for writing. His family's connections in the publishing world had helped secure her first book deal. She'd managed the rest by herself and was well on her way to fulfilling her new dream. That's what she needed to focus on, not her trip to the past.

She tightened her grasp on her carrying case as she stepped from the train onto the covered platform. Everett paused beside her and she followed his gaze to the looming three-story brick building that was Houston's Grand Central Station. He smiled. "As much as I enjoy chasing down a good story, there's nothing quite like coming home again. Why don't you go find your mother in the waiting room while I gather our luggage? We'll meet at the station entrance. That will save us some time, and we'll be home before we know it."

She worried her bottom lip. "And I'll have a few moments alone with Mother to tell her what happened on our trip."

"Exactly." He patted her arm and set off in the direction of the baggage claim.

Adelaide sighed, then gathered her courage and slipped through the bustling crowd. In the waiting room, Rose gave her a perfunctory hug, then asked, "Where's your stepfather?"

"He's going to meet us at the entrance with the luggage."

Rose scanned the crowd as they walked. "Well, I'll have a thing or two to say to him about taking you to Peppin."

"He didn't know. I mean, we never told him much about our history there. I...didn't visit father's grave."

"Why would you?" Rose pressed her lips together, then turned to look at Adelaide. "Did you see any of your old friends?"

"I saw Chris," Adelaide said, because that was really what her mother was asking. "He still works in his father's store."

"I don't suppose he's married."

"No."

"His kind hardly ever does marry, which is a mercy, really."

Adelaide pulled in a trembling breath. For a moment it was all she could do not to turn on her heel and board a train bound for anywhere out of here. She shook the notion from her head. What was wrong with her? Her mother hadn't said anything that wasn't true.

Yet, for the hundredth time, Adelaide wished she'd never breathed a word about why she'd broken off her engagement with Chris. She swallowed any further details of her time with Chris in Peppin and smiled. "I had dinner with Ellie and Lawson Williams while I was there."

Rose seemed to relax a little. "Did you? That sounds lovely. Now, tell me, did you get as much writing done as you'd hoped?"

"Yes. Well, almost." Adelaide had been too distracted to get much written while she was in Peppin. However, the rest of the trip made up for that. "The change of scenery helped me figure out what was wrong with my heroine."

"Good! Then you'll have plenty of time for all of our social engagements."

"Oh." Disappointment filled her voice, but Rose didn't seem to notice. Adelaide shook her head slightly. Why was it so hard to remember that her mother had no interest in Adelaide's books? Although Rose had never expressly said so, it was obvious the woman thought that writing dime novels was a waste of time and a borderline vulgar means of making money. Adelaide tried not to let that disdain affect her. After all, her mother had never read a single one of her stories, so Rose was hardly an authority on the subject.

"You do remember that we're having a garden party at our house this afternoon, don't you?"

She smiled as pleasantly as possible while wondering if her mother had truly mentioned this before. Sometimes Rose liked to spring things on her at the last minute so that she wouldn't have a chance to back out. Well, Adelaide could hardly back out of this since it was taking place at their house—no matter how much she might wish she could. As her mother went down the list of eligible gentlemen who were expected to attend, Adelaide stared out the window at the busy street outside the station. The energy of the city could be both exciting and overwhelming. Trolley cars zipped down the street, clanging their approach to each intersection with a jolly bell. The clop of horses' hooves sounded against brick-paved streets. Grand multistory buildings jutted toward a sky that seemed all the bigger and bolder for the city's lack of hills.

Everett greeted Rose with a hug and a circumspect kiss on the cheek. He whispered something that made Rose's tense shoulders ease completely. Finally, Rose laughed, then teased him back. Adelaide blinked at the transformation. Everett's effect on her mother was truly amazing. Somehow he knew just how to soften her edges and ease her anxiety. Even the cadence of her mother's voice was calmer now.

Why couldn't Rose relax that way around her? Adelaide blinked away the prickle of tears that threatened her vision. She had them firmly under control by the time she climbed into the carriage with her family. It wasn't long before they reached the Holden Mansion. Blossoming magnolia trees shaded the long sidewalk that led to the sprawling green-and-white two-story home. As soon as she entered, a maid rushed her upstairs where a hot bath waited. Adelaide washed away the dust of her travels, then barely had a chance to unpack a few essentials before it was time to dress for the party.

Clad in a mint green walking dress and flowered hat, Adelaide stood beside Rose and Everett on the back patio where they welcomed the guests to their extensive lawn and garden. Most of the attendees were far closer to being acquaintances than true friends. Part of that was her fault. Adelaide focused so much on the imaginary worlds she created with her pen and ink that she didn't pay much attention to the real one. It didn't help that she'd never felt as though she belonged in this world. Though society had been polite and welcoming, she was certain they knew it, too. After all, she wasn't a Holden like her mother. She was simply Adelaide Harper—the daughter of a no-good traveling salesman.

"I think most of our guests have arrived," Rose said, then nodded toward a small group of young men and women who were laughing together. "Adelaide, dear, why don't you join that nice group of young people? Try to make some friends and, please, for my sake, don't mention your books."

Adelaide stiffened, then watched her mother walk away.

Everett stayed behind to give her arm a gentle squeeze. "She means well, Adelaide."

Not in the mood for comfort or company, Adelaide shied from his touch and strode toward a hidden corner of the garden behind the greenhouse. This was her safe haven. An oak tree stretched its branches over an extremely comfortable wooden bench that she often curled up on to think or write or daydream. Today she paced in front of it. A familiar, slow-burning anger flickered to life inside her.

Why was it so hard to be the woman her mother wanted her to be? Perhaps it was because Adelaide didn't like that woman. She was weak, superficial and controllable. She never dared speak her mind. She was boring and vapid. She was nothing like the person Adelaide used to be. The one she'd been in Peppin.

A smile tugged at her lips at the memory of the way she'd behaved the previous day—horribly. She'd kissed the last man on earth she should've kissed, right in the middle of his family's store. She'd put up a fight when he'd dragged her into that alley. She'd certainly had no trouble venting her temper then. She'd come up with the idea to keep the story of their engagement going. And, great day in the morning, she'd enjoyed it—every bit of it. Well, except for the part where it had all come crashing down around her.

"Adelaide?"

She startled, then spun toward the voice to find one of her mother's guests had followed her. It wasn't just any guest, though. It was Bertrand Milney, the man Rose had been trying to pair her up with for the last three months. He fit all of her mother's requirements to a T. He was successful, well-known in Houston's elite circles, and…well, rather plain. Adelaide might not have minded that so much if they had some sort of innate connection, spark or even common interest. Unfortunately, that wasn't the case. However, he'd always been kind and respectful toward her, so she'd done her best to be pleasant without actually encouraging his attentions.

His pale gray eyes latched on to her with concern. "Are you all right?"

"I'm fine. Was there something you needed?"

"Just a moment of your time, if that's all right." He didn't wait for her answer. Instead, he clasped his hands behind his back and gazed at the stone pathway beneath his feet in deep contemplation. "You see, there comes a time in each man's life where he begins to think quite seriously about his future."

Oh, no.

"That future can never be complete without a proper companion—a wife."

She sank to the wooden bench and barely held back a sigh.

"I've come to regard you fondly." His lanky form bent down to one knee. "Your mother says that you've spoken of your feelings for me—"

"Oh, she did? I see. Did she happen to tell you what those feelings were?" Adelaide had told her mother more than once that she wasn't interested in anything more than friendship with Bertrand.

"She didn't have to say anything. I know you care for me, too, but please don't interrupt."

Her eyebrows rose. She bit her lip to hold back a laugh. This was the third proposal her mother had managed to procure for her in three years. So far, it was simultaneously the best and worst of the lot.

Adelaide was impressed by her mother's effort. Only three months into the year and already she'd prompted a suitor to propose. She was far ahead of schedule. At this rate, she might be able to up the average.

Bertrand seemed to realize he'd made a mistake, for he winced. "It's only that I've memorized everything. As I was saying…"

Suddenly, his words faded to mere background noise. Adelaide narrowed her eyes and tilted her head as she watched an intruder climb over the fence behind him, landing in the grass with a loud *oomph*. Straightening, the man brushed the dirt from his knees and the palms of his hands. She'd recognized him immediately, of course, and the flood of relief she felt upon being in his presence again was downright unsettling. She stood and walked toward him. "Chris Johansen, what in the world? What are you doing here? Why did you jump our fence?"

His blue eyes caught on hers. A sheepish grin tilted his lips. He lifted his chin in a quick greeting. "Hello there, Adelaide. Nice to see you again. Your servants refused to let me into the house without an invitation. My pa and I didn't hop a train and come all this way to get turned away at the door."

She shook her head. She wouldn't allow herself to entertain any silly notions about his intentions—no matter how fast her foolish heart tried to race. "I don't understand."

"He wants to apologize, is all. I told him—" The sound of a throat clearing interrupted him. He glanced behind her and lifted a brow. "Am I interrupting something?"

Adelaide whirled to find Bertrand still kneeling before the bench with his elbow resting against his knee. A sapphire ring gleamed in his hand. Bertrand stood, his chest puffing out a bit. "You most certainly are. You've ruined my proposal. I've forgotten the entire thing."

"Honestly, Bertrand, it doesn't matter. I'm sorry, but I wasn't going to accept your offer of marriage."

"Of course you were. Your mother gave me her blessing. She said you—"

Chris made a sound somewhere between a scoff

and a laugh. "Your mother gave *him* her blessing. That's rich."

"Excuse me?" Bertrand glared at Chris, then turned to Adelaide. "Is he why you're turning me down? Who is this man to you? Some secret beau? Is that why you were hiding back here? You were planning to meet him, weren't you?"

"I was…" Her adamant protests died a sudden death at the birth of a new idea. Oh, she shouldn't. She couldn't. Well, she could, but she *really* shouldn't.

It had worked for Chris, though, for almost four years. Imagine the progress she could make on her career in four long years! She'd be entirely independent by then. All she had to do was put on a convincing show while Chris was here, which surely wouldn't be for long. When he left, she'd be set. Her mother might not stop throwing other men at her. However, Adelaide would be able to tell those men she was taken, which should keep them from proposing. Rose would be absolutely livid about Adelaide's choice of beau and possible groom…so much so that having a daughter settled down to the quiet life of a spinster writer would seem far more palatable in comparison.

Doing her best to hide the smile playing at her lips, Adelaide lifted her chin. She allowed the tears she'd held at bay all morning to well in her eyes. That gave her a tragic air as she said, "I'm sorry you found out this way, Bertrand. But, I suppose it's only right that you know the truth. Just please…don't tell my mother."

Chapter Four

Chris narrowed his eyes and turned to stare at Adelaide in disbelief. Her beautiful green eyes glistened with unshed tears. A cool wind tugged at her copper curls and teased the lace swags of her skirt. She was vulnerability mixed with defiance. It was a downright distracting sight to behold. However, the hint of a smile on her rosy lips told Chris his ears hadn't deceived him. He knew exactly what she was doing, and he'd have no part in it. "Adelaide—"

She turned and cut off his warning with one of her own. "*Hush*, darling. It's all right. I'm sure Bertrand will keep our secret, especially once he knows there's no way my mother will ever approve of a courtship between you and me."

Catching her elbow, Chris tugged her closer to level her with his gaze. He lowered his voice so that she had to listen to him closely. "Listen here—"

"You will return the favor I paid you by playing along," she whispered before sending a pointed gaze down to his lips. "Don't make me kiss you, because I am not afraid to do it if you mess this up for me."

He tamped down the laughter rising within him, knowing she wouldn't appreciate it. "You are horrible at making threats. I hope you realize that. Besides, there's no need to waste your kisses on me. Your friend is gone."

"What?" She whirled away from him to stare at the empty spot where Bertrand had been. "We can't stay here."

"Of course we can't. My pa is waiting at the front door."

"No. What I meant is that Bertrand is probably on his way to tell my mother. If she finds us here... Well, let's just say it's better if she catches up to us in a more public place. There'll be less of a scene."

Chris shook his head in confusion, but let her grab his arm and lead him forward. "I thought you said Bertrand wouldn't say anything to her."

"I only said that because I knew he would."

"So you're trying to fool your mother. Why?"

"I'll explain in a minute." She slid her hand into the crook of his arm as they stepped from the shadows of the greenhouse into the party. "Oh, good. People are dancing now. I'll ask the band to play a slow waltz. That way we'll have plenty of time to talk on the dance floor."

Chris straightened the collar of his traveling suit. He'd dressed nicely in preparation for seeing Adelaide and her family again, but he still felt out of place among what seemed to be Houston's high society. The curious stares he garnered for having Adelaide on his arm didn't help. "Adelaide, my father is waiting. Why don't we find him? He'll apologize. Then he and I will leave before your mother finds us."

"Coward." She caught the attention of one of the servers, then instructed the man to find Olan and bring him to Everett.

"I'm not afraid of your mother," he said, but she ignored him and left his side to speak with the band. When she returned, he took her hand and tried to guide her toward the house, saying, "I just think my idea would be a more peaceful solution all around."

She tugged her hand free, escaping to the large wooden platform of a dance floor where she waited with her arms in a closed hold with the air. Chris couldn't let her stand there looking that ridiculous—even if she deserved it for attempting to manipulate him. He slid into position and pressed his hand against the back of her waist to ease her closer as they waltzed. "I thought you were trying not to cause a scene."

"No, I was trying to keep my *mother* from causing a scene." Her gaze scanned the garden. "I see her, and she looks purely ticked. She's spotted us."

He felt his shoulders tense and willed himself to relax. He truly wasn't afraid of her mother, but this whole situation was making him jumpy. "Where is she?"

"Near the house. No, don't look. We have to pretend we don't see her. That way she won't be able to motion us over to talk to us. She's approaching the dance floor with Bertrand. She's stopping." Adelaide's met his gaze and smiled. "I told you this would work. We're safe for now."

"Speak for yourself. I might as well be dancing with dynamite."

She laughed. "Why, thank you."

He shook his head. "How about you tell me why you think all of this is necessary."

"It's quite simple, really. I'm tired of fending off my mother's matchmaking attempts. I'm ready to focus on my work."

"Your work?"

"Yes. You see—" Her voice faded to a whisper as a blush swept across her cheeks. "I'm a writer. I've had several books published."

He squeezed her hand. "Adelaide, that's amazing. Congratulations! I'm actually not that surprised. You were always the best writer in our class at school."

She ducked her head. "Thank you, Chris."

"What kind of books do you write?"

She shrugged. "They're just dime novels."

"Really? That's pretty much how I learned English after coming to America."

"I know. You told me dime novels were exciting enough to keep your attention and made you want to learn how to read a new language."

"Exactly. I always have a stack of them on my nightstand. I even brought one or two along in my suitcase. Hey, I'm in charge of ordering the books for the store. I'd be happy to stock some of yours. Do you write under your real name?"

She gave a short laugh. "Absolutely not. My mother would never have put up with that. Actually, Ellie said Johansen's already stocks my books. I write under the pseudonym Joe Flanders."

Chris missed a step, causing Adelaide to stumble into him. "You're Joe Flanders?"

"Yes." She tilted her head. "Are you familiar with my books? I mean, have you read any of them?"

Every single one of them. What's more, his copies were dog-eared and worn out. Joe Flanders was one of his favorite authors. Those Wild West stories were filled with outlaws, gunfights, stampedes and stagecoach robberies. In essence, everything Chris had been disappointed not to experience when he'd moved to Texas from Norway as a child.

And there was one other part of Joe Flanders's fictionalized worlds that Chris had yet to experience. The hero always got the girl. That had always been Chris's favorite aspect of the books, even if it was completely unrealistic. He ought to know. He'd been rejected by three women within the last six months. Maybe the fault lay with him. After all, he was no hero. Especially not to "Joe Flanders" if her rejection four years ago was any indication. But she sure seemed to need him now. Perhaps he could be a hero yet, though he knew better than to think he could get—or rather, keep—this girl.

He shot a covert glance toward her mother. How much trouble could it be to pretend to be Adelaide's beau until he went back to Peppin? Judging by the past few days, a whole lot. Nevertheless, she'd done the same for him once, and he'd used her as an excuse for years, so surely he owed her something in return. He'd actually be doing himself a favor, as well. Olan was expecting Chris to spend time with Adelaide— enough to either get over her or decide to fight for her. If Chris went along with her scheme, it would appear that Chris was doing exactly that. Of course, deceiving his father had gotten him into this mess in the first place. Yet, as far as Chris could see, it was the only way to give Olan what he wanted. It was also the best way to keep a sensible perspective on the situation.

A tap on his shoulder jolted him from his thoughts. He released Adelaide and turned in time to see Everett offer them a tight smile.

"Family meeting in the library. Now." The man turned on his heel, offered his wife his arm and ushered her into the house.

Chris glanced down at Adelaide. "Um, am I family?"

"Apparently. We'd better follow them." She bit her lip. "Will you…?"

"Play along?" He'd already made his decision, so he nodded. "Absolutely."

Adelaide found Chris's sudden enthusiasm for her idea surprising and extremely suspicious. However, there wasn't any time to question it.

She wound her way through the curious guests with Chris on her heels and found Olan waiting outside the door of Everett's library. Olan glanced inside the room where presumably her parents were waiting before he met her gaze with concern. "I'm not entirely sure what's going on here. Before we find out, I'd like to apologize to you. I think I may have said something that hurt your feelings while you were in Peppin."

"I appreciate the apology, Mr. Johansen. Nevertheless…" She lifted one shoulder in a helpless shrug. "You didn't say anything that wasn't true."

"Perhaps, but—"

She placed a hand on his arm to still his words and smiled. "Truly, it's all right. We should go inside."

Chris's supportive hand on her back gave her the

courage she needed to step through the library door. She lifted her chin, prepared for a battle. Everett and Rose stood in front of his large walnut desk, speaking in low tones. Rose caught sight of them first. Adelaide blinked as her mother smiled warmly.

"Well, this is *quite* a surprise. Olan, it's so nice to see you again." She offered her hand to Olan, then nodded to Chris. "And Chris…you've certainly grown up, haven't you? Won't y'all sit down? I'm afraid we won't be able to speak for long with so many guests here, but Everett says you will be here for several days. Is that right?"

That was news to Adelaide. She glanced at Chris for confirmation of that while they settled side by side on the library's settee. He was too busy watching her mother with a mixture of curiosity and confusion to notice. Adelaide couldn't blame him. Her mother's warm greeting to the Johansens had taken Adelaide off guard a bit, too.

Olan nodded, claiming a seat in one of the leather chairs Rose had indicated. "I'll only be here a couple of days. After that, I've got to get back to my store. Chris is going to stay for a while longer."

"I hope you get to see some of Houston before you leave, Olan. It truly is a lovely city." Rose clasped her hands in front of her and turned Adelaide. "Now, Adelaide, my dear, Bertrand Milney told me the strangest thing a few minutes ago. He said that he caught you having a liaison with a man fitting Chris's description, a man you claimed as your beau. Of course, I told him that he must be mistaken. Please, tell me that he is."

Adelaide stared into Rose's piercing gray eyes and felt her resolve begin to waver. Maybe it wasn't such a good idea to antagonize her mother. Yet why should choosing her own beau be upsetting to Rose? True, her mother had never trusted Chris—for good reason it turned out. Yet, wasn't that the point? Adelaide had to do something drastic if she wanted any chance at gaining her mother's approval of her writing. That was all that mattered, wasn't it?

Chris's hand covered hers, steadying her topsy-turvy thoughts. She met his gaze. He gave her a supportive nod. Her mouth opened, but the words she wanted to say wouldn't come. He transferred her hand to his other and put his free arm along the back of the settee. "Adelaide and I reconnected when she visited Peppin."

That much was true, so Adelaide nodded. "Yes, we did."

"When my father decided to visit Houston, I knew I had to see her again, so here I am." Chris had already informed her he was here to do his father's bidding by arranging the opportunity for Olan to apologize. However, his tone was so earnest that even she almost believed he had romantic feelings for her. It was a bit unnerving to know he was so good at affecting emotions he didn't feel. How many times had her birth father done that very thing? Usually, it involved Hiram pretending to be sorry for something, only to go out and do that exact same thing again.

Adelaide pulled her hand from Chris's and placed it in her lap. "If that's all, Mother, we really should get back to the party."

Olan leaned forward. "Actually, I have a question. It's been bothering me for years. Rose, what have you got against my son? Why don't you approve of him?

He's a good man, responsible, kind. He makes an honest living. What more could you want for your daughter?"

"Pa," Chris chided, tensing beside her.

Olan frowned. "What? You've got a right to know."

Rose had never liked Chris because his charm and good looks reminded her of Hiram. The news of Chris's infidelity had confirmed Rose's suspicions and clinched that dislike. Adelaide knew her mother would never speak of Hiram to visitors. The less personal explanation for Rose was Chris's dealings with Amy. Rose had wanted Adelaide to confront Chris about his infidelity since they'd first heard of it. Not to give Chris a chance to defend himself, but so that he would know that he'd been caught. Rose had also wanted Adelaide to put Amy on her guard. Adelaide had been too upset and embarrassed by the whole thing to say a word. Plus, she couldn't have borne hearing Chris's attempts to justify or excuse himself the way Hiram always had.

Rose took in Adelaide's pleading look at a glance, then turned back to Olan. "I simply don't think they're well suited as a couple."

Olan nodded. "Well, on that, we can agree."

Adelaide's eyebrows lifted. She found herself scooting closer to Chris with her chin lifted in a mix of defiance and defensiveness. "Oh? And, how can y'all be so absolutely certain of that? Perhaps we would have made a perfect couple if anyone had ever given us a chance at it."

Olan gave her a skeptical look. "The two of you have had five years' worth of chances to figure this out."

"Five years when we lived over a hundred miles

apart," Chris countered. "Besides, Pa, I thought you said I should fight for her."

"He did?" Adelaide pressed a hand to her heart. "Mr. Johansen, that is the sweetest thing, but why?"

Olan didn't bother to explain. Instead, his mouth set in a line that looked downright ornery and he glanced away as if the ceiling was the most interesting thing he'd ever seen. Adelaide didn't have time to do more than tilt her head in confusion before her mother's amused voice distracted her. "Adelaide, dear, you do realize that it was probably in your best interest not to have spent more time as a couple. Don't you?"

Stymied, Adelaide's lashes fluttered at the memory of why she'd broken off her engagement in the first place. Her mother was right. Chris was everything she hadn't wanted in a husband—untrustworthy, unfaithful and too handsome for his own good. Her voice came out rather subdued. "I suppose."

Chris's dark blue gaze shot back and forth between Adelaide and her mother. "Why is that?"

"Perhaps Adelaide will tell you some other time. Meanwhile, I must say the very idea of this courtship is perfectly ridiculous to me. However, if the two of you insist on it, I can't stop you—or so Everett tells me."

Adelaide opened her mouth to speak, but was saved from herself when Everett clapped his hands together. "All right! Now that everything is settled, let's get back to the party." He extended his arm to Rose. "Come along, my sweet. Olan, I'll send your cab on its way. My carriage will take you and Chris back to your hotel later. First, you must have something to eat."

Olan stood with a grin. "Don't mind if I do."

Rose took Everett's arm as Olan walked with them toward the study door. As their parents' voices faded into the hallway, Adelaide realized just how close she was sitting to Chris. She slid farther away. He followed her. She turned her questioning eyes on him. He lifted an eyebrow. "I repeat. Why is that?"

She fluttered her lashes innocently. "Why is what?"

"Why was it in your best interest that we had no time together as a couple?"

"Aren't you hungry? I'm hungry. I think we should…" She tried to stand but he placed his hand on the arm of the settee to block her in. She poked him just below his right rib and had the pleasure of seeing him jump almost a foot. She had little time to smirk over the fact that he was still ticklish because he caught up with her as she attempted to break for the door. He lassoed her waist and drew her in until her back met his chest. Exasperation filled his voice. "How old are you?"

She had a smart answer prepared, but all that came out was an involuntary giggle as he tickled her elbow. She freed it from his grasp, then jabbed it into his stomach softly enough that it wouldn't do any real damage. He didn't even bother to wince. She turned so that she could glance up and properly aim her disdainful look. "The same age as you, apparently."

A half smile tugged at his lips. He glanced down at hers. She held her breath. Finally, he shrugged. "Let's call it even. Now, will you settle down so we can have an honest discussion for once?"

Her gaze lowered to the top button of his shirt. "Are you sure you want to do that?"

"No, but I think it's long overdue."

She pulled in a deep breath, then eased from his

hold to walk over to the window that looked out onto the back lawn. What did it matter if she told him? Everything had happened so long ago. Surely it wouldn't hurt to be straightforward with him now. Also, there was no danger of her being persuaded by him to continue their long-dead relationship. Her heart was safe. She sought his gaze as he joined her by the window. "My mother was referring to your previous courtship of Amy Bradley."

He frowned. "What does that have to do with this?"

She stared at him. "Then you don't deny that you courted her?"

"Why would I? Everyone in Peppin knows about it, and how she threw me over for the fellow she eventually married. What does any of that have to do with us?"

"Everything!"

"Look, if you didn't want me courting other girls, you should have married me."

She gave an astonished laugh. "As if that would have stopped you."

Confusion filled his eyes. "What?"

"Did you or did you not express an interest in Amy while you and I were still engaged?"

"Of course not."

"Did you walk her home from school? Did you take her to the harvest dance? Did you tell her she was pretty?"

He froze. "Yes. Now that I think of it, I did all of those things. I had to pass Bradley's Boardinghouse on the way home, so, since you weren't there, she and I walked with each other. Neither of us had anyone to go to the dance with so I didn't see the harm in us going together. I doubt I was a very good escort because I spent most of the night playing my fiddle with the band. As for me telling her she was pretty, any gentleman would say the same when a girl gets gussied up to go somewhere with him. I didn't actually start courting her until after you broke off our engagement."

She laughed. "Do you really expect me to believe that you didn't have any romantic feelings for her while you were doing all of that?"

"Believe what you want. The truth won't change. I only had friendly feelings for her until I needed..."

"Until you needed...?"

"To get over you," he finally admitted lowly.

Drawn in by his appearance of sincerity, she caught herself swaying toward him. She swallowed and forced herself to take a step back. *Oh, he* is *good.*

"Wait a minute." He searched her face. "Are you saying—is that why you broke our engagement? Because you thought something was going on between me and Amy?"

She clasped her hands behind her back, then lifted her chin. "Amy and I wrote to each other for a while after I moved to Houston. Like everyone else in Peppin, she didn't know about our engagement. I suppose that was why she had no qualms about sending me a detailed account of every indication you gave her of your romantic feelings for her."

He shook his head, a wry smile tilting his lips. "That sounds like Amy, all right. She was always pretty quick to believe every fellow was in love with her. Well, no matter. She liked being admired, but had no intention of marrying me. Turned me down flat when I proposed."

"You...proposed to her, too?"

"Who *haven't* I proposed to at this point?" Frustration filled his voice as he turned away to pace. That was probably a good thing since it took her a moment or two to close her gaping mouth. He ran his fingers through his hair. "I suppose Ruth. She's the seamstress in town now, but she's all business. How can you court a woman when you can't even get a smile out of her?"

Adelaide held up a stilling hand. "I'm sorry. I can't help being curious. Exactly who else have you proposed to besides me and Amy?"

"Let's see. There was Amy's younger sister Isabelle. You remember her, don't you? Before that, I proposed to Maddie, sort of in jest. She nearly dumped a coffeepot in my lap at the mere suggestion. Ellie didn't let me get as far as a proposal. Helen...you don't know her, but she married Quinn before I had a chance to ask her."

Adelaide shook her head in disbelief. "I thought your proposal to me was sincere."

"It was!"

"So were your proposals to all of these other women, I suppose."

"I told you I have to find a wife. I honestly don't understand why you seem so upset about this. Like I said, if you didn't want me wooing other women—"

"I should have married you?" She gave a mirthless laugh. "No, thank you."

His jaw tightened. "Yeah, you said that...once before, in a letter. I think I'm clear on that. I also think it was a mistake for me to agree to pre—"

Seeing a flash of movement near the door of the room, she caught the lapels of Chris's coat and tugged him closer for a silencing kiss. He stiffened slightly before hesitantly kissing her back. She released him at the sound of a throat clearing behind them.

Her stepfather glanced back and forth between them with his arms crossed. "I'm not a man who enjoys keeping secrets from his wife. She trusts me to tell her the truth. It took me a long time to build that trust, and I don't intend to lose it. If I find out the relationship between you is not what you've presented it to be, I *will* tell her. So…" A hint of a sparkle lit his otherwise stern gaze. "You'd better not let me find out, and you sure better not tell me anything you don't want her to know. Furthermore, this conversation never happened. Is that understood?"

"Yes, sir," they replied together.

He gave them a firm nod before leaving the room. Chris sank onto a nearby chair, then met Adelaide's gaze with a mix of uncertainty and amusement. "Our parents…"

She perched on the arm of the settee. "They are something else."

"For sure."

"I mean, I love them."

"Of course!"

"But…"

He sighed. "Yeah."

She shook her head, then reached across the expanse to place a hand on his arm. "We can handle this, though, if we work together. Are we? Working together, I mean."

He glanced from her hand to her eyes. "As far as I can see, I'm not getting much out of this agreement. However, I'll go through with it on one condition."

"What's that?"

"We have *got* to come up with a better signal to tell each other to stop talking."

She laughed. "Deal."

They shook on it, and, in that moment, the years seemed to melt away. She had her best friend back, her study partner, perhaps even her champion. One fateful kiss all those years ago had changed him into her fiancé and, subsequently, something that never should have been. Yes, kisses were powerful things when it came to Chris Johansen. She just had to remember that they were nothing uncommon. Even proposals from him were a dime a dozen. The only thing special about any of it was the heartache that came with it. She'd made it through their last courtship without experiencing too much of that. Next time, she might not be so fortunate. That was why there wouldn't be a next time—not for her, and definitely not with Chris.

Chapter Five

Hours later, Chris still couldn't understand what Adelaide had gotten so upset about. Why did it matter to her whom he wooed or courted or proposed to after their engagement was over? She'd given up her claim on him long ago and obviously hadn't changed her mind about that. And he was glad of that. The last thing he wanted was for either of them to start softening toward the other romantically. He'd been down that path once before and had no intention of venturing there again.

Of course, he'd also had no intention of accepting her mother's invitation for him and his father to stay at the Holdens' house while they were in Houston, either. Now here he was lugging suitcases up to the rooms she'd assigned to them. Chris paused at the top of the stairs to glance down at Olan, who was only a few steps behind him. Keeping his voice to a low whisper, Chris asked, "Don't you think it's a little strange that Mrs. Holden is being so nice about all of this?"

"Who can understand the workings of a woman's mind?" Olan passed him to open the door to the first bedroom. "She seemed so insulted by my initial refusal to stay here that I thought it prudent to agree. It probably worked out for the best, since this will give you plenty of time to spend with Adelaide and a chance to get to know her again."

Chris gave a reluctant nod, not altogether sure that spending more time with Adelaide was such a good idea. They seemed to have a talent for getting each other into trouble whenever they were together. As far as getting to know her better...there was already so much about her he hadn't forgotten that he wasn't entirely sure that was necessary or wise.

Shaking the thoughts from his head, he deposited his father's suitcase on the bed, then turned a concerned gaze to Olan, noticing that the man seemed a bit out of breath. "How are you feeling, Pa?"

Olan waved aside Chris's concern and sat on the bed to open his suitcase. "I'm a little tired from our travels, but I'll be fine after a good night's sleep."

"All right. If you start feeling poorly or need anything at all during the night, I'll be in the room across the hall. Don't be afraid to wake me."

"Fine. Fine. Now, off you go. Have a good night."

Chris wished his father the same, but soon found himself tossing and turning in a comfortable yet unfamiliar bed. He turned the gas-lit sconce beside the bed on low and reached for one of the books he'd placed on the nightstand. Of course it turned out to be one written by Joe Flanders—hardly the distraction he was looking for. His stomach provided that with a rumble that reminded him of how little he'd eaten at the Holden's party earlier. He'd been too busy being introduced to all of Adelaide's lady friends, then joining them all in what had seemed to be a never-ending game of croquet. The Holdens had encouraged them to feel right at home so Chris tossed aside his covers, grabbed a robe and went in search of the kitchen. Once he found it, he hesitated at the sight of Everett standing at the counter near the ice box. The man glanced up from the plate of food he was making. "Hungry?"

"Yes, sir."

Everett nodded to a large oak kitchen table that was probably where the Holdens' staff took their meals. "Have a seat. There are plenty of leftovers for the both of us. I never do manage to eat much at those parties. Too busy socializing with advertisers, I suppose."

"Adelaide told me you run a newspaper here in Houston."

"Yes, I'm the owner and editor of the *Houston Gazette*. I was in Peppin to do a little research for a story I'm working on. I was surprised to find a town of that size didn't have a newspaper of its own."

"I guess most folks get their news at the café in town. Of course, a good portion of that is just gossip. We do have a bulletin board in the mercantile for people to put up—well, I guess you'd call them classifieds." Chris took the plate Everett offered him with a quick word of thanks before continuing. "If there is anything major going on in town, I put up a little notice about it for folks and try to spread the news through word of mouth. That usually works pretty well because most folks have to stop in at the mercantile at some point."

Everett lifted a brow and took a seat across the table. "So, you're a bit of newsman yourself."

"Oh, I don't know about that."

"Why not? It sounds like you're disseminating facts to the masses in writing and by word of mouth. That isn't any different than what I do every day. What's the most exciting thing you've told people about in the last few months?"

Chris bit his lip thoughtfully. "We had a fire in town on New Year's Eve. Afterward, some folks decided to hold a benefit concert to raise money to buy the town a new fire engine. I helped spread the word about that. Pretty much the whole town showed up. We raised enough money for the fire engine. It was great."

Everett smiled a faraway look in his eyes. "That would have made an interesting news story."

"It might have, at that, but who would read it? Pretty much everyone in town was there. They already know what happened."

"There's little that people like more than seeing their own names in print. Better yet, the story would serve as a record keeper for the town so that future generations could look back and see how their parents and grandparents came together to do something positive in the face of tragedy. You could even do a follow-up story that answers some of the unresolved questions. For instance, what kind of fire engine is the town going to purchase? Why was that model chosen? When is it going to be purchased? When will it arrive? Who is going to be responsible for its upkeep and use? Where will it be stored? Don't you think the public deserves to know the answer to those questions since they are the ones paying for it?"

Obviously, the answer was yes, but Chris couldn't seem to form the word. His mind was too busy grappling with all of the questions Everett had just asked.

Chris realized that he wanted to know the answers. What's more, he wanted to be the one doing the asking. He leaned forward. "How did you come up with all of those questions so quickly?"

"I've had a lot of practice at this." Everett paused to give him a gentle yet measuring look before leaning forward, as well. "I think you could come up with a few questions yourself. Tap into your own curiosity. What concerns you or interests you about this topic?"

Chris thought about it for a moment, then shrugged. "I guess the main thing I've been wondering about is how the new fire engine will affect the volunteer firefighters. How is it going to change the protocols they already have? Who is going to train them to use the engine? That sort of thing."

Everett grinned. "You're a natural. I'd like you to come by my newspaper on Monday to take a look around. While you're here, let's see if we can teach you the basics of the trade and send you back to Peppin as a reporter equipped to write the next big story. Who knows? Maybe one day you'll be the one to start your town's first newspaper."

"Mr. Holden, I'm not sure that's a good idea."

"Why wouldn't it be?"

"Because..." Chris was going to run Johansen's Mercantile one day. That was the plan. It had been the plan for nearly a decade. While he was still trying to find a way out of marrying a mail-order bride, he knew that taking over the mercantile was nonnegotiable. Olan's health was questionable at best and his brothers were too young to shoulder the responsibility of running the store, so Chris needed to be ready to take over if or when the doctors advised his father to stop working. He couldn't allow himself to be distracted by an outside interest like newspaper reporting. Not when his family's main source of income was at stake.

Everett stood and clasped Chris's shoulder. "Just go for a tour. Anything you decide to do or not do after that is up to you. I won't pressure you. I simply like to encourage talent when I see it. I'd better get back to my room now. When you're finished eating, simply leave your plate in the sink and someone will take care of it. I'll see you in the morning for breakfast, then church."

Chris offered a parting smile and a nod. Talent. No one had ever used that word in regard to him except when it came to his fiddle. That was a safe talent—something encouraged by his parents. He couldn't see them approving of him becoming a newspaperman. The idea was completely impractical. He knew nothing about newspapers and even if he learned something while he was here, it didn't mean he'd ever be able to start a newspaper in Peppin. No, it'd be far more worthwhile to focus on the slightly more attainable goal of finding himself a wife. In all the hoopla surrounding Adelaide's return, he'd managed to forget something. He was still running out of options and time. The Bachelor List had been no help. Neither had its matchmaking author. Who else was there to appeal to?

The answer that arose within him seemed to resound in the stillness. God. He could appeal to God. That was the one thing he hadn't done, the one Person he hadn't talked to about this. Why? Because he was more than a little afraid that God was on his parents' side in this. The Bible did say that Chris should honor his father and mother. What if marriage to Brigitte Salomon—or whatever her name might be—really was God's plan for him and for her?

Chris shook his head, unable to even consider that. Perhaps he'd wait awhile and exhaust what few possibilities were left for him. Then, if he was truly desperate, he'd take the chance of asking God for help in finding a wife. First he had to make it through the rest of his stay in Houston. That was a situation Chris didn't mind bringing to God because he had a feeling he was going to need all the help he could get.

Morning fog still clung to the ground when Adelaide stepped onto the veranda after an early breakfast with her family and the Johansens. She eased her shawl closer around her shoulders while waiting for the carriage to be brought around to take them all to church. The front door opened behind her. She turned, only realizing when she saw Olan that she'd hoped it would be Chris. Olan caught sight of her and offered her a smile. "A little chillier than normal for Texas, isn't it?"

"Hopefully the sun will come out and warm things up." She paused for a second. Then, because Everett had long since taught her the value of being direct, she addressed something that had been bothering her since the so-called family meeting yesterday. "Mr. Johansen, you asked my mother to be honest about the misgivings she had about Chris. I'd like you to extend the same courtesy to me. Why did you encourage Chris to fight for me if you don't think we're a good match?"

After a long, quiet moment, he finally shrugged. "You asked for honesty, so I'll give it to you. I can tell him until I'm blue in the face that the two of you aren't suited, but he won't believe it until he discovers it himself. The more time y'all spend with each other, the faster he'll figure it out. Once he does, he'll be able to move on and find happiness with someone else."

She longed to ask him why he thought Chris hadn't moved on, but she had little doubt that Olan was using what he'd seen in Peppin and Houston as his evidence—evidence she knew was false. Surely Chris couldn't still have feelings for her when he'd pursued so many women in her absence. He'd been trying to find a bride of his own choosing so she had to grant that he hadn't done anything dishonorable—once their engagement was over. However, all that meant was that he'd been prepared to marry another woman multiple times. Those weren't exactly the actions of a man pining for a lost love. Perhaps that simply meant her mother had been right all along, and whatever emotions Adelaide and Chris had felt for each other had been immature and underdeveloped. A childish infatuation rather than love.

As though conjured by her thoughts, Chris stepped onto the porch looking debonair in a Sunday-go-to-meeting suit. His vibrant, navy blue eyes glanced black and forth between her and his father as he picked up on the tension in the air. "What are y'all talking about?"

"You, of course," she said, not even realizing she was reaching for his hand until he caught her hand in his. Chris's inquiring look went unanswered, for Rose stepped onto the porch, still putting on her gloves.

Her gaze immediately settled on their joined hands. Adelaide battled the urge to remove her hand from Chris's gentle hold. That would, after all, defeat the entire purpose of the exhibition. However, she couldn't help feeling the uncomfortable prickles of warmth that spread across her cheeks until Rose focused on something over Adelaide's shoulder.

"Ah, here comes the carriage. It's right on time… and so is the buggy." Rose turned to look at her husband as he stepped through the door. "You don't think we'll all fit in the carriage?"

"I thought Chris and Adelaide might want to do a little courting."

Adelaide felt her eyebrows rise at the realization that her stepfather was matchmaking. In fact, he had been since the moment she'd divulged the truth about her past with Chris to him in Peppin. That's why he hadn't tried to dissuade her during the Johansen's put-together wedding ceremony. It was why he hadn't blown the whistle on this second attempt at a faux courtship. What's more, she wasn't the only one who'd come to that conclusion if the thick, uncomfortable silence descending on the veranda was any indication. She nearly cringed at the utter awkwardness of it all. Finally the silence was broken by Olan's resigned sigh. Everett grinned at Chris as though impervious to the disapproving glare of his wife. "You don't mind driving, do you, son?"

Chris's face looked almost frozen—a sure sign that he was desperately trying to keep a straight face. "No, sir. I don't mind."

"Good. Just follow the carriage, then. If we get separated, Adelaide knows the way. Let's get going, shall we?" Everett led the way down the front steps. After a regal lift of her chin, Rose swept down the steps behind him. Olan shook his head as he followed them, murmuring something in Norwegian. Adelaide waited until the carriage door had closed before daring to meet Chris's laughing gaze. "It isn't funny. They're driving me crazy. There's enough tension in the air to put the humidity to shame. I'm like a sponge soaking it all up."

He caught her arms and squeezed them gently. "Don't let it get to you. Remember why you're doing this."

"For my writing and to stop my mother's match-making attempts."

"Right. Wait. How does this help your writing? I don't think you ever explained that."

It didn't seem particularly nice to tell him that she was counting on the fact that her mother would put up with anything—even Adelaide's writing career—rather than see Adelaide married to him. Instead, she shrugged. "It's complicated, but I'm certain what we're doing is going to help."

She thought it prudent to head for the buggy before he could ask any more questions. He helped her into it, then took the reins, hurrying to ease into line behind the carriage, which was waiting for them at the front gate. After they turned onto the street, he sent her a sideways glance. "I'm debating whether or not I want to know what you and my father were discussing earlier. On one hand, forewarned is forearmed. On the other, I think we need to stop trying to figure out what our parents are up to and stay focused on what it is that we're trying to accomplish."

"Well, I for one think it might be refreshing not to talk or think about them at least until we get out of church."

He shot her a heart-fluttering grin. "Deal."

She leaned her shoulder into the cushioned seat-back to survey him. "What are you going to do when you go back to Peppin? You still don't have a bride."

"I reckon I'll just have to keep going down my list of possibilities. There are still a few women left on it, though I think my chances with them might be slim."

She narrowed her eyes, unable to decide which was worse—that he'd made a list of women to woo or that there were only a "few" left in town that he hadn't gotten to yet. In the end, she decided that she didn't have the energy to challenge him on either statement. Even so, she couldn't help but wonder if the friends she'd left behind in Peppin were blind, deaf or dumb. For all of his maddening qualities, Chris was still a catch. How could he still be unmarried? Of course, there was the possibility that they'd known exactly what they were doing by rejecting his suit. Adelaide might not have warned Amy about Chris's wandering ways, but that didn't mean the women in town hadn't warned each other.

She sighed and barely resisted the urge to reach over and pat his knee in sympathy. She really shouldn't feel badly for him, given his roguish tendencies. However, it was undeniable that he was in a just as sticky a situation as she was. Perhaps that was why it was so easy for her to feel an affinity for him. The least she could do was try to take his mind off his troubles for a moment. "So, tell me, what do you do for amusement in Peppin when you aren't chasing—uh, I mean *looking* for a bride?"

"Well, the mercantile hasn't left me much free time lately. When I do have a moment of my own I like to play my fiddle, spend time with family and friends, and attend whatever social the town might be putting on." He glanced around at the grand buildings lining the street. "I guess that must sound pretty boring to you after living here for so long. You've got such a full life here."

She gave a soft laugh of disbelief. "What makes you say that?"

"The books you write. The house you live in. All of those friends at the social. I could go on."

"Please don't. The books I write have nothing to do with where I live. In fact, I write better when I'm away from home. That house belongs to my stepfather. As nice as it is, I've no claim on it besides what he allows me. Those people at the social are more acquaintances than friends. I don't have any close friends here. All of those women around my age who wouldn't leave us alone last night were far more interested in you than they were in me."

He frowned as he slowly turned into the church's lot. "Why would they be interested in me? Because they were curious about your new beau?"

"No. I mean, I'm sure they were a little curious, but that wasn't the whole reason. You know that." The blank look he sent as he set the brake surely had to be manufactured. She shook her head at him. "You're going to make me say it, aren't you?"

"Say what?"

She rolled her eyes. "That you are ridiculously handsome."

His eyebrows rose. His neck and cheeks flushed. He glanced away, then back at her. "I'm—what—you think I'm—really?"

She stared at him, finding his genuine surprise and embarrassment confusing to say the least. It was almost as though he wasn't aware of the effect he had on women. That didn't make any sense. For a rogue to use his charm to his advantage, he had to know that he possessed it and understand how to wield it. Either way, it couldn't hurt to tell the truth. "Of course I do."

His somewhat bashful smile was absolutely heart-melting. "Thank you, but that doesn't explain why you don't have any close friends here."

"I didn't see the point of making any at first. After all, I was planning to return to Peppin in a few short months to..." She stopped herself from continuing, but the words hovered between them anyway. She almost wanted to speak them after all, to finally acknowledge exactly how much of her life she'd sabotaged by clinging to the idea that they would marry one day. Looking back, she could see the foolishness of it all. Perhaps if she'd been friendlier, more willing to really settle into Houston, then she wouldn't feel so alone now. At the very least, society would have been more accepting of her if she'd allowed Everett to go through with his plan to formally adopt her before she legally became an adult. It had seemed unnecessary to become a Holden since she'd thought her last name would soon be changing to Johansen.

Lost in her reverie, she was barely aware of Chris hopping from the buggy and tying the reins to a hitch-

ing post before he was at her side to help her step
down. She made the mistake of meeting his gaze and
couldn't look away. Up close, it was easy to be mes-
merized by the way his eyes darkened to a rich midnight as they searched hers. His voice was quiet and
deep. "What changed your mind about us, Adelaide?
Your letter said that this city had made you outgrow
us—outgrow me. From what you've said on the ride
here, that doesn't seem to be the case. Surely that small
misunderstanding about Amy wasn't reason enough
to call everything off."

"I think we have different definitions of what quali-
fies as 'small,' but no." She stepped past him toward
the church, glancing back to say, "That wasn't the
only reason."

It had been, instead, the tipping point. She'd become convinced that Chris was not a man of integ-
rity and that a life with him would only be another
version of what she'd grown up watching. She hadn't
wanted to end up like her mother, who'd been married at sixteen to a man who'd made marriage nearly
unbearable. Adelaide wasn't sixteen now, though. She
wasn't seventeen, either, which was the age she'd been
when Chris had proposed. Enough time had passed
for her to become someone she didn't altogether recognize. And Chris? His words often seemed to confirm her fears that he'd grown into exactly the kind of
man she'd feared he would. But sometimes the honesty in his voice and the uncertainty in his eyes made
her think there was a possibility she was doing him a
disservice by assuming the worst.

Now, *that* was a fearsome thought, and one she
wasn't sure she had the courage to entertain. It would

be much safer to continue believing the worst. However, to be absolutely honest with herself, she had to admit that she couldn't make out his character at all. For now, it was best to leave it that.

Chapter Six

A slow, steady drizzle pattered on the windowpane, almost drowning out the ticking of the large grandfather clock that stood sentry in the corner of the doctor's waiting room. A spectacled young man sat at a desk to greet visitors and direct patients through the doors to the appropriate specialist.

Chris had never been this nervous—not even when proposing to all of those women back home. He wished Olan hadn't insisted on seeing the doctor alone. The waiting was becoming unbearable. He'd flipped through every magazine on the low-slung table in front of his chair, including the *Ladies' Home Journal*. None of them had made the last hour and a half pass any faster. He transferred his attention to the other family members waiting for loved ones and found a fashionably attired woman stealing a covert look at him. She blushed at being caught, then turned her attention back to whatever she was reading. Chris rubbed his jaw as if that would hide the heat rising there. Ever since Adelaide had said that bit about him being handsome he'd suddenly become aware of the fact that women looked at him a lot. He wasn't sure how he'd failed to notice that before, but now he couldn't stop and it was downright disconcerting.

Yesterday had been the most uncomfortable experience he'd had in a while. At first, Rose's suggestion that they all attend a performance by the Faust Opera Company had seemed like the perfect way to spend an afternoon in a big city. However, halfway through the first act of *Romeo and Juliet*, Chris had realized her suggestion might not have entirely been prompted by the Johansens' well-known love of music. After sitting through the tragic tale of star-crossed lovers who defy their family's expectations and eventually commit suicide, Chris had once again found himself besieged by Adelaide's "friends." He'd done his best to use the attention they paid to him as an opportunity to foster what he'd hoped could be the start of a friendship between her and the other women in her society. Unfortunately, most of their questions and comments seemed to revolve around him and his visit to Houston. At some point, Adelaide had slipped away. He'd eventually spotted her with his father, discussing music if Olan's animated expression was any indication. Eventually, Everett had been kind enough to extricated him from the conversation.

Adelaide hadn't said much on the carriage ride to her house. Chris hadn't been sure what the thoughtful look in her eye meant, and certainly hadn't wanted to broach the subject in front of their parents. All in all, he'd be happy to never speak of it.

Chris jumped to his feet as his father finally stepped into the waiting room. With only a quick glance at Chris, Olan headed straight for the hat rack near the front door. Chris caught up with him in the hallway. "Pa, slow down. What's going on? Did you see the specialist? What did he say?"

Olan turned to face Chris with blue eyes flashing in anger. "He told me to go get my head examined."

"What?"

"He did. Look." Olan pulled a folded paper from his pocket. "He referred me to a psychiatrist."

"A psychiatrist?" Chris took the paper his father offered and frowned at it. "There must be some mistake."

"The mistake was me coming to Houston to see a specialist. He was supposed to help. Instead, he's acting like it's all in my head. Well, I'm not going to any psychiatrist. I've got a wife and five young'uns who need a father. I'm not going let them put in me in an asylum just because I'm having heart flutters."

"Pa, no one is going to put you in an asylum. You know that. He must have misunderstood something you said. We didn't come all this way to leave without any real answers. I'll go talk to him and figure out what this is all about. Meanwhile, why don't you order some dinner at the restaurant we saw on the first floor? I'll join you there in a few minutes."

Olan wavered for a second before nodding abruptly. Then he turned on his heel and headed down the stairs. Chris went back into the waiting room and persuaded the man at the front desk to tell him where to find his father's doctor. A moment later, Chris knocked on the doctor's half-open office door. "Dr. Morrison, I'm Olan Johansen's son Chris. I wanted to speak with you about the referral you gave him."

Caution warred with concern on the young doctor's face, but he stood and waved Chris into his office. "Yes, please come in. Have a seat. Is your father all right? He seemed agitated when he left."

"He's still agitated, but I'm hoping this is all some sort of misunderstanding." Chris sat in one of the chairs beside the examining table. "He says you told him to see a psychiatrist about his heart flutters."

"That true, I did." Dr. Morrison smiled and held up a hand to ward off Chris's next question. "Thankfully, your father gave me leave to talk to you about his condition so I'm free to explain what I was trying to tell him. As you may know, I've been in correspondence with Dr. Williams, your father's regular doctor in Peppin, so I am fully aware of your father's health history. I conducted my own examination, including a few extra tests that Dr. Williams didn't have access to in Peppin. My resulting opinion corroborates Dr. Williams's original diagnosis."

This was the first Chris had heard of Doc diagnosing Olan with anything. His father had always said Doc Williams hadn't been able to figure out what was wrong with him. Chris frowned. "What diagnosis is that?"

"Mr. Johansen has a healthy heart—especially for a man his age."

"Then why does he have heart pains and flutters and shortness of breath when stressful things happen?"

Dr. Morrison leaned forward, excited. "Ah, you see? There it is. You've discovered the cause on your own. It's anxiety. Now, everyone at one time or another experiences a sense of panic or feels the strain of stress on their body. However, your father stays in such a high state of stress on a normal basis that anything out of the ordinary compounds the problem and displays itself as a physical symptom. His heart rate goes up suddenly. The change of pace creates the feeling of a flutter. He starts breathing more rapidly, not giving his lungs a chance to expand fully. Less air gets in, leading to less oxygen in his blood so he starts to feel dizzy and light-headed. I went down the list of symptoms with your father. He's experienced every one of them. Yet, for some reason, he refuses to believe that the problem is anxiety and is convinced it's his heart."

"Is that why you referred him to a psychiatrist?"

"My intention was to send him to someone who can help him deal with managing stress. That person doesn't have to be a psychiatrist, but it needs to be someone whom he will talk to, someone he'll allow to help him get to the root of his problem. If he can lower his general state of stress, he won't experience as many physical symptoms when he faces new or unexpected stressors."

"So he isn't dying?"

"No, he isn't. However, staying in a constant state of anxiety can eventually have a negative impact on his health."

"I understand." Chris shook his head, then ran his fingers through his hair. "Thank you for explaining all of this. This has certainly been an eye-opening discussion for me."

"You're more than welcome. I'm going to send my findings to Dr. Williams. I'm sure he will continue helping your father to the best of his ability. I hope you and your father find a way to work through this."

"So do I." Chris shook the man's hand, then took

his time making his way downstairs. He couldn't quite seem to grasp everything he'd just heard. His father wasn't dying. That was a huge relief. However, it seemed that Doc Williams had been telling Olan that from the beginning. Why hadn't Olan believed him? Why hadn't he told the family the doctor's true opinion even if he thought it to be wrong? They'd all been so worried, fearing the worst. It didn't make a lick of sense.

Chris's thoughts must have shown on his face as he joined his father because Olan immediately became defensive. "You can't believe what that doctor said. I know the problem must have to do with my heart. There's no way my health is acting up just because I'm facing a little trouble."

"What kind of trouble are you facing, Pa? I mean, besides what you're getting right now from me because you let us all think you were dying."

"Don't take that tone with me, young man." Olan placed a hand on his heart. The angrier Olan got the more Texan his vocabulary became, even as his Norwegian accent thickened. "Ridiculous flutters. I'm no swoony woman. I can handle my life without any interference from young whippersnappers like you and that no-good doctor."

"Don't get excited. Just calm down and—"

"Stop telling me that. Apparently, I'm not going to die from it, so I'll get excited if I want to get excite—" Olan ran out of breath and grabbed the table to steady himself.

"Pa." It would never stop being scary seeing his father like this, regardless of what explanation the doctors gave him. "Please, just take a deep breath."

"I'm going home to Peppin. Stay here if you want. Court that girl. Get her out your system. Then come home."

As if Chris would let his father travel all that way alone. "I'll go with you. You were right about Adelaide and me. She and I aren't going to last. I see that now. We're going to go back to Peppin and figure out what to do from there. Let's have lunch first, all right? It's better than eating on the train."

"Fine," Olan said, but the look in his eye showed he wasn't fooled. He knew Chris was only trying to give him time to compose himself.

Motioning to the waiter, Chris ordered before his father had a chance to get any more ideas about leaving the restaurant. Chris was relieved to see Olan slowly begin to relax as they talked about the opera they'd seen the night before. Eventually, Chris's gaze strayed to the streetcars and hansom cabs that splashed through Houston's streets at what seemed to be a frenzied pace. It had been an interesting visit, to say the least, and he was sorry that he wouldn't have the chance to explore the city more. As for Adelaide, she should be able to follow through on the rest of whatever her plan might be without his help. So he'd served his purpose here. This was a good time to leave—before he got too attached to anything or anyone in this city.

Adelaide had been more than a little surprised when the Johansens returned from the doctor's appointment to announce that they wanted to leave for Peppin right away. Since her stepfather was working at the paper and her mother had gone to one of her committee meetings, Adelaide had quickly arranged for their luggage to be loaded into the carriage before riding along to see them off. The reality of their leaving was just setting in now that they had their tickets and were waiting for their train. She eased closer to Chris to be heard over the rain. "I know your pa has to go, but are you sure you have to leave? I thought he said you'd be staying a few days after he left to take care of some business."

A hint of a smile warmed his eyes. "That was simply a fancy way for him to say I would be sticking around to court you. I told him that I'd realized you and I weren't going to last. He seemed satisfied."

Adelaide wasn't entirely sure how to respond graciously to that, so she didn't try. Instead, she glanced over Chris's shoulder to where Olan sat on a bench several feet away. He'd been rather taciturn since returning from the doctor. Adelaide tugged at the lapel of Chris's coat until he leaned down enough to hear her whisper. "Is he all right? I mean, the doctor's report. I've been afraid to ask, but was it very discouraging?"

"What?" He pulled back slightly to look at her as realization lit his blue eyes. "Oh, no. Not at all. I should have told you as soon as he and I got back to your house, but he was so set on leaving quickly that I guess I forgot to mention it. My pa going to be fine. He isn't dying after all."

"Chris," she exclaimed, stepping forward to give him a jubilant hug. "That is *wonderful* news!"

His hands lingered at her waist to give it a quick squeeze in return before releasing her. "It certainly is."

She narrowed her eyes in confusion. "Wait. So does

that mean Doc Williams was wrong about your pa's condition the whole time?"

"No, he wasn't wrong. I guess you could say there was a misunderstanding." He pulled in a deep breath and shook his head. "It's all pretty confusing, which is why I think it's important that Pa and I go home to discuss what the specialist said with the rest of our family."

"Of course."

He slid his hands into his pockets, then caught her gaze. "Listen, about our pretend courtship... If you're having second thoughts, this would be a good time to end it."

She tried not to look at him as though he was crazy, but she wasn't entirely sure that she succeeded. No way was she turning back now. Not after having spent one of the most uncomfortable weekends of her life trying to convince her mother that the courtship was legitimate. "I'm not having second thoughts, but don't worry about me. I'm sure I can manage the rest on my own."

"I don't doubt that you can. It's just that I've been down that road. I know it doesn't seem like it's going to hurt anyone or anything, but shortchanging the truth...it's going to have consequences. I wouldn't encourage you to try to keep this facade going long-term."

"Why not? It seems to me that it worked out pretty well for you."

He gave her a disbelieving look. "Adelaide, it didn't work out for me at all."

"But you bought yourself more time."

"For all the good it did me. I'm still in the same

situation I started out in, except I've lost one pretend fiancée and my parents' trust."

"Your parents found out? You didn't tell me that."

"They didn't have to find out. They suspected the truth from the moment you broke off our engagement. I guess I wasn't very good at hiding my broken heart."

She tilted her head and searched his gaze. "You were heartbroken?"

He froze. A flash of panic filled his eyes followed by resignation. He glanced away before meeting her gaze again. "I was for a while. Why? Weren't you?"

"That doesn't make any sense," she said, ignoring the challenge in his voice, certain it was only meant to deflect her attention. "That last letter you sent me made it seem as though you didn't care one way or another about—"

"I didn't want you to know I was upset." His jaw tightened even as he gently caught hold of her arm, probably in an attempt to make her refocus. "Listen, that isn't the point. What I'm trying to say is…"

She nodded every so often as he kept talking. Hopefully that would be enough to make him think she was listening while giving her a chance to sort through her tangled thoughts. Chris Johansen had been heartbroken over her—so much so that his parents noticed, even when he tried to hide it. That didn't fit into the neat little box where she kept all of the facts and her feelings concerning her engagement to Chris. Before this conversation, she'd taken his lack of emotion in that final letter as a confirmation that he no longer—and perhaps never had—cared for her deeply. If that wasn't the case, what else had she gotten wrong?

She refocused on his voice just as he was finishing

up his argument. "So we agree that you aren't going to go through with it, then?"

"Don't be ridiculous. Of course I'm going through with it."

"But you were nodding the whole time."

"I see how that could be misleading...just like your letter to me."

"What?" He sighed. "You weren't listening to a word I said, were you?"

"Did you love me?" She was suddenly aware that she'd been wondering that for a long time. "I mean, did you really love me?"

Confusion filled his gaze as if he still didn't quite understand the question. She watched his jaw clench as he seemed to battle with the idea of letting his defenses down enough to answer her. Finally he took a small step closer. His voice was filled with certainty and a hint of aggravation. "You know I did."

Truthfully, she hadn't been sure. She was now, but it was too late for that to make a difference. Realizing she'd lost herself in Chris's blue eyes, she glanced away to watch a train pull into the station. Chris checked his ticket. "That's my train."

Olan must have realized the same thing for she saw him stand and begin talking to a porter. She should probably say her goodbyes now. "Chris, I—"

"I could write to you, if you'd like...to help you keep up appearances with your parents."

She waved away his offer. "Oh, you don't have to— Actually, that would be wonderful as long as it isn't an imposition to you. I'm sure once you find a bride... Well, I wouldn't want you to get in any trouble with her for writing to me. Not that there's any reason why our letters would—"

He caught her waist and tugged her into a hug. He placed a kiss on her temple before he stepped back to offer something just shy of a smile. "Goodbye, Adelaide."

"Goodbye," she whispered back as he began to turn away. Her lashes fluttered against a sudden sting of tears. What was wrong with her? Chris's departure was a good thing. She didn't need him here making her wonder about the past. An occasional letter just for show would be so much easier to contend with than living, breathing trouble. Yet his goodbye had been so final. It had felt as though he truly intended to never see her again. That possibility prompted her to do something she should have done long ago. She hurried across the short distance between them to catch his arm. As soon as he turned to her, she said, "There's something I have to give you. I left it in the carriage. I promise I'll be back before your train leaves."

He called her name in confusion, but she was already threading through the crowd and back into the station. It would only take a moment to retrieve the satchel. It held a copy of the first dime novel she'd ever completed—the one she'd never tried to have published because she'd written it for Chris. She'd cast him as the hero, and had meant it to be a present to him for his eighteenth birthday. Despite her best intentions, she hadn't gotten up the courage to send it to him before they'd broken off their engagement. Each year it had gotten buried deeper in her desk drawer until she'd pulled it out this morning. She'd been uncertain as to whether or not she should give it to him, but now it seemed right. After all, it truly had been meant for him. She just had to make sure he got it before his train left the station.

She hurried through the baggage claim area and the waiting room before she made it out the front door. She peered through the rain until she spotted the carriage, then hopped across the puddles already forming on the sidewalk to get to it. The overcast sky did little to light the dim interior as she climbed inside. Her hand had just settled upon the satchel when the carriage door opened. She stiffened in alarm at the sight of a strange man entering the carriage. Before she had time to think or move, he'd pinned her to the seat and placed a cloth over her face. She pulled in a gasping breath to scream. Instead, her voice came out in a weak cry. She tried to struggle, but numbness crawled across her limbs. Finally, the world clouded over and everything faded to black.

Chapter Seven

"All aboard!"

Chris took another step backward toward the train while searching the crowd for any sign of Adelaide. It had been six minutes since she'd told him to wait for her. That was more than enough time for her to make it to the carriage and back, especially as fast as she'd been moving. What if something had happened to her?

"Chris," Olan called from the train steps. "I don't think she's coming."

Chris shook his head. "Something must be wrong."

"Gentlemen, I'm sorry, but this is the last chance I can give y'all to get on this train," the porter said. "What's it going to be?"

Chris met his father's tired gaze and made a decision. "Pa, I know you're eager to go home so why don't you get on the train? You can be in Peppin in a couple of hours. I'll stay here, make sure Adelaide is all right, then take the next train headed for home."

Olan frowned. "If something really is wrong, then maybe I should stay and help."

"Whatever's wrong, I'll handle it. All I want is for you to relax and have a nice trip home. All right?"

Olan gave a hesitant nod, then boarded, much to the porter's relief. Chris thanked the porter for being so patient with them and returned his father's wave as the train began a slow chug out of the station. Grabbing his suitcase, he glanced down at his pocket watch. He waited exactly two more minutes for Adelaide to appear. When she didn't, Chris slowly walked back through the station, carefully scanning the crowd as he went. He held the door open for a rain-soaked man, then stepped outside only to stop and turn around.

The other man did the same. "Mr. Johansen?"

"You're the Holdens' driver." Chris searched his mind, then pointed at the man. "Ezra, right? I need your help. I'm trying to find Adelaide. Have you seen her?"

Alarm filled Ezra's features. "I thought she was seeing you off inside the station."

"She was, but at the last minute she said she needed something from the carriage. That was several minutes ago. She hasn't returned and I haven't been able to find her."

"In that case, we might have a problem. The carriage is gone. I was standing by that overhang to get out of the rain and keep an eye on it. A man stopped to ask me for the time. I looked down, and the next thing I knew I was waking up in an alleyway. I figured whoever did that to me was intending to steal that carriage. Now, I'm thinking—"

"They took Adelaide." Chris's stomach tightened at Ezra's nod. "We need to notify the police."

"All due respect, sir, it might be better to speak

with Mr. Holden first. He's got some powerful enemies in this city. It could be that one of them had something to do with it. If so, he'd have a better idea of who might be responsible. That could help us find her more quickly."

Chris frowned. "How could he possibly be faster than the police?"

"He has contacts. The police wouldn't know where to start, other than asking if anyone saw anything—which we can do ourselves. These men were stealthy enough that I didn't see or hear them coming. I doubt they would have made it easy for anyone to identify them later. Even if they did, that won't necessarily help us find Adelaide or the carriage. The best thing we can do is let Mr. Holden handle this."

If this had happened in Peppin, Chris would have strapped on his Smith & Wesson before helping Sheriff O'Brien round up a search party to canvas the town and its outlying areas for any trace of Adelaide. This wasn't Peppin, though. This was Houston—a much bigger, unfamiliar place where one wrong turn could render him completely lost. He'd never missed his hometown more. He couldn't wait to get back there. But first, he was going to do everything in his power to find Adelaide. Right now, that meant agreeing to let her stepfather handle the search, so Chris finally agreed to Ezra's plan.

No one in the immediate vicinity admitted to having seen anything, so Ezra flagged down a hansom cab, which they took to the *Houston Gazette* office. Ezra insisted on being the one to go in to Everett's office to break the news. After the driver left, Chris entered to find Everett standing at his desk gathering a few papers. The man looked pale, but determined. "Chris, thank you for not getting on that train. It would have taken us much longer to figure out Adelaide was taken. Are you going to stay and help us find her?"

Chris nodded. "I'll do whatever I can."

Everett rounded the desk and clasped Chris's shoulder. "I knew I could count on you."

"Did you know she was in danger?" The question was out before he could stop it.

"There was no threat to her specifically."

"But there were general threats."

"To me and the paper. That's nothing unusual. I can't take them all seriously because most of them aren't. I do try to be watchful and careful. That's why I hired Ezra. I'm sure you've figured out he's more than just a driver. He's a bodyguard. And, no. Adelaide had no idea. I'm sure you have plenty more questions, but now is not the time. C'mon, son. We're going to rally the troops and find our girl."

Adelaide awakened slowly, vaguely aware that for some reason it was very hard to move. She tried to open her eyes, but her lashes felt too heavy to lift. She groaned. Realizing something was covering her mouth, she reached up in an effort to pull it away. A hand caught hers before she could. A calm voice reached her ears. "Everything is all right, Miss Harper. Just stay calm. I won't hurt you."

Hurt me? Why would he hurt me? A murky memory filled her mind, then slowly cleared until she recalled a man climbing into her carriage and pinning her down. She jolted upright in the seat she'd been slumped against. Her left wrist jerked painfully and she realized it was bound to something immovable. The reason she couldn't open her eyes was because she was blindfolded. The gag in her mouth promised to muffle any sound, though she was too groggy to emit anything more than a questioning moan.

"Take a deep breath, and focus on my voice." He waited for her to still before continuing. "We're still in your carriage. We simply went for a little drive. You haven't been touched except for what was necessary to restrain you. I ask that you return our courtesy by listening closely to what I'm about to tell you. Are you awake enough to do that?"

She finally took the deep breath he recommended and found that it helped to clear the last vestiges of fog clinging to her mind. She still felt disoriented, but she had a feeling that had more to do with the fact that she was bound, gagged and blindfolded than anything else. Oddly enough, this situation felt rather familiar. Perhaps that was because she'd written a scene similar to this for one of her books. The setting had been only slightly different—a stagecoach rather than a carriage. One of the outlaws had ridden along as a passenger, then used chloroform to incapacitate the hero. She was relieved to find she'd described the smell of the chemical accurately, even though no one had agreed to provide a sample for her.

"Miss Harper?"

She snapped to attention with an indiscernibly mumbled, "Yes?"

"Take this warning to your stepfather…"

Relief filled her at the realization that she could only take a message to her stepfather if her assailant planned to release her. Since he'd explained how careful he'd been with her while she'd been unconscious and since she felt uninjured, she'd even go so far as to say he planned to keep his word about not hurting her and releasing her soon. She allowed herself to relax a little.

"If he continues to investigate the charity house in Peppin, you will be the one punished for it."

She grunted her displeasure. "That hardly seems fair."

"I can't understand you."

"Then ungag me so I can tell you that you're a lout. A gentlemanly lout, but a lout nonetheless. I would like to punch you in the nose."

"Stop talking," he said loudly before he leaned closer and lowered his voice. "Listen, I don't cotton to manhandling women, but I'm not the only one here right now. My boss has men working for him who wouldn't think twice about hurting you whether he ordered it or not. If Everett Holden doesn't heed this warning, those men will be coming after you and your mother. Do you understand?"

She nodded, then slowly eased her hand from his to point at her gag.

"You won't scream?"

She shook her head. He removed her gag. She licked her lips, then twisted her mouth from side to side just because she had the freedom to do so. "Thank you for your careful treatment of me. I do appreciate it."

"Uh...you're, um, welcome... I guess."

"I understand your warning and the threat you want me to communicate to my stepfather. I don't, however, understand you as a person. You sound educated, so I can't help wondering how you got into this life of crime. Are you being blackmailed? Or are you doing this of your own free will? It would be more compelling if you were being blackmailed. Have you ever killed someone? No. Don't tell me that. I don't want to know. Well, I do, but still don't tell me. You really are most interesting, though. In fact, I—" The gag slipped back into place muffling the rest completely. "That was just rude. I was going to make you a misunderstood antihero, but now you're going to be a cold, calculating, one-dimensional villain."

Keeping hold of her wrist, he eased over to one side of the carriage and opened the door. "There is a pair of scissors on the seat beside you to cut the ties."

"Come back here! I've never met a criminal before, and I'm not done—" She growled in frustration when the door slammed shut. Realizing she was wasting time, she used the hand he'd released to push at her blindfold. It was so tight that she only managed to free one eye from the darkness. She slid toward the door where he'd exited only to be reminded that she was still tethered to the other side of the carriage. Finding the scissors he'd left, she rid herself of all her restraints and halfway stumbled out of the coach in her haste. She found herself alone in a dead-end alley.

"Obnoxious, rude criminals, why'd you have to leave so fast?" She kicked at the carriage wheel of the abandoned carriage, then felt her stomach roil. "Uh-oh."

She'd researched chloroform enough to know that nausea was normal. She needed to lie down for a while if she didn't want to lose the contents of her stomach. She could try to recline in the carriage. However, hanging around in an alleyway didn't seem like a smart idea. Despite her protests to the contrary, she'd met enough dangerous men for one day. Dangerous men… Chris! She hadn't had a chance to give him the manuscript. She supposed she could always mail it to him. Why hadn't she thought of that before? She'd been too caught up in the moment, in his final good-bye. Well, it didn't matter. He was long gone by now.

An unexpected sadness washed over her at the thought. She shook her shoulders in a vain attempt to rid herself of it. Turning to the waiting horses, she crooned, "Where is your driver, darlings? I hope he wasn't hurt. We need to get out of here and find out, don't we?"

One of the horses neighed, which seemed to indicate they agreed with her plan. Unfortunately she wasn't entirely sure if she was capable of implementing it. She hadn't driven herself in almost five years. Even before then, she'd only driven in Peppin, which had fewer intimidating roads and much less traffic. It would help if she knew how far she had to go. She walked to the opening of the alleyway and sagged onto the nearby building in relief. She was only one block away from her stepfather's newspaper offices. She had no delusions that she'd been left in this spot by accident.

She went back to the carriage to gather her reticule and satchel, then gave each of the horses a reassuring pat before she stepped out of the alleyway. She suddenly realized it was entirely possible that her captor was still out there somewhere, hoping to watch her take his message to Everett. She lifted her chin and threw back her shoulders to show them she'd not been intimidated by their tactics. All the while, she willed her stomach to stop inching toward her throat.

The moment she entered through the employee's entrance she found herself rushing to the mercifully unoccupied restroom where she emptied the contents of her stomach in short order. Once she felt it was safe to do so, she rather shakily made the seemingly end-less journey up the stairs to her stepfather's office. Thankfully, everyone in the office seemed too busy to notice her so she didn't have to speak with anyone. Everett's office was empty, which meant he was prob-ably downstairs speaking with one of his reporters. No matter. He'd be back soon enough, and she'd tell him what had happened to her. Until then, she'd lie down on his divan to settle her stomach and rest her eyes...

Adelaide had been missing for more than three hours. The reporters of the *Houston Gazette* had hit the street in pursuit of answers. They'd found the Holden's carriage in an alleyway nearby with evi-dence suggesting that Adelaide had been bound and gagged. The police were canvasing the area, but so far nothing more had been found. Everett left to find Rose and inform her of what was happening. Chris stayed at the newspaper making notes as reporters checked in to report where they'd been before leaving to get back to the search. Everett returned and immediately looked to Chris. "Any new leads?"

"No, sir."

Everett's mouth pressed into a firm line before he yelled, "Smalls, is the press ready?"

A man who couldn't be much over five feet tall

popped out of the back room. "Ready, chief. You have the copy?"

"And the illustration Brehm worked up for me." Everett handed all of that to the Smalls. "I want those circulars printed and out the door in twenty minutes. Smalls? Smalls, what wrong with you? Stop stopping and go."

Despite the crisis they were facing, Chris couldn't help being impressed by Everett's authoritative demeanor. He couldn't imagine where Smalls found the gall to stand there shaking his head in defiance of his boss. The man must have lost his mind. Chris froze as the sound of Adelaide's voice filled the silence. "Pa, I'm sorry to interrupt, but could I speak to you for a moment?"

Relief filled Chris. Before he could take a step toward her, Everett had already crossed the room to take his stepdaughter in his arms for a hug. Realizing he didn't have a right to do the same, especially after he'd all but said his final goodbyes to Adelaide at the station, Chris hung back and waited for Everett to start asking the questions begging for answers. He wasn't disappointed, for the man stepped back to look at Adelaide in concern. "Are you all right? What happened? We've been so worried."

He caught a glimpse of her reassuring smile over Everett's shoulder. However, Chris couldn't help being concerned despite her insistence that she was fine. She might be trying not to worry them. Or she might not fully know the extent of her injuries if the criminals had used the same tactics with her as they had with Ezra. Chris waited until Everett finished hugging her before quietly suggesting, "She should still see a doctor just to make sure."

Adelaide's light-green eyes landed on him and widened even as her smile grew. "Chris! I thought you'd be long gone by now."

He crossed his arms and offered a shrug. "You didn't come back, so I didn't leave."

"Chris has been helping us try to track you down," Everett said. "He's right. We'll have a doctor look you over to be safe."

"If y'all insist, but I really do feel fine. The nap I took helped. Thanks for letting me borrow your office."

Chris shared a confused look with Everett who frowned. "You were in my office? For how long?"

"That depends. What time is it now?"

Chris glanced down at his pocket watch. "A quarter to four."

"Well, I walked over here right after…what I need to talk to you about so I guess three hours or so." Her eyes widened. "Oh, Ezra and the horses! Pa—"

"We found them, and they're fine. But, three hours!"

The men exchanged glanced with each other until Smalls finally said what they were all thinking. "She was right under our noses almost the whole time."

"You mean y'all didn't know I was here?" Adelaide grimaced. "I'm so sorry! No wonder y'all were worried. I guess I should have said something when I came in. I wasn't feeling very well and everyone seemed so busy that I didn't want to bother anyone."

"For the record," Chris drawled. "You wouldn't have been a bother."

A hint of amusement sparked in her eyes. He did his best to curtail his smile because they were the only ones who seemed to think the situation was the least bit funny. Everett shook his head as he slowly sank into the nearest chair. "Don't worry about it, Adelaide. It wasn't your fault. We had a roomful of reporters and policemen. Someone should have noticed. The fact that we didn't doesn't speak well for our observation skills. We'll be the laughingstock of Texas if this gets out."

"The circular never went out," Smalls said as he returned the papers Everett had handed him earlier. "That means the public doesn't need to know this ever happened."

"True." Everett squared his shoulders and offered a nod. "The police will want to know for their investigation, of course, but I doubt they'll do anything to publicize this. Their reputations are just as much at stake as the newspaper's is. Let's not worry about that now, though. Smalls, if you'll stay and inform everyone that Adelaide is safe, I'll go ahead and take her to see a doctor."

"Sure thing, Chief."

"Thank you. Chris, will you join my family for supper?"

Chris glanced down at the suitcase which he'd set beside his borrowed desk. He'd promised his father that he'd return to Peppin as soon as Adelaide was safe. On the other hand, a man had to eat. Besides, the next train wouldn't leave until almost eight o'clock anyway. He'd probably have plenty of time to make it to the station. Right?

Wrong. Supper was delayed by Adelaide's visit to

the doctor and an interview with the police chief. By the time they did eat, Everett had convinced Chris to stay in Houston one more night. After the household retired, Chris still hadn't been able to settle down enough to even change into his sleeping clothes. Realizing that his uneasiness was probably nothing compared to what Adelaide must be feeling, he slipped from his room and down the stairs. As he'd expected, he found her pacing back and forth in the candlelit library.

He stepped inside, quietly calling her name so as not to startle her. She jumped anyway. After placing a calming hand over her heart, she rushed into his arms. He caught her to his chest and buried his face in the free-spilling waves of her hair. He suddenly knew this was why he'd stayed. He'd needed a chance to hold her in his arms, offer what comfort he could and know that she was truly out of harm's way.

She shifted to rest her cheek against his chest, but didn't let go.

"I was fine. I was fine all day, when I talked to the police—even while it was happening. I managed to stay calm. Now, I'm shaking like a leaf. Every time I close my eyes I see that man lunging at me in the carriage." She shuddered. "My heart starts beating so fast."

He rubbed calming circles on her back. "Hey, it's all right. You're all right. Take a deep breath."

She did as he said, then pushed away slightly to meet his gaze. Tears pooled in her eyes but she sounded somewhat calmer. "Do you know what the scariest part of all this is? I was bound, gagged, blindfolded and unconscious. Anything could have happened to me. I wouldn't have been able to defend myself."

"You're right that it could have been worse, but it wasn't. You know the end of the story so don't let the unknowable bother you. You were released. You're unharmed. Let's focus on that, all right?"

She nodded, which knocked a tear loose. He brushed it away, then led her to sit beside him on the settee. She bit her lip and stared into the empty fireplace across the room. "There is something I haven't told anyone about what happened."

He covered her hand with his. "What's that?"

"After I figured out that the abductor wasn't going to hurt me, I convinced him to remove my gag, then I tried to question him…" She met his gaze guiltily. "So I could use him as a character in one of my books."

That was so far from the realm of anything Chris had expected her to confess that it took a moment for him to process. He grinned. "That whole situation is exactly like something that would happen in one of your books."

"I know!" She leaned forward. "That's what I was thinking the whole time. In fact, it was very similar to what happened to—"

They finished together, "Chet Ryder in *The Outlaw Ranger.*"

They stared at each other for a moment before a soft but delighted smile touched her lip. "That's absolutely right, Chris."

Of course it was. He'd read that book more times than he could count. "So did you learn anything from the abductor?"

"No." She rolled her eyes. "He wouldn't cooperate—

didn't answer a single one of my questions, then he put the gag back on."

"How rude."

She laughed. "I thought so."

It was Chris's turn to pull in a deep breath. "I'm glad you're safe."

"So am I." Her green eyes sobered. "And I'm glad you stayed."

Chris took her hand as he smiled and nodded in agreement. He wouldn't have wanted to be anywhere else during this time than by her side and helping her family. However, that, in and of itself, was a frightening admission. He didn't want to care for her. Yet, couldn't seem to stop himself. That was fine. Caring was one thing—a manageable thing, something he could walk away from if need be. He wouldn't allow it to go any deeper than that.

Chapter Eight

When had Chris released her hand? Adelaide opened her eyes in search of it, in search of *him*, only to find herself alone in the library. Morning light eased through the heavy curtains to softly illuminate the room. She must have drifted to sleep while they were talking.

She shook her head to banish the lingering sleepiness, then sat up, accidentally knocking the throw that covered her onto the floor. A smile drifted across her lips as she imagined him laying it over her. She wasn't entirely sure how long they'd stayed up talking last night. All she knew was that it had been wonderful... like having a best friend again. It had been so long since she'd connected with anyone who truly seemed to understand what made her tick—five long years to be exact. She remembered now how Chris had always been willing to listen and ready to help. She'd made herself forget that and so many other things because it had been too painful keep those memories close.

Chris was everything she remembered. The frightening thing was that she was starting to forget why she'd let him go in the first place. She closed her eyes and took the opportunity to remind herself. She could believe that his feeling for her had been genuine and maybe even deep when he'd first proposed. However, that didn't mean that hers had been. Everything had happened so fast that rainy evening she'd left Peppin. All because a single kiss had transformed their friendship into something more. How could she possibly have risked basing the entirety of her future on that?

A soft knock on the library door interrupted her thoughts just before her mother entered the room. "Oh, good. You're awake. How are you feeling?"

"I'm feeling fine. I think I slept off all the effects of the chloroform in Pa's office yesterday." Adelaide's eyebrows rose at the sight of the breakfast tray Rose carried. "What's all this?"

"I thought you deserved a bit of pampering today." Rose placed the tray table in front of the settee.

"Really? That's sweet," Adelaide said, hating that she was unable to stop the hint of confusion entering her voice. There had been a time before Hiram had died, and even before they'd moved to Houston, when she and her mother had been a team with the same goals and objectives. Somewhere along the way, they'd become adversaries, whether her mother knew it or not. However, for right now, the tension that usually filled the air between them seemed to have lessened considerably. Adelaide offered her mother a tentative smile. "Thank you."

"You're very welcome. Now, eat up while we talk about next steps."

"Next steps to what?"

"Keeping you safe, of course. Your stepfather and

I were absolutely terrified at the idea of anything happening to you yesterday. We don't want to take any chances when it comes to your safety. Everett plans to work with the police to launch a full investigation into the person or people behind your abduction. Now that he knows you were targeted as a way to threaten him about one specific story, he's been able to narrow the field of suspects considerably. It shouldn't be long before they find proof of whatever it is those men wanted to hide. Until then, he and I agree that it's best you leave town until it's safe for you to return."

"Leave town? Where would I go?"

"To Peppin with Chris. I'll be going with you as a chaperone and also because your stepfather is concerned about my safety, as well. It's all been arranged. The train leaves in about two hours. I have a maid packing some of your belongings right now. After you eat, you can go up to see if there's anything you want to take with you that she's missed."

Adelaide shook her head. "There are so many things I don't understand about what is happening right now. How is traveling to Peppin any safer than staying right here? I can just stick close to the house until whoever did this is caught."

"You know Everett. The fact that these people threatened him through you has only made him more determined to expose whatever they're doing. But he doesn't want you or me in the line of fire."

"Peppin isn't entirely safe, either. Is it? That's where the charity house is that started all the problems."

"To hear Everett describe it, that place is nothing more than an empty false front. He talked to the sheriff while he was in Peppin and there's been no activity around the property. Besides, the town is so small that it will be easier to spot anyone who is out of place or acting suspicious. If we let it be known that we're in danger, the whole town will look out for us. We lived there long enough, and you kept in touch with enough of your friends, that they consider you one of their own."

That was because she had been one of their own. Perhaps a part of her always would be. Peppin was the one place in all of their travels that had felt like home to her. Despite the changes it had been through in the five years since she'd left, it had still felt that way when she'd visited there. She wasn't entirely sure her mother shared that feeling. "You must be pretty convinced this is the right thing to do if you're willing to return to Peppin."

"What I'm not willing to do is lose you again." The emotion in Rose's voice made Adelaide reach out to take her hand. To Adelaide's surprise, Rose clung to it. "I know we don't always get along, but that is truly something I couldn't bear. Those few hours you were missing were some of the hardest I've ever lived. Now, it's going to be difficult to let you out of my sight. So, you see? Even if Everett wasn't concerned about my safety, as well, I'd still insist on going to Peppin with you. However, I do find it encouraging that you didn't immediately agree. I thought for sure you'd jump at the chance to spend more time with Chris. Is it possible that you're beginning to see him for who he really is?"

Adelaide pulled her hand free. "Actually I think I am."

Granted, she still found the situation with Amy suspicious, and the string of women he'd shamelessly admitted to pursuing after she left town was disconcerting. However, he'd had a relatively believable explanation for that with the whole mail-order bride problem. She could hardly fault him for trying to find some way to avoid his father's matchmaking. Wasn't she trying to do the same with her mother? Maybe so, but she hadn't involved herself with a bunch of men to do so. She'd only involved one.

Relief filled her mother's voice. "I'm so glad you're coming to your senses. Trust me. Marrying a man like that would be worse than never marrying at all."

Adelaide couldn't believe her ears. Had her plan worked already? She offered a disbelieving smile and somehow managed to keep her tone casual. "You mean you'd rather I become a spinster?"

Rose laughed. "Oh, my dear, that will hardly be necessary. I'm sure I can find the perfect man for you. I don't think Bertrand is quite out of our reach yet."

"Mother, I'm not marrying him. I told him that. I told *you* that."

"Well, we can talk about it later. Now, tell me about you and Chris. When are you going to break things off again? Your stepfather insists we travel with him for safety's sake, so it would probably be better to do it after we arrive in Peppin. Don't you think so?"

"I think you sound far too giddy about the prospect of this. I don't understand how you can continue to be so hard on Chris when he's been nothing but kind and respectful to you. Isn't it time to ease up a little—especially after everything he did to help us yesterday?"

"I do appreciate his help. However, that doesn't change his lack of character in other ways. Nor does it make up for the negative impact he's had on my relationship with you."

"Negative impact?" Adelaide shook her head in confusion. "What are you talking about?"

"You resented me for encouraging you to break off your engagement with him. I know you did. That's why there's so much distance between us now..."

"That isn't... I mean, yes. It was frustrating that you constantly belittled him to me and discounted whatever feeling I thought I had for him. But that is only one small part of why there's so much distance between us."

"But the distance started after I made you leave him."

"After you made me leave *Peppin*," Adelaide corrected. "You made Papa promise not to uproot me again, then you did exactly that out of the blue and only weeks before graduation. When we arrived in Houston, you expected me to start over in a new city as though I hadn't left my friends, my home—and, yes, my fiancé—behind in Peppin. You married Everett, who I admit, has been a blessing, but decided that I wasn't good enough to fit in his world. At least, I assume that's why you made such a concerted effort to turn me into your idea of a perfect socialite. Well, I'm not a socialite, Mother. It isn't who I am. It isn't who you raised me to be. I can't just change on a whim to suit your purposes."

"My purpose is to make sure you marry a man who is dependable, financially secure, and too busy loving you to even glance at another woman."

"I don't want that."

Rose laughed in disbelief, then shook her head. "Of

course not. You want a man like Chris, who sparks another girl the second you leave town. A man who, according to his father, has a bride standing by in Norway in case he finally gets bored enough to marry her."

Adelaide bit her lip to rein in her temper before responding. "I meant that I don't want to get married. Why would I, after watching what you went through with Papa? Oh, for a while I thought that things would be different with me and Chris, but I think some part of me always has been and maybe always will be skeptical of him. I know that I can't risk marrying him. That doesn't mean that I don't…" She swallowed hard, not entirely sure of where she'd been going with that statement and completely unwilling to find out. Her mother had no such compunction.

"You have feelings for him."

"What? No. I…" Everything within her seemed to freeze as her mother's words reached her heart and reverberated their truth. Flabbergasted, Adelaide sank onto the settee without a sound. How could this have happened?

Her dismay was echoed in Rose's eyes. Rather than the condescending tone Adelaide might have expected, her mother's words were filled with empathy. "Oh, Adelaide, already? It's only been five days." Rose shook her head. "This is more serious than I thought."

Now that was something they could agree on. Adelaide bit her lip and glanced away. This wasn't only serious. It was unacceptable. She still didn't want to get married. She especially didn't want to marry Chris. That meant any feeling she might have for him were pointless. In that case, she wouldn't have feelings for

him anymore. There. She'd decided. Crisis averted…
right?

"Adelaide, please keep your head about you and
your eyes open. We're going back to Peppin. This is
your chance to find out who he really is—good or bad.
If there's something about him that isn't aboveboard,
we'll find out. There's no hiding a bad reputation in
a small town. Agreed?"

Adelaide nodded. "Agreed."

Now, how on earth was she going to convince Chris
to keep their pretend courtship going in Peppin when
he'd already told his father that their relationship was
over? More important, how was she going to keep
him from discovering the inconvenient inclination
she felt toward him? It was imperative that he didn't
find out. It would be too mortifying for him to know
that the only person their little deception had worked
on was her.

Chris's eyebrows lifted at the sound of raised voices
that drifted through the house. The words were too
muffled by all of the walls between the library and
the breakfast room for him to decipher the specifics
of what was being said, but it didn't sound pretty. Lifting his cup of coffee, he met Everett's gaze. The man
offered him a comforting nod. "It's all right. This has
been a long time coming."

So Chris hadn't been imagining the tension that
filled the air when Adelaide and her mother were in
the same room. "How do you handle—" he stopped
himself just short of saying "them" and settled for
"—all of this?"

Everett shrugged. "I just love them, I suppose. And

wait for the day when they work out their differences. Trust me. This is far better than their usual silence. At least they're finally talking to each other."

That was certainly one way to look at it. His heart went out to Adelaide, though. After what had happened yesterday and the tough time she'd had last night, an argument with her mother hardly seemed an ideal way to recover.

While waiting for the women to end their discussion and finish packing their bags, Chris and Everett went over the plan one more time. It was a simple one. The Holdens and Adelaide would escort Chris to the train station with his suitcase. He would buy two extra tickets at the ticket booth, then at the last moment Adelaide and Rose would join him on the train. Their luggage would be sent along later. All of this was arranged to make it harder for them to be followed. It also meant that the women's real goodbyes to Everett would have to be said at the house instead of the train station. Chris waited by the front door to give them the privacy to do just that.

Adelaide went first, then hurried over to join him. Placing her hand on his arm, she kept her voice and her gaze lowered. "Chris, my mother still thinks that you and I are a couple. I don't suppose—I mean, I know you already told your father—"

"I'll do it."

Surprise lit her eyes as she finally met his gaze. "Really?"

"Of course. My father might not like it, but he'll just have to deal with it for a little while. What matters is that this will give me a good reason to stay close to you while you're in Peppin." It wasn't until her eyes widened that he realized he should probably explain. "For your safety, of course."

"Right. Safety," she said, as though reminding herself.

He was about to ask if she was all right when Everett decided it was time to hurry them all out of the house. Noticing Adelaide's slight hesitation as she first caught sight of the carriage, Chris caught her hand and threaded his fingers through hers. She eased closer to his side and held on until they reached the station. Once they stood beside the waiting train, Everett put an arm around the waist of each of the ladies. "Let's all face Chris as though we're saying goodbye to him. Now, I want both of you to listen to me. Everything has been arranged. As soon as y'all arrive Chris will take you to the sheriff's office so that the local law enforcement will be aware of our situation. Chris will then move to his parents' house so that y'all can stay in his apartment above the mercantile. Neither Chris nor I will accept any arguments about that. This arrangement will be far safer than having y'all stay at the hotel where strangers can come and go as they please."

Chris gave the women a reassuring nod. "We know our customers well at Johansen's Mercantile. We do get a lot of out-of-towners passing through, but those people will be obvious to us, so we'll have a better chance at spotting anyone suspicious. There will always be someone from my family in the store to keep watch when it's open. I'm sure Sheriff O'Brien and Deputy Bridger will be willing to keep an eye on the place when it's closed."

"Stay in Peppin with Chris until I come for you myself. Don't leave with anyone besides me. I won't ask anyone to bring you back to Houston—not even Chris. Understood?" He waited for them each to agree before continuing. "Good. Now, enjoy your break from the city. Visit with your old friends. Try to relax."

Rose lifted her chin. "You be careful while we're gone. Don't take any unnecessary chances. Do you hear me, Everett Holden?"

"I hear you, sweetheart." Everett shook Chris's hand as the conductor called all aboard. "Take care of my girls."

"Yes, sir." With a final nod, Chris ushered Adelaide and her mother onto the train. They had just enough time to take their seats before their journey began. The tall buildings of the city gave way to rural fields of rice and cotton, then pure wilderness. Finally, the train wound through the rolling meadows that made up the foothills of the Hill Country before pulling to a stop in Peppin.

Chris left the women to get settled in his apartment while he walked over to his parents' house, carrying everything he anticipated needing for the next few days. He'd already seen Sophia and August at the mercantile. The younger two boys were still in school. That meant his parents were the only ones to greet him when he stepped inside their colorful Queen Anne house. He set his suitcases down in the foyer to receive his mother's hug. She didn't let go any too quickly. "It's so good to have our boy back in town, and staying with us, too! It will be like old times."

"Yes, but hopefully it will only be for a few days. I'm sure August will be glad to have our old room back to himself after that." Chris reached out to shake his father's hand. Olan used his grip to pull Chris forward for a quick hug. Afterward, Chris searched his father's face. "Pa, how are you feeling?"

Olan waved Chris's concern away. "I'm fine. I told your ma that the doctor said my heart condition wasn't as serious as we thought."

Chris sent his father an exasperated, disbelieving look while Marta slipped an arm around her husband's waist to grin. "Isn't that a blessing?"

Chris ignored his father's warning look to say, "It's a blessing that Pa doesn't have a heart condition at all."

"What?" Marta looked back and forth between them in confusion.

Chris sighed. "Do you want me to explain, Pa?"

Olan grimaced. "I reckon you might as well now that you've betrayed my confidence. Besides, I don't remember much of what the doctor told me. I was too busy being angry to listen, I guess."

They moved to the parlor where Chris pulled one of the chairs closer to the settee where his parents sat. He explained the specialist's findings to both of them and was relieved to see that his father was actually listening this time. Once Chris finished, Marta stared at Olan with tears in her eyes. "How could you not tell me this?"

"I'm sorry, Marta." Olan ran his fingers through his hair, then captured his wife's hand in his. "I know I should have said something, but what man wants to admit to his wife that he's been fluttery and swoony like a woman?"

She lifted her chin. "One who is honest? And, for the record, I have never fluttered or swooned so it has nothing to do with being a woman. No, there is something else going on here—something else you're keeping from me, from all of us. Otherwise, you wouldn't be so anxious. What is it?"

Olan pressed his lips together, staying stubbornly silent.

Marta crossed her arm. "Take your time, dear. I'll wait as long as it takes."

Olan released a sigh, then began a reluctant explanation. "Remember how much damage that hailstorm did to the house and the mercantile back in October? Well, it took all of our savings to repair everything. Once our savings were gone, our personal finances got pretty tight. I didn't want to do anything to the business that might weaken it for when Chris takes over. Unfortunately, that meant I fell behind on the mortgage payments for our house. Mr. Wilkins at the bank has been nice about everything. With his help, I've managed to catch up somewhat so we're only a month behind now."

Taking the news in stride, Marta softened. "Olan, that isn't so bad. We were in far worse spots than this back in Norway."

"I know. That's why I didn't want it to happen again here." Olan rubbed his reddening eyes. "Our whole family has worked so hard and done so well, even the little ones. I didn't want anything to jeopardize that. If I'd just been more frugal, saved more and maybe been a bit more hard-nosed when it came to giving money away to charities and extending credit at the store, then we wouldn't be in this spot."

Chris shook his head and leaned forward to capture his father's gaze. "Don't do that to yourself, Pa. You did what you thought was best at the time, and that's all anyone can do. It's all anyone can expect from you, including yourself. What's more, I'm so proud of you for your compassion. It is a gift to have a generous heart. This town respects you for that. Maybe it's time to be a bit more generous to yourself by not so judging yourself so harshly...and by keeping a little more of your own money."

His father laughed despite the tears in his eyes. "*Ja*, maybe I can do that."

"I will help you," Marta said. "We are a team. That means you don't have to bear this alone. We'll figure out all of it together. Agreed?"

"I agree."

"The specialist said he was going to send his notes to Doc Williams, so you might want to follow up with him in a couple of days," Chris added. "He also said that it's important that you talk to someone about what's troubling you. I think that's a good idea in general for you to do that regularly. I know you can always talk to Ma." Chris smiled when Marta vigorously nodded. "You can talk to me, too, especially if it has something to do with the store. Also, I think Doc would be a good listener. He has to keep everything you say confidential, anyway. Hopefully, he can also help you find some healthy ways to manage your anxiety."

"I'll ask him about it, to be sure." Olan took a deep breath. "Thank y'all for being so understanding. I truly am sorry for not telling y'all everything to begin with, especially about my health. However, despite what Doc said, I honestly was convinced that I was dying."

Marta smiled. "Well, we are overjoyed that you aren't."

"Hear, hear," Chris said with a nod. "Sophia and the other boys are going to be so relieved."

Olan nodded. "I'll tell them this evening."

Chris stood. "Now, if you'll excuse me, I promised I'd take Adelaide and her mother to the café for a late dinner."

He left before his father could offer more than a frown. He wasn't ready to get into any discussions about his relationship with Adelaide quite yet. He'd wired his parents ahead of time so they already had a general idea of what was going on. The specifics could wait…but only a couple of hours, because Sophia had already extended their mother's invitation for Adelaide and Rose to join them for supper later that evening. Keeping in mind what had happened the last time Adelaide had come over for supper, Chris didn't want to give his parents any ideas.

He had to admit that, despite his parents' probable disapproval, part of him was looking forward to continuing this charade of a courtship with Adelaide. Perhaps that was why he'd agreed to it so easily even though it was taking time from his increasingly urgent search for a bride. That woman wouldn't be Adelaide. He simply had to keep that in mind and not let his heart get tangled in the web they'd begun to weave.

Chapter Nine

As soon as Adelaide entered Chris's apartment she knew that her stay in Peppin would be painful at worst and bittersweet at best. What else could it be when she'd all but stepped into the reality of what her life would have been if she'd married Chris as she'd promised? His apartment over the mercantile was exactly where they would have lived.

She'd expected little more than the quintessential bachelor's house. Instead, it actually looked and felt like a home. All of the furnishings had to be a bit small to fit, which gave a charming air to the three-bedroom apartment. Rich, amber hardwood floors stretched throughout while large windows filled each room with light. The kitchen was small, but functional with a shiny white stove that contrasted with the china-blue painted cupboard and cabinets.

"Adelaide, please sit down," Rose said from where she sat on the brown velvet settee in the parlor. "You're making me nervous."

Realizing she'd been pacing, Adelaide wrung her hands together. "I can't sit down."

A hint of amusement filled her mother's voice. "We've been in this apartment for less than an hour. How can you possibly have cabin fever already?"

"We can leave, right? The apartment, I mean. We don't have to stay in here all the time, do we?"

"Oh, there is no way that we are staying in here constantly. We would go crazy."

Relieved that for once she and her mother were on the same page, Adelaide finally sank onto the comfortable white chair across from the settee. "Or we'd kill each other."

Rose laughed. "Or go crazy, then kill each other."

"So we can walk about freely?"

"With company," her mother amended. "There's safety in numbers, so if you aren't with me, make sure you're with someone else you know you can trust."

A knock sounded at the door that connected the apartment to the mercantile and Adelaide jumped up to answer it. She opened the door slightly to make sure it was Chris before fumbling with the lock and chain. Finally managing to get it open, she sighed and shook her head as Chris stepped inside. "Honestly, these safety precautions are making me more jittery than that abduction ever did."

"You'll get the hang of it in a little while." Chris caught her hand and gave it a little squeeze.

She didn't want to get the hang of it. Right now she just wanted to get out of there. Fortunately that was why Chris had arrived—to escort them to dinner. "I'm famished. Let's go."

"Yes, please." Her mother seconded as she grabbed her reticule. "Chris, did Everett tell you when our luggage was arriving?"

"It should be here pretty soon. I'll check on it after we eat." He guided Adelaide toward the steps so that she preceded him downstairs while he hung back to lock the door and speak with her mother.

Seeing Sophia gathering her reticule and hat in the employees' back room, Adelaide invited her to join them at the café. Sophia hesitated a moment before falling into step with Adelaide. "I'm afraid I won't be able to stay long since my break is only twenty minutes, but I'd love to join y'all. Are you and your ma settling in all right upstairs?"

"I have to admit I've been a little antsy. The past several days were so busy for me that it's hard to settle down sometimes."

Sophia gave her a sympathetic look as they exited the store. "I'm sure. Well, if you ever want to come down to the mercantile, you're more than welcome. We can always use another hand around the place."

"I just might do that." Adelaide laughed. "Other than my nervousness, everything is fine. More than fine, actually. Chris's apartment is lovely—definitely not what I was expecting from a bachelor."

"That's because he wasn't expecting to…" Sophia's words stumbled to a halt before continuing more slowly and gently. "When he moved in, he wasn't expecting to be a bachelor for long."

"Oh." They crossed the street while Adelaide went over the string of women he'd said he'd proposed to. "Who was he going to marry?"

Sophia's brow furrowed in confusion. "You, Adelaide. He was going to marry you. I helped him a little with the decorating, but every choice he made was with you in mind. We were putting the finishing touches on the place when he got that last letter breaking the engagement."

Adelaide couldn't find the words to respond as her heart sank in her chest. An apology rose to her lips, but didn't escape. Why should she apologize? She was the one who'd been wronged. Yet her anger had deserted her. All she felt in its absence was loss. How was it possible that she was only now starting to truly feel the effects of their long-ago breakup? Perhaps because once she'd heard about him and Amy she had refused to acknowledge that she'd ever cared for him as more than a friend. If she had, then how weak would it have made her to have fallen in love with a man with the same deplorable characteristics as her father?

Now she was faced with a new dilemma. If by some chance Chris didn't have the same tendencies, then she'd hurt a good man and walked away from the possibility of a happy future with him…and for what? Either way, it hardly mattered now. The damage had been done to both of them. Regardless of how it might feel to live in the apartment he'd prepared for her, there was no going back.

She forced herself to snap back to the present. Meeting Sophia's concerned blue eyes, a hint of a smile and a nod was the best she could offer the woman who would have been her sister-in-law. "That sounds like something Chris would do."

"What sounds like something I would do?" Chris asked as he placed a proprietary hand on her back.

Adelaide realized her eyes were a bit misty and avoided his gaze, hoping Sophia would think of something to say. They were distracted instead by Rose's happy gasp. "Is that Amelia Greene inside the café? Oh, it is."

Mrs. Greene glanced up from her table on the other side of the café's large picture window. The woman's mouth fell open before mouthing *Rose*. Mrs. Greene gestured wildly for Rose to join them. Rose glanced back at them. "You don't mind if I join her, do y'all?"

"Of course not," Adelaide said, knowing that Mrs. Greene had been one of her mother's closest friends when they lived in Peppin. At the time, Mrs. Greene was known to be the mouthpiece of the town's grapevine, which was exactly why Rose had started a friendship with her. Rose always believed that gossips were less likely to spread rumors about their friends than they were mere acquaintances. It was a plan Rose implemented in every town they'd lived in, since Hiram had always given people plenty to talk about. Here in Peppin, Rose's resulting friendship with Mrs. Greene had deepened into something genuine.

Adelaide and Rose agreed to meet back at the apartment later, then split up as soon as they entered the café. Adelaide was afraid that Chris might try to pick up their previous vein of conversation. However, once Adelaide finished catching up with Maddie, Sophia kept the conversation moving until her break was over. By the time Adelaide and Chris finished lunch and walked over to the train station, he seemed to have forgotten all about it.

He waved at one of the railroad men walking into the station. "Hey, Wes. This is Adelaide Harper. We're looking for some luggage that was supposed to come in by train this afternoon for her and her mother, Rose Holden. Can you help us?"

"Sure thing." Wes pulled off his gloves and nodded to Adelaide. "Nice to meet you, Miss Harper. I think I know which ones are yours. Two fancy-looking trunks, right? The train dropped them off only a few minutes ago, so I put them in the back. I'll bring them out to you in just a moment."

True to his word, Wes returned quickly with the trunks on a wooden pushcart.

"Miss Harper, if I could have you sign something saying you've picked up the luggage, I can get you on your way."

Wes led the way inside the station. He pulled a tablet from behind a counter near the door beneath it and began to make a few notations. "So, you're from Houston?"

Her eyes narrowed. "How did you know that?"

He glanced up to grin. "The tags on your luggage gave you away."

"Oh." She laughed. "I guess they did. Actually, I used to live in Peppin."

"You don't say. When did you move away?"

"About five years ago."

"That's right about the time I was getting here. We must have just missed each other." He turned the tablet around. Pointing to the place for her to sign, he asked, "Are you back here for good or just visiting?"

"I'm just visiting."

"Well, I hope you have a nice time while you're here—"

"Excuse me." A young woman with dark blond hair stepped up to the counter. She offered them an apologetic look before continuing in a demure and heavily accented voice. "I'm sorry to interrupt. I am new. I do not know a lot of English. Can you help me? I'm looking for Johansens."

The woman pronounced the J in Johansen with a soft Y sound, so it took Adelaide a moment to figure out what she meant. "Johansen's? The mercantile?"

"No. Um…Chris or Olan? Marta?"

"Oh, the Johansen family," Wes said. "Chris is right outside."

"Chris is here?" Somehow the girl seemed to pale and flush at the same time. "Where?"

Wes rounded the counter to point out the window. "There he is, moving that luggage into a little wagon. See him?"

"*That* is Chris Johansen?"

Adelaide glanced out the window and decided the awe in the girl's voice was more than a little justified by the sight of Chris hefting the last piece of luggage. However, the squeal that followed seemed a bit excessive. Chris turned to look toward the station, almost as if he'd heard the sound. He was probably looking for Adelaide. She, however, stayed inside watching from a safe distance as the other girl hurried toward him. The girl said something. He nodded hesitantly. That was enough for the girl to launch herself into his arms.

Chris caught her, which was probably a good thing, since she would have ended up facedown in the dirt if he hadn't. He set her down and began to step back but she went in for a kiss. Adelaide felt her eyebrows lift as she counted the seconds it took him to disentangle himself. Precisely three. A little too long for her liking.

Wes leaned forward for a better look. "How does he get all of these girls to kiss him out of the blue?"

She spared a quick glance over her shoulder at him. "Exactly how many times has this happened?"

"This is the second that I know about. The first one was last week. Some woman walked into the mercantile and kissed him—"

"*He* kissed *me*, thank you very much."

"Oh. Uh…sorry. I'll be sure to clear that up next time I hear the rumor. Meanwhile, don't you want to go out there and break that up? Or at least find out who that is?"

Adelaide bit her lip. She was pretty sure she knew exactly who that was. Well, not *exactly*. Chris never had told her the name of his Norwegian mail-order bride-to-be. A smart woman, a woman who wasn't trying to relive the past, would take this opportunity to concede defeat and bow out gracefully. Of course, to do that she would have had to have been fighting for something—which she most certainly wasn't. Chris's panicked gaze seemed to find hers despite the distance as he kept his hands on the mail-order bride's shoulders to hold her off. Helping him out was the least she could do after everything he'd done for her and her family for the over the past several days. Adelaide heaved a sigh. "I guess I'd better. Are you coming?"

"I wouldn't miss it."

"I figured."

"That's what friends are for."

He didn't seem to notice the startled look she gave him. He was too busy trying to explain the correct form for a right uppercut punch just in case she needed to defend herself or Chris from the "mystery woman" as he called her. Meanwhile, Adelaide marveled at the fact that she'd made a friend in less than five minutes.

That was something she hadn't been able to do in five years while living in Houston.

Keeping the woman who'd kissed him at arm's length, Chris glanced desperately over her shoulder in time to see Adelaide and Wes exit the station. They walked toward him as though completely oblivious to his situation, even though he'd seen them watching from inside. They kept jabbing the air. Finally, they laughed together and an unfamiliar feeling coiled in his stomach.

Why had he never considered that Adelaide might meet someone else and fall in love? Just because she didn't want to marry him or the men her mother had picked out for her, didn't mean she never wanted to get married to someone of her own choosing. Wasn't that what Chris wanted for himself? Adelaide could do a lot worse than Wesley Brice…

But that was not the point. They had a deal. There was no way he was letting her out of it now. He forced himself to refocus on what the woman in front of him was saying in rapid Norwegian. She sounded exhausted and overexcited, which made all her words run together in an incomprehensible babble.

"Slow down," he said. "I can't understand you. Who are you?"

"I told you," she responded. "I am Britta Solberg. Your bride-to-be."

Chris shook his head. "There has been a mistake."

"You are Chris Johansen. I am Britta Solberg. Your parents arranged a marriage between us. I know that I am here earlier than they planned, but I could not wait a moment longer. You are more handsome than I thought you would be."

Chris felt his cheeks redden. What was it with women and his looks lately? This was getting uncomfortable and not just because she'd already kissed him. Britta was pretty with her dark blond hair and gray eyes, but she looked young—really young. "How old are you?"

"Nineteen."

Chris frowned.

"Eighteen."

He lifted a brow.

"Seventeen." She held up a hand to stop him from narrowing his eyes. "I am seventeen. I promise. That is more than old enough to get married."

He would have said the same thing once. Now, standing face-to-face with a seventeen-year-old who *did* want to marry him, he realized that Adelaide had been a little young to become a bride back when he'd proposed. And back then, he'd been seventeen about to turn eighteen. Now he was twenty-four. The six-year difference between him and Britta seemed huge. To be honest, the way she stared at him now with such adoration reminded him of a younger version of Sophia. He found himself slipping into overprotective brother mode. "Did you travel here alone? Where is your chaperone?"

"She went on to Clifton—the Norwegian settlement to the north. She left me here. I have my bags. Where is your family? When do we get married?" She shifted from one foot to the other with nervous energy until she appeared to be wagging like an overzealous puppy. How was it, then, that he was the one who felt

like whimpering? The sound of a throat clearing behind Britta shifted the girl's focus from him to Adelaide. Chris took advantage of Britta's distraction to
catch Adelaide's arm and guide her to his side. Britta
smiled at her. "Sophia?"

Adelaide gave her a sympathetic if guarded smile
in return. "No, I'm afraid not."

It almost seemed as if Britta understood her, for
both women looked to him. Adelaide was giving him
a choice. He recognized that. He was going to try to
go about this the honest way if he could. "Britta, I
can't marry you."

Her smiled dimmed. "We are promised."

"I did not promise anything."

"Your parents did. That is enough."

Adelaide leaned closer to whisper. "She speaks
English, Chris, and I'd prefer to know what y'all are
saying."

He tested it out. "I know what my parents promised, but I made a promise to Adelaide many years
ago that I'd marry her."

"Chris…" Adelaide began, no doubt protesting their
sudden jump from a courtship back to an implied engagement. However, one pointed glance at her lips
was enough to silence her.

Britta frowned and proved that she could speak
English with two words. "Speak Norwegian."

He repeated himself.

"This is the Adelaide to whom you have promised
yourself?" At his nod, Britta's gaze surveyed Adelaide
as though thoroughly unimpressed and unthreatened.
"I will speak to your parents, then we will marry."
Chris didn't even realize Wes was still standing there

until Britta switched to English to speak to the man. "I want to see Olan and Marta Johansen. Will you take me there and help me with my things?"

Chris shrugged. "I'll take you. It's the least I can do. Which bags are yours?"

She pointed them out. He hefted them into the push-cart next to Adelaide's and Rose's trunks. Looking at their luggage all mingled together, he realized that Britta was going to need someplace to stay. She probably didn't have money for a hotel. She could hardly stay with his parents—in the same house as him. That meant there was only one place for her to stay. He sent Adelaide an apologetic look even though she didn't seem to realize her fate yet. Wes kept Britta distracted while Adelaide joined Chris beside the cart.

"You do know that no one can make you marry a woman against your will," she whispered to him. "Engaged to me or not. You have to stand up for yourself and tell your father no."

"Says the woman who refuses to tell her mother that exact same word."

"Hey, I've told her *no* plenty of times. She just completely ignores me. It's annoying as all get-out, but you don't see me about to walk down the aisle with someone I don't want to marry. Do you?"

"Well, you are engaged to me so…" He caught her hand before she could poke his stomach. "None of that. I've been manhandled by enough women today. I've reached my quota." Her gaze fell to his lips and lingered there long enough to make his thinking go a little haywire. Why else would he be considering suggesting that he and Adelaide put this whole issue to rest by simply getting married to each other? It was a logical solution that would solve both their problems.

He shook those thoughts away. The true solution to his problem was a simple one. It was time to tell his parents no. There was no reason not to now that Olan's health wasn't nearly as precarious as they'd once feared. Besides, having finally come face-to-face with his parents' plan for his future, Chris was more certain than ever that he wouldn't have gone through with marrying Britta no matter how badly he wanted to honor their wishes.

Britta approached with her chin lifted. "Chris, I am ready to go."

"One minute." He glanced from Adelaide to Wes and knew there was no getting around it. She needed a trustworthy escort back to the mercantile. "Wes, would you do me a favor by delivering Adelaide's luggage to my... Uh, where she's staying? She can show you the way."

"My pleasure." Wes grabbed the handle of the push-cart. "After you, Miss Adelaide."

She glanced from Chris to Britta, then back again. Her voice was for his ears only. "Be strong."

Britta grabbed her suitcases from the cart as it passed. She grinned up at Chris. "Ready."

"This way." Chris took the luggage from her and began walking toward his parents' house. After all of her earlier chatter, Britta's thoughtful silence was a bit unnerving. He searched for a safe topic. "How was your trip?"

"Your parents' letter did not say anything about you being promised to another girl. Do they know?" Chris glanced over to meet her watchful, too insightful stare. He wasn't entirely sure how to answer her question. Before he could try, she continued, "If they do know, they do not approve. How could they? She is not Norwegian. They want you to marry someone from the home country. Their letters said you were a good Norwegian son—first born, at that. How can you go against their wishes?"

"Because I am a grown man who makes his own decisions." Or, at the very least, he was trying to be.

Britta frowned but waited until they crossed Main Street into the residential section of town before asking, "Do you mean to tell me that you do not intend to run your father's business as he wishes?"

"Of course I do." Even as he said it, the memory of sitting in the *Houston Gazette* newsroom filled his mind along with Everett's prediction that he would make a good newspaperman.

"Are you not the strong, responsible, compassionate, smart man they said that they have tried to raise you to be?"

"I hope so."

She stepped into his path, bringing them both to a stop as she leveled her stormy gray eyes at him. "You have always done exactly what they want you to do. Why do you suddenly want to draw a line in the sand when it comes to marrying me?"

A vision of Adelaide filled his mind. Without a doubt, she'd been the reason originally. However, after she'd broken their engagement, what had stopped him from giving into his parents' wish that he consider a mail-order bride? Certainly not his need for independence, because as Britta and even Everett had pointed out, he'd never sought the freedom to make his own choice—except when it came to marriage.

Was Adelaide still the answer after all these years? Had some part of him been waiting for her to return? Why else had he restricted his proposals to women he knew only considered him to be a friend? Had he actually been hoping they'd reject him so that he'd have yet another reason to postpone marrying anyone but her?

Britta's hand touched his arm, pulling his attention back to her. He had no desire to talk to her about his apparently unresolved feelings for Adelaide. He'd have to try something new and be completely honest. "I am sure you are a nice girl, Britta, but I do not want to marry you. I do not even know you."

Placing a hand on his chest, her sultry gaze never left his as she eased a step closer. Her voice softened. "We could get to know each other, Chris. It would be quite easy, I am sure, once we are married."

"Britta," he began, making sure he kept his voice low so that she had to listen closely. "Whatever you're trying to do here isn't going to work. Take your hands off me. I am not your husband or your betrothed, so your affection is unseemly. I apologize for the confusion, but you are here as a guest of my family and that is all. You will respect my boundaries. You will respect Adelaide. Is that understood?"

Britta closed her gaping mouth, then took a step back and pressed her lips into a firm line. They remained that way for the remainder of their short journey. Chris set her suitcases on the porch and knocked. Olan opened the door. "Chris, back so soon? I— Oh, hello, Miss…"

Catching his father's questioning gaze, Chris nodded toward the woman beside her. "Pa, may introduce Miss Britta Solberg? Also, you and I? We need to have a talk."

Chapter Ten

Adelaide had barely begun to unpack her trunk when Chris had shown up at the door of his apartment with an unhappy Britta in tow. The girl's frown had deepened at the sight of Adelaide. However, once Britta had stepped inside Chris's apartment, the mail-order bride's mood had improved considerably. Britta had nearly swooned as she hurried from room to room. She kept repeating the word *bedårende*, which according to Sophia meant "adorable."

It was a good thing Britta liked the apartment, because she sure didn't seem to like anything else about the situation. Adelaide couldn't really blame her. After all, the girl had traveled thousands of miles only to discover that her intended groom was dead set against marrying her and, by all appearances, quite ready to marry someone else. Keeping that in mind, Adelaide almost felt deserving of the icy glare Britta so often tossed her way. Still, the stony silence seemed a bit excessive, especially now that they'd all had three days to reconcile themselves to their uncomfortable new living arrangement.

Sophia had joined them at the same time as Britta. Her presence was invaluable. Not only did she serve as an interpreter when needed, but her joyful spirit helped lighten the strained atmosphere. Adelaide tried to do the same by remaining positive and friendly. However, she couldn't deny that it was challenging at times—especially since there seemed to be a disconcerting alliance forming between Rose and Britta. Adelaide had caught them speaking in low tones with their heads together more than once. Even now, her mother was out with Britta and Mrs. Johansen helping the girl to look for employment. Adelaide didn't begrudge them that. She'd just thought that after the conversation she'd had with Rose before they'd left Houston… Well, she wasn't entirely sure what she'd thought.

As it was, she was grateful that the sleeping arrangements had been decided so that Rose and Britta each had a room to themselves while she and Sophia shared the room containing a pair of twin beds. Sophia, being more sociable, kept mostly to the common room. She also continued to work downstairs at the store. That gave Adelaide plenty of time and privacy to write. In turn, her writing gave her a legitimate reason to stay out of everyone's way.

A knock on the bedroom door made Adelaide jump just as Sophia leaned inside. "I'm sorry, Adelaide. I didn't mean to startle you."

"That's all right. I was just lost in thought." She glanced down at the rather barren-looking page she'd been working on, ready for a distraction. "What are you up to?"

"It's such a nice day that I thought we might have it

picnic-style on the lawn in front of the church. Chris said he could join us in about ten minutes when he has his break from the store. Or, if you'd rather keep writing, we can eat here. What do you think?"

Adelaide placed a hand on her stomach which gave a little growl at the mere mention of food. "I think that sounds like a lovely idea. I can't remember the last time I had a picnic."

"Well, it's time to change that. Everything is ready. We just need to grab the basket on the way out."

"Perfect." As they walked to the church, Adelaide allowed herself to enjoy the friendship that had begun to deepen between them since they'd started sharing a room. They'd always been friendly to each other in the past. However, Adelaide had also always been Chris's particular friend, so she and Sophia hadn't interacted quite as much back then. The past two nights they'd stay up talking long after they'd turned out the lights. It was refreshing, but Adelaide wasn't entirely sure how close she should allow herself to get to Sophia or anyone else in Peppin. Sooner rather than later she would be going back to Houston. She'd have to say goodbye to them all over again.

Adelaide held back a sigh as she helped Sophia spread the blanket on the thick layer of green grass that was the church lawn. Chris met up with them just as they were laying out the food. He took one look into Adelaide's eyes and asked, "What's troubling you?"

She smiled at his perceptiveness and Sophia's surprise before offering a shrug. "It's hard not knowing what's going on in Houston with my pa. I know he hasn't contacted us because he wants to keep our whereabouts unknown. I'm sure he'll come to tell us everything himself as soon as he can. But not knowing when that's going to be makes it hard to..."

Sophia reached over to touch her hand. "Makes it hard to what?"

"Not get attached to Peppin again." She avoided the intense searching in Chris's gaze by focusing on his sister. "I know it probably sounds bad to say that, but I moved so often as a child that I learned to remain sort of detached. Peppin was different. I had every intention of spending the rest of my life here. Being back in Peppin... Well, part of me wishes my pa would hurry up and get here so that I can leave already. The longer I stay, the more it will hurt when I finally have to go."

Chris tilted his head with a doubtful frown. "So you want to rush back to your life in Houston? The one where you seemed to have no interest in what was happening around you, no real friends and were completely under your mother's thumb? You deserve better."

Sophia rolled her eyes. "Land sakes, Chris! Don't hold back, now. Tell us how you really feel."

"He's right. I was pretty miserable. However, it isn't as though I have much of a choice."

"Of course you do." Sophia frowned. "You and Chris can get married. There's no reason to put it off any longer."

Awkward silence descended upon their picnic as Sophia glanced back and forth between them while they looked anywhere but at her. Adelaide finally met Sophia's gaze in time to see realization fill the woman's blue eyes. That was quickly followed by disappointment and exasperation. "Oh, come on. Really?

Again? Why can't y'all just be a normal couple? Either get together, or break up once and for all."

"Listen, princess—"

She didn't. "You know what? I stand by my previous statement. Y'all should get married. It's obvious that y'all care for each other—always have and probably always will. However, I respect the fact that it's completely your decision so that's all I'm going to say on that matter. Strawberries, anyone?"

Adelaide glanced at Chris and they both burst out laughing. Adelaide scooted over to give Sophia a sideways hug, crying out softly, "Oh, no. I'm already attached."

Sophia grinned and hugged her back. "Good. You should be. Maybe we can find a way for you to stay here, with or without you marrying my brother."

"I don't know," Adelaide said, altogether unsure if it was really a good idea to live in the same town as Chris for the rest of her life. She had promised herself that she would get over her feelings for him. Surely that would be far easier from a distance. Yet, if her goal was to be a spinster author one day, why not try to find a way to do that in a town she loved? Was that feasible?

She made a respectable income from her writing, but she wasn't sure it was enough to allow her to be totally independent. She certainly couldn't see her mother supporting that lifestyle, or her stepfather for that matter. He was far too concerned with her safety to be amenable to the idea of her living in another town by herself. She shook her head. "I simply don't see how it's possible."

"Then we should pray about it, and ask God to show

us a way." Sophia tilted her head when Adelaide didn't immediately respond. "Why do I feel as though I said the wrong thing again?"

"I stopped praying a long time ago."

Concern furrowed Chris's brow. "Why?"

"The church we go to in Houston isn't genuine like the one here. It's more for show. All the *right* people go there. I guess it never really appealed to me because I don't consider myself one of them. I know you aren't supposed to go to church for the people, but..." She stopped because Chris was already shaking his head. "What?"

"Sweetheart, the people *are* the church. Sermons can be excellent and helpful and all of that. However, fellowship with other believers is extremely important. That's why the Bible talks about 'iron sharpening iron.' I'm guessing you haven't had that."

"I suppose not."

"Well," Sophia said. "Now you do. Chris, would you lead us in prayer?"

Chris seemed to hesitate slightly before he nodded and offered one hand to each of them. Adelaide stared at his hand for a moment as something inside her rebelled. Something stronger filled her eyes with tears and then prompted her to slide her hand into his. Sophia completed their circle. Chris's words were slow and deliberate. "Lord, we thank You for the time You've given us with Adelaide. I know that You're using it to strengthen her faith and mine. I ask that while she's here You allow us all to be an encouragement to each other. Help us to remember that You have a plan here, Lord, even though we can't always see it."

He pulled in a deep breath, then sped up considerably. "Most of all, we ask that You reveal Your love to Adelaide and draw her closer to You. Plant her in a body of believers who will help her faith to grow. If that place should be Peppin, then we ask and believe that You will make a way for that to happen. We ask this all in Jesus' name, amen."

Chris released their hands almost before they'd finished echoing his amen. "I'd better get back to the store."

Sophia frowned. "But, you've barely eaten anything."

"I know, but there's something I forgot to do."

Adelaide wrapped one of the sandwiches in a napkin for him. "Here. At least take this with you."

He accepted it with a quick "Thank you," then set off toward the mercantile. Adelaide turned to watch him go, certain that his departure had very little to do with the store. Something was definitely bothering him. She just didn't know if it was something about the prayer...or something about her.

This was all wrong. Chris shouldn't have been the one to pray for Adelaide. As she'd talked he'd realized he was struggling with the same thing except that his problem was worse. Unlike Adelaide, who'd slowly drifted away from God, Chris had purposefully disconnected himself. He'd shut down every line of communication with his Maker because he hadn't wanted to give God a chance to lead him to do something he didn't want to do. Well, that was exactly what God had done as soon as Chris had started praying. The simple act of actually thanking God for bringing Adelaide back into his life had been difficult. Admitting that

God had a plan in all this, some purpose that Chris himself might not be aware of was downright scary. Yet, as he'd said the words he'd known that they were true and that he meant them.

He'd also realized that the huge act of obedience he'd been wrestling with wasn't to his parents. It was to God. It had nothing to do with the mail-order bride and everything to do with Adelaide. What God wanted was so simple and obvious that Chris knew the only reason he hadn't been aware of it before was because he hadn't wanted to be. God was asking him to forgive Adelaide. To release the anger he'd held against her like a guard around his heart. To recognize the fact that the choices she'd made years ago might have been hurtful but they weren't unhealable—unless he chose for them to be, as he had for so long.

Before she'd returned to Peppin he'd had a much easier time ignoring the pain he felt. Now that she was here, living in the home he'd prepared for her, he couldn't ignore it anymore. Chris was beginning to suspect that the only true relief would come by doing exactly what God was asking of him. So right there in the business office of Johansen's mercantile where he'd retreated for lack of anywhere else to go, Chris bowed his head.

"Father, I'm sorry for ignoring You, avoiding You and disregarding Your direction in my life. I know the things You ask me to do are out of love for me and for a good purpose. I put down the pride that says I know what's best for my life. I submit myself to You again. Help me to be more sensitive to Your voice and eager to do Your will. Right now, I bring myself back into obedience to You by forgiving Adelaide." He swallowed hard. Now that he'd started down this path, the words seemed to come more naturally. "I do forgive her, Lord. I forgive her for breaking our engagement all those years ago. I forgive her for rejecting me. Help me to live out that decision."

He was right about to say amen when a knock sounded on the closed office door. He held his breath hoping that, if he was quiet, whoever it was would walk away. Instead, the person knocked more loudly. Whispering the ending to his prayer, Chris was about to bid the knocker to enter when the door opened on its own. Britta peeked into the room before stepping inside and closing the door behind her. "There you are. Why did you not answer?"

"I was busy with something." He watched her gaze sweep the empty presidential-style desk before it returned to where he stood by the window. Britta had adhered to his No Touching policy so far. However, he'd caught a predatory glint in her eyes a couple of times over the past few days. She was definitely up to something. He just wasn't sure what. He also wasn't entirely sure whether it would be safer to stay where he was, which was far away from her but in a corner, or sit behind the desk, which would put an object between them while limiting his mobility. He settled for standing behind the desk and crossing his arms. "How can I help you?"

"You can congratulate me." She stepped forward before offering a small smile. "I have a job at the café. I am going to be a waitress."

"That's wonderful, Britta! That is an excellent place to work. I am sure Maddie will be a great employer."

"Thank you. She seems nice. I am certain the job

will be adequate." She paced to the window, presumably to look across the street at the café. "Naturally, that is not what I had hoped for when I set out for America. However, as Mrs. Holden says, one must do the best with what one is given."

Chris frowned. "You've been talking to Mrs. Holden?"

"We live in the same flat," Britta said, as though that made it a given. In Chris's opinion, it didn't. Mrs. Holden wasn't even all that friendly with her own daughter most of the time. Why would she be so to Britta? Furthermore, Chris knew being in the same flat with someone didn't mean Britta would talk to them. According to Sophia, the girl hadn't said a word to Adelaide since they'd all moved in together. Chris hadn't said anything about it because he'd figured Adelaide might not necessarily mind the silence.

Britta turned to face him. Her gray eyes were sober. "The other reason I came here was to apologize. I realize now that you were not expecting me and that is was silly for me to expect you to receive me with open arms."

Chris couldn't help glancing down at his tightly crossed arms. "I suppose you could not have known that I hadn't agreed to my parents' arrangement."

She gave a shallow nod. "I am also sorry that I offended you by touching you too much. My family is very affectionate, so that is just how I was raised. I fear it is something of a habit. However, I am doing my best to curtail it."

"I have noticed, and I appreciate that."

She smiled hesitantly. "Then you accept my apology?"

"Certainly."

"Good. Perhaps now we can relax and be friends. It seems the thing to do, does it not? After all, I will be staying here for an uncertain amount of time and—"

Amused at her exuberance, he finally laughed. "Yes. Yes. We can be friends. Now, you know that you will have to practice your English in order to be able to do your job. You can't tell everyone the daily specials in Norwegian."

"Oh, I will practice my English, of course! Your mother said she would help me. I will go find her now so we can begin." She chattered on as Chris walked her to the office door. He closed it behind her with a relieved sigh that immediately made him feel guilty. Britta had seemed genuine in her apology, so surely there was no need to remain on his guard. However, something told him there was. After promising he'd be more sensitive to God's leading, Chris intended to take that gut feeling seriously. He straightened from the door intending to finally eat the sandwich Adelaide had given him. A knock sounded on the door again. Holding back a groan, he opened the door. "Britta, I— Oh. Adelaide."

Laughter filled her eyes at the obvious relief in his voice. She lifted an eyebrow as a hint of a smile tugged at her lips. "Sorry to disappoint."

"Funny." He caught her hands and tugged her inside, backing up until he was able to lean against the desk. "What can I do for you?"

"Nothing. I wanted to check on you. You left the picnic so abruptly that I thought something might be wrong."

"No." Chris paused to consider whether or not he

should tell about his decision to forgive her. Admitting such a thing might make her feel obligated to do the same—something she might not be ready for yet. Or she might not feel that she'd done anything warranting his forgiveness and be offended that he was offering it. No, it would be far better for him to keep quiet about it for now. Perhaps he'd tell her one day. Until then, he could try to show his change of attitude through his actions. Refocusing on her, he said, "I just need a minute alone to do a little praying of my own."

She searched his eyes for a moment as though sensing there was more to it than that. "All right. Well, in the future, feel free to let me know if anything is bothering you. Since you prayed for me, it only seems fair I return the favor—especially now that I'm learning to do it again."

"I will."

"Good. I'll let you get back to work." She took a step backward, but stopped when he didn't release her hands. He drew her back over the distance she'd created. Standing, he glanced down at their joined hands. He wasn't entirely sure why he couldn't let go except for the fact that he wanted to test this out. He wanted to see if forgiveness had managed to ease that dull ache that filled his chest when he was in her presence—the one he'd been constantly trying to ignore or avoid. He found that the pain was gone.

In its place was wariness.

He might have forgiven her for hurting him before, but that didn't mean he wanted to have his heart broken again. At the same time, he was so tired of being on the defensive around her. He'd waited years for her to return. Now that she was here all he'd done was keep his distance. He ought to keep doing it, pain or no pain. It was the right thing to do. The smart thing to do. The safe thing to do.

He'd just released her hands when a throat cleared near the office door. He glanced up find Mrs. Holden waiting for their full attention. Once she had it, she announced. "Everett is here. He wants to talk to the three of us. Brace yourselves. He looks… Well, I don't think he's bringing good news."

Chapter Eleven

Adelaide had to agree with her mother. Everett looked rough. Stubble littered his normally clean-shaven face. Dark circles revealed how rare sleep had been since they'd left him in Houston. After giving her a long hug in greeting he settled onto the settee in Chris's apartment with Rose at his side. Adelaide and Chris claimed the set of matching turquoise chairs cattycorner to it. Unable to bear the tension any longer, Adelaide asked, "Pa, what is it? What happened? What's wrong?"

He sighed and washed his hand over his face. "The story I was investigating turned out to be a fake. The whole thing was set up by a powerful man in an effort to discredit me by tricking me into publishing a false story. A police investigation revealed the truth. Unfortunately, that happened *after* I printed my article. My competition was quick to capitalize on my error and I can't blame them for it. I never should have fallen for such a ridiculous trick. I was just so eager to shut that network down that I fell into their trap. I sensed something might be wrong because all of the information was a tad too easy to find. However, after they dared to threaten my family, I let emotion cloud my judgment by going ahead with the story despite my misgivings. I suppose that was exactly what they were counting on, and I played right into their hands."

He shook his head. "I printed a retraction, but the damage has already been done. The *Gazette's* major advertisers all threatened to pull out if I don't resign from my position as editor-in-chief. I hired someone from the outside to serve in the interim. I hope that the quick change in leadership will keep the finances from taking too much of a hit. I know it sounds bad, but it could have been much worse. The newspaper could have folded completely. Or I could have been forced to sell. As it is now, I've maintained ownership, but agreed to keep my public involvement to a minimum until it all blows over. I'm afraid that may take a while." He took his wife's hand in his. "I don't know how many of our friends will stand by us. However, I do know that Houston is going to be an uncomfortable place for us. My reputation may never fully recover. I'm afraid that's going to affect your standing as well."

"My standing is of little consequence at the moment. I'm just sorry you had to go through this. I don't take the idea of pulling up stakes lightly, but I think this might be a case when starting over somewhere new truly is the best option." Rose turned to Adelaide. "What do you think, dear?"

This was the first time any of her parents had solicited her opinion on where they ought to live. Caught off guard by the deference, it took Adelaide a moment to respond. She'd hoped to say something profound, but all that came out was, "I agree."

Chris met her gaze with a quick, silent question. She gave a small nod and he smiled before turning to her parents. "In that case, may I formally put in Peppin's bid to become the new location of the Holden-Harper household? We are, after all, a growing town without a newspaper."

Rose laughed. "Move to Peppin? There is no possible way..." She trailed off, most likely realizing that Everett wasn't laughing with her. In fact, he looked positively intrigued. Rose frowned. "Everett, you can't be seriously considering this."

"I am. In fact, I can't say the idea hasn't occurred to me before."

"I can. And, now that I'm thinking it, I don't like it."

Everett nodded toward Adelaide. "Look at our daughter, Rose. She's got color in her cheeks and a spark in her eyes. I've only been here a few minutes, but I can already tell she feels at home here. When was the last time you saw her like that? For me, it was a week ago when she and I came through Peppin."

Conscious of everyone's sudden stare, Adelaide lowered her gaze to her clasped hands in her lap. The ensuing silence finally made her lift her eyes to meet her mother's. Rose's mouth softened with a hint of a smile that only lasted until she looked past Adelaide to Chris and narrowed her eyes. "What makes you think Peppin is responsible for that and not—"

Adelaide shot to her feet, caught Chris's hand and dragged him along with her toward the door that led to the alleyway. "I think it's best that we give y'all some privacy to discuss this. We'll be right outside."

Stepping out onto the landing, she closed the door

behind Chris, then leaned back against it. Chris lifted a brow. "I wanted to hear what she was going to say."

"Trust me. You only think you did." Rose would never empower Chris by divulging anything she knew about Adelaide's feelings for him. She most likely had been about to say something negative about Chris. With a sigh, Adelaide sat on the first step of the stairs that wound down into the alley. He sat beside her.

"What does your mother have against this town?" He gently bumped her shoulder with his. "I mean, besides the fact that I live here. Or is that enough?"

She offered him a sympathetic smile. "I don't think it's entirely about you. There are a few other things involved. We lived here with my father for a while, so the town carries unhappy memories of him. He's also buried here. As you know, we made a living by taking in laundry after he died. I'm guessing she might be a little ashamed of it now that she's had a chance to rise to high society in Houston. Plus, Mr. Stolvins was always pestering her to marry him, which was unpleasant."

"Mr. Stolvins. Now, that's a name I haven't heard in a while. He used to own the saloon a while back, didn't he?"

"Yes, along with the building that housed our laundry and rooms. According to Mrs. Greene, he moved away not long after we left." She bit her lip and glanced toward the slice of Main Street that was framed by the shadowed alleyway. "In hindsight, I suppose my mother didn't have nearly as pleasant a time here as I did. I can understand her not being eager to return. Maybe I shouldn't have asked her to."

"You didn't ask. I did."

She angled herself so that she could look him directly in the eye. "Thank you for that, by the way. I truly appreciate everything you've done to help me and my family over the past week."

"I was glad to do it."

"I know. That's what is so amazing to me. You didn't have to do any of this. Yet you gave up your home, your time and I don't doubt some of your peace of mind without a single complaint or moment of impatience. On top of that, you did it for someone who…"

She couldn't decide how to finish that statement. There were too many options. She'd been someone he hadn't seen in years, someone who'd broken his heart, someone who wouldn't even have been considered his friend. Tears spilled into her lashes, pooling like dewdrops. She did her best to blink them away, but Chris caught sight of them anyway. He put his arm around her waist and drew her to his side until her head rested against his shoulder. "Hey, now. There's no need for all of that."

"Yes, there is." She pulled in a shuddering breath. "Please stop being so wonderful. It's very disconcerting."

She could tell he was smiling even though she couldn't see it. "It took me a while to get this way, so I think I'd better keep it up."

He was trying to make her laugh, but she didn't want to laugh. She wanted to be angry. It was all so unfair. She was trying exceedingly hard not to like him, and he wasn't helping her cause at all. She tilted her head back, intending to give him an irritated look. Unfortunately, her gaze got a little hung up on his smile. It was so warm and sweet and playful that she completely forgot everything else. She forced her attention to his eyes, hoping he hadn't noticed where hers had lingered. He had. Of course he had. His smile slipped away. His blue eyes darkened. She waited, hardly breathing until he dipped his head to kiss her.

Nothing about this kiss was for show. It was gentle. It was testing. It was brief. When he pulled away, a beat of frozen silence stretched between them. Then, as one, they turned toward each other, his hand pressed against her back to guide her into another kiss. Keeping one hand on the landing for balance, her other arm went around his shoulder while his free hand landed on his waist. The kiss deepened until her hand slid down to his chest and she forced herself to push away. "Whoa. Wait. What are we doing?"

Chris's fingers traced the curve of her chin. Realizing that her words weren't processing for him, she caught his hand. "Chris, focus."

His gaze honed in on hers with an intensity that left her a little woozy. She closed her eyes and shook her head. This was bad. This was really bad. She'd gone too far. She needed to pull back completely if she intended to have any success at ridding herself of her infatuation with this man. "Chris, we should stop pretending that we're courting."

"I'm pretty sure we just did."

He'd misunderstood her completely. He thought she meant she wanted their courtship to be real. She opened her eyes to tell him differently, but she couldn't do it. She'd wanted this to happen. She knew that now. Otherwise, she wouldn't have allowed him to kiss her in the first place. She certainly wouldn't have kissed him back. But she couldn't bring herself to feel happy when she was too busy being scared.

What if her mother was right about Chris? Adelaide still had her own suspicions. Then there was Britta. The girl hadn't given up on capturing Chris's heart. Britta certainly wouldn't have any second thoughts about kissing Chris. How much of her pursuit could Chris take before succumbing and agreeing to marry her? Was Adelaide really willing to fight for Chris? If she won, wasn't there still a chance she'd lose out to someone else later?

Refocusing on him, she found a way to smile and agree with his assessment even though she knew she could be taking the first step toward a lifetime of heartache.

Chris hadn't intended to go from forgiving Adelaide to actually, officially, courting her in the span of a few minutes. Yet there had been an undeniable sense of inevitability to it all. He knew that history could easily repeat itself. There was a good chance that he could find himself alone, rejected and heartbroken. But he couldn't cheat himself out of the opportunity to find out once and for all if he could make a relationship work with Adelaide.

A little over a week later, he was feeling less confident. Adelaide and her parents had returned to Houston to pack up their belongings. They were due back any day now and planning to move into a house on one of the more affluent streets in town. Meanwhile, Chris was feeling rather like that seventeen-year-old boy who'd been left behind to wait and wonder if or when Adelaide would return. That feeling had brought on many doubts and the same old fears.

"She's going to break my heart. Man, she's going to break my heart. I know she is. What was I *thinking*? It's her kiss. There's something about it that makes me temporarily insane. The first time I kissed her…the *very first time*… I proposed. Who does that?" Exasperated at himself, Chris shook his head and melted onto one of the moss-green chairs in the parlor of Rhett Granger's new house. The room, with its cream walls and large windows that looked onto the flower-filled garden, was far too cheerful to match Chris's dark mood. Then again, perhaps his mood was what needed changing. "You know what? Forget I mentioned anything. We're here to practice music. Not talk about women."

Rhett sent Chris a skeptical look while claiming his own chair. "When have we ever had a practice session without talking about women at some point? This is the girl who Ellie paired with you on the Bachelor List, isn't it? Quinn, I gave Chris the list."

Quinn Tucker who, according to Rhett, had been the first bachelor to use the list, stopped in his tracks to grin. "Oh, yeah, boy. You're in for it now."

"In for what?"

"Love." Quinn and Rhett answered together, both drawing out the word for a ridiculously long amount of time. The two men grinned at each other before Rhett crossed the room to extend his hand to Chris. "I suppose I should officially welcome you to the club."

Chris set his violin case down to shake Rhett's hand. "Wait. What do you mean? There's a club?"

Rhett said "Yes" at the same time that Quinn said "No." Quinn frowned. "Since when is there a club?"

"*Why* is there a club?" Chris asked.

"There's a club because we need to support each other. We already are anyway. I helped Quinn out when he had the list. Quinn definitely helped me. Now we're both helping you." Rhett turned to Quinn. "I founded the club right after Ellie created the Bachelor List. Lawson and I made her president, but she hasn't done anything with the organization so I'm moving that we dispense with the formalities of offices. Now, all in favor say aye."

"Wait!" Isabelle cried before entering the room with a carafe of coffee. She pinned her husband with her emerald gaze. "Rhett, you can't just vote someone out of their own club—especially if they aren't around to speak for themselves. It isn't right."

Rhett lifted a brow. "I thought you said you were going down the block to visit your folks with Helen."

"I'll make it there eventually." She lifted the carafe, then placed it on the low table. "First, I was going to bring y'all some coffee. Then I started eavesdropping. I'd apologize to y'all, but I wouldn't mean it, so I won't."

Quinn called out to his wife, "Helen, you might as well come in, too."

She at least had the grace to look a little guilty. However, that cleared up as she realized her husband was more interested in wrapping his arm around her waist and pressing a kiss to her hair than he was in the conversation. Helen shrugged. "Honestly, I don't see anything wrong with the men banding together to support each other. However, it would be nice of y'all to give Ellie back her list since it belongs to her."

"She doesn't need it anymore," Quinn insisted. "She made her match with Lawson."

Rhett crossed his arms. "She let me go around thinking my match was Amy instead of Isabelle."

Isabelle shook her head at them. "Listen to yourselves. She's helped all of y'all find love in one way or another even if it was only through a point in the right direction. Y'all aren't *entitled* to her help. She's given it because she considers you her friends. These attitudes are no way to repay her. Rhett, as nervous as you were around Amy when you thought she was your match, I can understand why she wouldn't tell you about me. If y'all don't think she's involved enough in your club, then invite her to be. She might appreciate having at least a little control over something she set in motion."

Chris exchanged glances with Rhett and Quinn, feeling just as taken to task as they looked. Rhett was the first to admit what they were all thinking. "Isabelle is right."

Quinn rubbed his jaw. "I guess we ought to find a way to thank Ellie."

Realizing everyone was looking at him with expectation, Chris searched his mind for something to say. "I'll try to make sure Ellie knows I appreciate all she's done. It's just…uh… Well, I'm not entirely certain I should be in this club. I mean, the list does say that Adelaide is my match, but that doesn't really help me all that much."

Quinn sat on the settee and tugged his wife down beside him. "Maybe you aren't using it right. Have you told Adelaide she's your match? That's what made Helen agree to marry me."

"No, it isn't."

Quinn caught Chris's eye and nodded while silently mouthing *the list*.

Helen caught him and placed a stilling hand on her husband's chest. "Stop it. You'll give Chris false expectations. The list may have given you the courage to ask me, but we both know I originally agreed only because I wanted to be a mother to the nieces and nephews you were raising."

Isabelle grinned. "And she was attracted to you. She told me that herself."

"Did she, now?"

"Uh-oh," Chris teased. "Helen had a crush on Quinn."

A blush rose in Helen's cheeks even as she shook her head at them. "Y'all are ridiculous. How can this possibly be new information to anyone? Especially you, Quinn."

"It isn't new...just mighty interesting," Quinn winked at her before turning back to the subject at hand. "Chris, I still think you should use the list to help you propose."

Rhett shook his head. "You don't have to use the list for anything. It's there to confirm that it's time to go after the woman you're matched with. Stop worrying about her breaking your heart. Focus on wooing her so hard and so well she wouldn't even think of it."

Helen smiled. "Is that what you did, Rhett?"

Isabelle's heart showed in her eyes as she looked at her husband. "That's what he's still doing."

Chris felt his heart melt a little as he glanced back

and forth between the two couples before him. The love and trust they had for each other was so deep and genuine that it felt almost tangible. He wished he could bottle it up and apply it directly to his relationship. However, it was impossible to shortcut his way to what these couples had. He knew their stories. They'd built what they had now from the ground up through courage, commitment and perseverance. If that's what he wanted, he'd have to go about it the same way. He only wished he could be more certain that he and Adelaide were up to the challenge.

Chapter Twelve

Sunlight streamed through the windows onto the bare wood floor of Adelaide's new bedroom in Peppin. She followed its path to kneel on the broad window seat. She raised the pane up as high as it would go. A gust of wind filled the room, teasing at her hair and bringing with it the heady scent of honeysuckle. She took a deep breath of it before leaving the bedroom and heading down the stairs.

She edged past the servants who were on the way up with the headboard for her parents' room. This was most of the staff's last day, since their services wouldn't be needed in Peppin. They would each receive a bonus at the end of the day and a train ticket back to Houston. That's why Rose stood on the front porch directing traffic with the finesse of a seasoned policeman. Adelaide gathered her courage, then ran over to give her mother a quick hug. "Thank you for changing your mind."

Rose froze in surprise before hugging her back. "You're welcome, dear. Although I'm altogether convinced I'm going to regret this decision."

"Uh-uh. It's too late to change your mind now."

"Don't I know it?" Rose's focus shifted over Adelaide's shoulder into the house. "Wait! You can't leave the settee in the dining room."

Adelaide stepped aside to let her mother rush off to deal with the latest crisis. Taking the brick-paved path across the front lawn, Adelaide met up with Everett beside the wagons parked on the street. He took the hug and thanks she offered before nodding toward the front porch. "That was nice to see. I'm hoping that moving here will allow us to spend more time together as a family and help us grow closer."

Wondering if that actually might be possible, she glanced back at the two-story Queen Anne–style house. Painted in shades of blue with white trim, it had a porch that spanned the entire front of the house. It was substantially smaller than the house they'd had in Houston, but there was still plenty of room for the three of them. It represented a fresh slate and brand-new memories. She figured those memories might as well be good ones, so she nodded. "I hope so, too."

"Speaking of family, or perhaps I should say possible future family, where's Chris? I thought for sure he'd meet us at the station."

She bit her lip. "I didn't tell him we were coming. He's done so much for us already. I didn't want him to think he had to help us move in, too."

"You mean he doesn't know you're here?" Everett waved a hand in the general direction of Main Street. "Go find him. He'll want to see you. If he offers to help, just tell him we have it covered."

"Shouldn't I stay and help, though?"

"There isn't much that you can do while we're unloading the wagons. We'll need you to tell us how you want your furniture set up in your room, but we're a couple of hours away from that stage. Go on, now. Get going."

"All right, I'm going." She laughed as she set off down the street. It only took a few minutes to reach Johansen's Mercantile. Olan was the first to greet her so she went over to lean against the front counter. "Mr. Johansen, you're looking well. It's good to see you behind the counter again."

"It's good to be back and thank you. You're the second person who has told me that today. I guess all that resting Doc Williams told me to do must be paying off. Does Chris know you're back in town?"

"No. I was looking for him." She glanced around the store, but only saw August near the back helping a customer. "Is he working right now?"

"He's off today, but he did pass through on the way to the café a few minutes ago. I think he's still there."

She thanked him and hurried across the street. The moment she stepped into the café she spotted Chris facing away from her at one of the tables across the room. A flurry of butterflies took flight in her belly. She hadn't seen him in nearly two weeks. What if he'd changed his mind about courting her? Well, she still had every intention of going through with a real courtship even though it didn't seem one bit less terrifying or foolhardy than it had when she'd first agreed to it.

She swallowed hard, lifted her chin and tried to ignore the curious glances she drew. If the folks in this wonderful, nosy town expected another exhibition like the one they'd seen in the mercantile, they would be sorely disappointed. Noticing that he was

intent on his newspaper, she paused, trying to decide
how to best approach him without startling him. She
could simply call his name, but that was such a boring way to surprise someone. And now folks in the
café were really staring.

Decision made, she backed up a few feet to ask
Maddie for a little help. The woman loaned her a pencil and a page out of her small order book. Adelaide
scribbled a quick message, then handed it to Maddie
before slipping outside to wait in the soft shadows of
the alleyway beside the café. Maddie must have de-
livered it immediately for Adelaide heard the hollow
ring of footsteps on the wooden sidewalk in a matter
of seconds. Chris stepped into the alley, caught sight of
her and grinned. "Well, it's about time. Get over here."

She laughed and stepped right into his waiting
embrace for a tight hug. She finally eased back just
enough to look into his eyes. The relief there made
her realize that he hadn't been entirely sure she'd actually return. She was glad that he'd actually wanted
her to. Her hands slid down to wrap around his waist
while she let her head rest on his shoulder. His deep
voice rumbled in her ear with a hint of uncertainty.
"You're here to stay?"

She took a step backward out of his embrace, but
he caught her hands so she couldn't go much farther
than that. She nodded. Her knees began to bounce
with nervous energy to a happy beat only she could
hear. Swinging their hands back and forth, she widened her eyes. "I'm so excited!"

He laughed, then leaned down to place a feather-
light kiss on her mouth. "We should go back inside."

"But there are so many people in there."

"Exactly. There's safety in numbers." He stepped behind her to catch her waist in his hands and propel her toward the sidewalk. "Have you eaten dinner?"

"No." She leaned back against his chest, using her weight to bring them to a stop before they reached the sunlight. "Wait!"

"What?"

She placed her hands over his. "We can't step out there like this. We have to at least pretend to be respectable."

"Says the woman who sent me a note in front of the entire café that told me to meet her in an alleyway." He released her waist with a light squeeze. He guided her onto the sidewalk and back into the café where he pulled out her chair for her, then seated himself. "All right. Tell me everything. When did you get here?"

"We arrived about twenty minutes ago on the train. Pa had sent the wagons ahead with our things so we met up with the drivers at the livery. We brought almost our entire house staff down for the move. They're all unloading the wagons now, but they leave tomorrow, so that's when the fun begins for my family when it comes to unpacking. Right now, everything is pretty hectic. I think part of the reason Pa shooed me off to find you was so I'd be out of the way."

"Well, I'm glad he did." His smile turned into a concern frown. "How were things in Houston?"

Adelaide shrugged. "Honestly, I was too busy packing to see much of the fallout from the newspaper crisis while I was there. Mother went on a few farewell visits, but she didn't tell me how they went. Pa had so much to do that I could barely catch him coming and going. Speaking of fathers, I saw yours a few minutes ago at the mercantile. He seems to be doing better."

"We're still working through a few things, but you're right. He is improving. In general, he's more relaxed now, which means he can rest better and actually get some sleep. Apparently he wasn't doing much of that before, which only made his symptoms worse. All of that means he doesn't have nervous spells as often."

"Good. I'm so glad to hear that." She bit her lip. "What about us? I mean, has he said anything?"

He grinned. "Not a word. I think he kind of ended up scaring himself with that whole mail-order bride scheme. I'm guessing it seemed like a good idea in theory but it became too real too quickly when the actual stranger showed up at his door wanting to marry his son. It didn't help that Britta was a little different than how she'd been presented in the letters."

"Different how?"

"She's younger for one thing. The letters said she was nineteen. She admitted to seventeen, but I wouldn't put it past her to be only sixteen. She also said she had a better command of English than she actually does. However, I can't really fault her on that because learning a new language and having to live immersed in it are two different things. Besides, you know how much I struggled with the transition myself. I guess the main thing is…" He stopped himself with a shake of his head. "I probably shouldn't say all of this. I feel like I'm gossiping about her."

She took his hand. "You aren't gossiping. You're informing me, and it's only right that I know. After all, she was brought here for you."

"All right. Well, this isn't a big problem anymore because I talked to her about it, but when she first

came…" He lowered his voice. "She was a little bold."
He shrugged. "You saw her kiss me at the station so
you know what I mean."

"Yes, I do," she said, battling the ridiculous urge
to wipe his mouth with a napkin as though that would
erase her memory of that kiss. "Has she done anything since then?"

"Not really. At least, nothing I couldn't handle."

That did not sound good. She frowned. "Chris, girls
like that don't need to be 'handled.' They need to be
avoided."

"That's kind of hard to do since my mother is giving her English lessons. She eats supper with my family most nights. If I avoid her, it means avoiding my
family. They feel responsible for her since she came to
America in response to my parents' erroneous promise. She has no family of her own here, no one else
to look after her. We tried contacting the chaperone
she traveled with, but haven't heard anything back
yet. The situation isn't ideal by any means. I've got it
under control, though. Trust me."

Adelaide met his honest blue eyes and didn't doubt
for a second that he *thought* he had everything under
control. Whether he truly did or not was still to be
seen. Her past actually didn't give her much guidance
on how to deal with this. As far as she knew, her father had been the one chasing women. But with Chris,
women simply came chasing after him. She wanted
to trust him, but how long could a man in his position
hold out when a woman like Britta had set her sights
on him? She could only hope the answer to that question was *forever.* She just wasn't sure she could trust
that it would be.

* * *

Chris was determined to follow Rhett's advice by wooing Adelaide to the best of his abilities. He hadn't had much of a chance to do so in the week since she'd arrived. He'd had work and she'd needed a chance to settle in to her new house. Today was his first real opportunity, so after his shift at the mercantile ended, he made sure to pick her up on time for Rhett and Isabelle's housewarming party. Chris introduced her to the few people she didn't already know. Then Rhett and Isabelle asked for everyone's attention.

Rhett put an arm around his wife's waist. "We just wanted to take the chance to thank all of y'all for coming and for your gifts."

Isabelle added, "Violet begged me to let her be in charge of our first game today. I think most of you already know this, but my little sister has a flare for the dramatic so I apologize in advance for any theatrics." Isabelle lowered her voice to a stage whisper. "She also wanted to make an entrance so… Violet, we're ready!"

The sixteen-year-old stepped into the parlor, setting off a twitter of laughter. She'd donned a long coat, a policeman's cap and a handlebar mustache. She affected a deep Scottish brogue. "My name is Inspector Bradley of Scotland Yard."

"Good accent, Vi," Wes called before elbowing Gabe Nolan who was standing next to him. "I helped her with that. Got in touch with my roots."

The dark-haired artist rolled his eyes. "I know. I was there visiting the Bradleys with you."

Violet lifted her chin and glared at them. "Gents, please. Simply because you were boarders in the former Bradley Boardinghouse does not mean you get to interrupt."

Nearby, Britta shook her head and leaned toward Chris's brother August to ask in Norwegian, "Is that English? What is she saying?"

Britta listened intently to August's quiet translation as Violet continued. "The name of the game is Murder. In my hands are the cards that hold your fate. Take one and pass them on. If you receive an ace, that makes you the murderer. Your weapon of choice? A simple, stealthy wink. Everyone else, I'm afraid you're potential victims. When you're winked at you must silently count to five and then die without revealing the murderer. I get three guesses. If I fail, then I'm afraid you're all dead. Y'all are all standing pretty much in a circle so the game can begin once all the cards have been dispersed. Just keep talking amongst yourselves, and keep an eye out for the murderer."

Chris took one of the cards, then glanced down at it to find he had the ace. Sticking it in his pocket, he passed the remaining two to Adelaide. She passed the last one to Helen, who stood beside her. The two women seemed to have hit it off immediately. Since Helen had grown up in Austin, they'd spent the last few minutes comparing experiences of society life in the big city. Chris had been content to stay by Adelaide's side and listen to them chat. He knew how important it was to Adelaide that she make new friends at this party. Now he was too busy locking eyes with potential victims to listen. His first two winks went to Rhett and Isabelle. Five seconds later, they cried out in unison. They looked at each other in surprise, then embraced and collapsed to the floor as one. Violet hurried toward them to investigate, then scanned the circle of suspects with narrowed eyes.

Adelaide shook her head and glanced around the circle. "Now, that's just rude."

Chris caught Lawson Williams's eye and winked. "What is?"

"Murdering the host and hostess after they went to the trouble of inviting you."

Chris shook his head. "Some people have no scruples."

Lawson grabbed his stomach as though he'd been hit by a bullet, then dropped to his knees before landing on his side. Chris's brother Viktor was next. The boy stumbled into the circle and grabbed on to the hem of Violet's coat before meeting his demise. Lorelei O'Brien, the sheriff's wife, chose to carefully stagger backward to sit on the settee rather than fall to the floor as everyone else had, which made Chris wonder if there was some truth to the rumor that she might be expecting. As Chris searched for his next victim, his gaze fell on Adelaide, only to find her already watching him. They stared at each other for a second and he knew that she knew he was the murderer.

There was something else in her look, though. Something he couldn't quite identify—and didn't like. For a second, it made him feel as though a distance had suddenly come between them. But how could that be? They were only playing a game. He couldn't think of anything to do but wink.

A few seconds later she gasped, then turned and swooned backward into his arms. She locked her desperate eyes on him before going completely limp. He gently lowered her to the floor. Kneeling beside her still form, a strange sense of foreboding stole over him like a soft breeze. That lessened the game's fun for him. He purposefully took more risks in choosing his victims. Much to his relief, the game ended only a few minutes later when Violet caught on to him.

He helped Adelaide off the floor and swallowed the strange urge to apologize to her since he wasn't sure what specifically he'd be apologizing for. He was grateful when Isabelle suggested they start an indoor game of hide-and-seek. Having been to the Grangers' house several times before, Chris immediately thought of the perfect place to hide. He caught Adelaide's hand and rushed from the room amidst the other scrambling guests. Muffled laughter filled the air at the many near collisions. Chris turned a corner and nearly knocked over Britta, who covered a small yelp a moment too late, then rushed up the stairs with August. Finally making it to the spot he had in mind, Chris pushed a large coat-and-hat rack out of the way to reveal the door to a slim coat closet in the foyer. He gestured Adelaide to go inside. She slipped inside, thanked him for finding a spot for her and closed herself inside. He frowned at the closet door for a second, then opened it and ducked inside. Adelaide's whisper sounded over Rhett's counting. "Chris, you aren't seriously trying to hide in here with me, are you?"

"Hey, this is a great spot. Trust me. I play this game with my brothers all the time. I'm a master at it. Scoot in farther. Try to hide behind a coat. That way, even if someone opens the door, they won't see us."

"This is as far as I can scoot. Be realistic." She elbowed him in the side—and probably not accidently, either—as he did his best to turn around.

"I am being realistic." He left the door open a crack to let in some air and light, hoping the rack in front of the door would cover it. "I'm also being strategic."

She didn't seem to notice that he'd caged her in with his hands resting on the wall on either side of her. "Chris, how can you possibly think there's enough room in here for both of—?"

"Very, very strategic." He lowered his head so that they were in kissing range.

She froze. Her gaze fell to his mouth before her thick lashes lifted. Her green eyes deepened as she captured his gaze. The realization he saw there shifted to an amused admonition. She lifted her chin. "You and I ought to have another talk about respectability, Mr. Johansen."

Something in her words triggered a flash of memory—Britta rushing upstairs with August. That was followed by recalling Britta's gaze on August's mouth as he lowly translated the rules for her. What if they were hiding together...the way Chris and Adelaide were? He stiffened.

"Chris, I was teasing. Or I suppose maybe I was flirting. I don't know. Apparently, I'm not very good at it."

"It isn't you. It's...we've got a problem. Come on." He helped her out of the closet, which in retrospect, and as Adelaide had pointed out, hadn't been the most respectable choice of a hiding spot for an unmarried couple. He'd only meant to steal a kiss. That plan had been prompted at least partially by his desire to erase the memory of that strange feeling of distance he'd experienced between them during the game. They made it to the parlor just as Rhett finished counting. Chris wasted no time in saying, "We have to stop the game."

Rhett frowned. "Why? What's wrong? Did someone cheat?"

"There are a lot of unmarried people at this party."

"So?"

Chris rolled his eyes. "So if you weren't 'it,' who would you hide with?"

"Isabelle," Rhett said without hesitation.

"Right." Chris nodded. "And what would you be doing?"

"I'd be… Uh-oh." Rhett stepped into the hallway. "Olly olly oxen free! Everyone come back. We're going to change the rules."

There was grumbling and questions as everyone filtered back into the parlor. Chris's suspicions proved correct when Britta returned walking arm and arm with… Viktor? She was with Viktor now. August entered a second later with Violet in tow. However, Violet went to stand beside Viktor while Britta and August shared a smile. Chris tilted his head in confusion. What was going on there?

He wasn't worried about Violet. She and his brothers had been friends for a long time. She'd also befriended Britta, which was probably how the mail-order bride had been invited to the party. He shook his head. He shouldn't let himself think so badly of Britta. It made sense for her to be friends with his brothers since she spent so much time at their house. She'd been bold with him in an attempt to persuade him into marriage. That didn't mean she'd try the same tactic on his little brothers, who would be more innocent, unworldly, unsuspecting and immature in their responses to any wiles she might… Oh, man. He was going to need to have a talk with his brothers and his parents. Maybe Sophia should listen, too. She could help keep an eye on…

He froze. Where was Sophia?

She finally entered alone and came to stand beside him. He looped her into his side for a quick hug. She smiled at him even as she gave him a questioning look. He didn't bother to explain his relief about having at least one sibling present whom he didn't have to worry about.

He changed his mind about that only thirty minutes later when he watched Gabe whirl her around the parlor's improvised dance floor. The two of them weren't saying a word to each other. Gabe was staring at Sophia as though trying to memorize her every feature. Granted, Chris had seen the artist look at people like that before. Gabe had explained his creative process to Chris on one of his visits to the mercantile to pick up art supplies, so Chris knew that look meant the man was getting an idea for a painting. However, Chris didn't appreciate the man getting ideas about Sophia, creative or otherwise. It didn't help matters that, although Sophia avoided the man's gaze at first, she eventually returned it in full measure and even agreed to another dance.

Chris would have cut in, but doing so would have meant stopping the music altogether since his fiddle was carrying the melody. That would embarrass his sister, which he had no desire to do. He had to content himself with glaring at Gabe. Chris couldn't even manage to keep that up for long because his attention kept being drawn across the room to where Britta was flirting with not one, but two of his brothers. They each reciprocated without seeming to realize the girl's attentions were split. Meanwhile, he saw Wes ask Adelaide to dance. She accepted and Chris watched them twirl and laugh around the floor.

It was all Chris could do not to throw his beloved violin in its case and drag all of his people home by their ears. Well, not Adelaide. He'd hold her hand, but the rest of them deserved no less. Suddenly Chris realized that, in his overprotectiveness, he was turning into his father. The scariest part was that he didn't care a whit. In fact, he completely understood why Olan had been so anxious. Chris's hands were sweating so hard that he could hardly grip the bow. One more song. He'd play one more song, then the party was going to be over for him, his family, Britta and Adelaide if no one else.

Chapter Thirteen

Chris excused himself from the music making. Any guilt he might have felt for doing so was assuaged when Quinn and Rhett immediately challenged each other to a musical duel. Meanwhile, Chris had set his sights on his little brothers and was making a beeline toward them when Adelaide stepped right into his path.

Catching his arms, she turned him around and propelled him out of the parlor. She seemed to be searching for a secluded place, but all the rooms downstairs were filled with partygoers. They finally found a quiet spot in the back garden. He shook his head. "Adelaide, I'm sorry, but I can't steal kisses with you right now. I've got go back inside."

She rolled her eyes. "Oh, honestly! Don't you think about anything besides kissing?"

"Yes, I do. As a matter of fact, right now I'm thinking about—" he wanted to say *knocking some heads together* but settled for "—something I've got to do."

He tried to pass her, but she stepped in front of him

again. "You can't talk sense into your brothers while you're in this state. It won't work. They won't listen."

His gaze found hers. He realized that somehow she had figured out exactly what was going on and how much it was bothering him without so much as a word or look from him. He wasn't in this alone. Relief filled him and made him sink to a nearby stone bench. "They're my baby brothers."

She leaned over to squeeze his shoulders. "I know you think of them that way, Chris. Maybe you always will. But you can't treat them like they're still little boys. It will do more harm than good."

"You don't think I should talk to them, then?"

"Oh, you should definitely talk to them. Just make sure they know it's coming from a place of love and experience. Express your concern, but don't make it into a lecture."

He frowned. "What about Sophia and Gabe? Did you see them dancing?"

"Yes, and I already asked her about it." She grinned. "Her response was actually really funny. She said, 'He's a strange one. It was like he was peering into my soul without actually seeing me as a person at all. Eventually I stared back to see if I could make him as uncomfortable as he was making me. I'm pretty sure I failed.'"

Chris laughed. "All right, I guess she's still safe."

"Safe from what?" Her head tilted as she narrowed her eyes. "Chris, have you been scaring suitors away from your sister?"

"Only since she was knee-high to a grasshopper. Of course, I've had some help from my brothers and my pa. Don't look at me like that. She's too pretty and friendly and precious and sweet. She's our princess. Look, let's not get sidetracked. I'm airing my grievances and..." He considered holding his tongue, but she lifted a prodding brow so he let loose as nicely as possible. "Wes is friendly."

She stared at him in confusion. "All right. It's nice to know you think so."

"To you, I mean. He's friendly to you."

"Wes was the first new friend I made in Peppin. Actually, he's the first new friend I've made in years. That's all there is to it. He has no designs on me. I know because he keeps giving me pointers on how to win my fight against Britta for you. He suggests a nice right uppercut." She ever-so-gently pushed her fist up under his chin.

He caught her hand and captured her gaze to make sure she was listening. "Hey, you are *not* fighting Britta for me. You've already won my..." His words ran dry as he realized he was heading into dangerous territory. He wasn't entirely sure what he'd been about to say. Whatever it was, he had no business saying it. He wasn't ready to make any declarations to her until he was more certain of her feelings for him. "What I mean is I should probably grab one of my brothers to begin straightening things out. Why don't you stay here? I'll go get him. We can talk to him together, and you can confirm the fact that she's flirting with both of them. I'll be right back."

He ducked inside the house before she could respond. He returned momentarily with August. Chris cautiously related when he'd seen happening with Britta while August listened with a furrowed brow. When Chris was done, August offered a genuine grin.

He stepped forward to pound Chris on the back. "You are such a good brother for telling me all of this, but none of that was new information to me."

Chris frowned. "What? You mean you already knew she was flirting with both of y'all?"

"Sure, I did. Viktor knows it, too."

"Then why…?"

August turned his hands palm up as though that should be obvious. "To keep her away from you."

"Aw." Adelaide's hand covered her heart. "Isn't that the nicest, sweetest thing?"

Chris clasped his brother on the shoulder. "The nicest and sweetest, but maybe not the smartest. Playing with fire isn't a good idea, little brother."

"There's no danger for us here. Viktor and I have a pact to knock some sense into each other if we start going moon-eyed. Besides that, I hate to break this to you, but she only flirts with us when you're around. Best we can figure, she's trying to make you jealous."

"And that," Adelaide said, "is not so nice."

"The only thing she's doing is making me angry so her plan isn't working out that well." Chris frowned. "I think I should talk to our parents about this."

August shrugged. "It's up to you. Don't worry about Viktor and me, though. We're fine. Now, if you'll excuse me, I've got to relieve Viktor."

"Hey," Chris said, "avoid being alone with her. Include Violet in your group and as many other people as you can manage. That ought to slow her down. Got it?"

"Sure thing." August gave them a quick wave and slipped back inside.

Chris took the seat beside Adelaide. "This has been the most stressful party I've ever been to." He shook his head. "I don't know about you, but I've had enough of all this for one day. Come on. I'll walk you home."

Adelaide couldn't help feeling a little disappointed at Chris's suggestion that they leave. She'd been having a wonderful time making new friends and reconnecting with old ones. However, he seemed so frazzled that she didn't have the heart to suggest they stay any longer. They said a quick round of goodbyes before heading out. They were both quiet as they strolled down the sidewalk. Adelaide was content with the silence for it gave her time to savor the memories she'd just created—the least favorite of them being the winking game. The actual game itself had been fun. Discovering that Chris was the "murderer" had been disconcerting, to say the least. She'd stood right beside him for nearly half the game without being even vaguely aware of his actions.

She hadn't enjoyed the reminder of how easily he could deceive her. She'd forced herself to put it behind her at the party and she was determined to do the same now. After all, it had only been a game. It didn't have to have a deeper meaning unless she assigned one to it. With so many lovely things to focus on, there was no reason to give it a second thought.

"How do you like your new house so far?" Chris asked as it came into view.

"I think out of all the places I've lived, this is probably my second favorite."

He glanced down at her with interest. "What's your most favorite, then?"

"Your apartment," she said without hesitation before feeling a blush rise in her cheeks. "That sounds far more scandalous than I intended it to, now that I've said it out loud."

Chris laughed, but sent her a searching look. "You mean it, though? My apartment was your favorite?"

"Absolutely. It was like a dream of…" *What might have been and of what perhaps still could be.* But those words couldn't find their way past her lips. In fact, they probably shouldn't. She settled for. "It was like a dream home."

"That's good. That's how I had hoped you'd feel."

She knew what he truly meant was that was how he'd felt five years ago when he was decorating the apartment for her. Then she saw the way his jaw had tightened. She noticed the faraway look in his eye. That's when she realized he wasn't thinking about dreams. He was thinking about the reality of receiving her rejection back then. She couldn't help thinking about it, too.

She'd worked so hard on that letter. She'd wanted to give him the final say in the matter. Truth be told, she'd hoped he'd show up at her door with her crumpled letter in hand, demanding answers. Refusing to let her go. She would have had a few questions of her own. There was no mistaking that. Even so, at least it would have shown her that he still cared enough to fight. Well, she cared enough to fight now, and that meant bringing both of them back to the present. She nudged his arm with her shoulder. "I have to say that I was thoroughly impressed by your fiddle playing. You were always good but you've improved a lot since I left five years ago."

He shrugged. "Thanks. We were just kind of mess-ing around today, though. I wish you could have heard us at the benefit concert for the fire engine."

"I'm sure y'all were wonderful, but I wasn't complimenting your group. I was complimenting *you*." She grinned as she watched that realization flush his neck and cheeks with a hint of red. She slid her hand into his and squeezed his arm with the other. "Will you play for me sometime, just you? It's only fair, you know, since you've read my books."

"If you like." A moment later he nodded toward the far end of the porch as they climbed the steps. Lowering his voice, he said, "Speaking of reading your books…"

Adelaide followed his gaze to find her mother seated in one of the rocking chairs. Her shawl was falling from her shoulders but she seemed far too absorbed in what she was reading to notice that or note their approach. Adelaide tilted her head for a better look and found that the book was, indeed, one of her works. Rose startled when Chris greeted her, then turned the book over to hide the cover before offering a bright smile. "Y'all are back earlier than I expected. How was the party?"

"Lovely." Adelaide smiled as she sent a pointed glance to the book. "What have you got there?"

Rose bit her lip. "I have a feeling you already know. You don't mind me reading it, do you?"

"Of course not."

"Good, because I read all the others and it would be a shame not to finish this one."

"You…what? When?"

"Chris lent them to me. Well, *lent* is a generous term. You know how I had Chris's room when we stayed at his apartment? He had all of them on his bookshelf, so I started reading them then. He was kind enough to let me continue borrowing them. I bought this one myself at the mercantile. I thought it was about time I did something to support your writing. I see Chris has been doing it all along."

Chris shrugged. "Not intentionally."

Confusion filled Rose's eyes. "What do you mean?"

"I didn't know Adelaide was Joe Flanders until she told me a couple of weeks ago. I guess I just have good taste in books." His dark blue gaze captured Adelaide's. "Women, too, apparently."

Adelaide pulled in a sharp breath as her heart somehow managed to simultaneous flutter and melt. For a moment, she was absolutely certain that she was going to swoon. No. She wouldn't even think it. She was not the swooning type. However, between Chris's obvious determination to continue being wonderful and her mother's sudden show of support, Adelaide didn't know what to do with herself.

Chris placed a hand on the back of Adelaide's waist and kissed her cheek before stepping back. "I'll leave y'all to discuss good ole Joe. Is Everett around?"

Rose shook her head. "He's at his newly acquired newspaper office setting up the printing press. He tried to explain what that would entail but it sounded pretty technical so I thought it best not to get in the way. Adelaide and I are going to help him arrange his office tomorrow."

"Well, that's exciting. I'll drop by tomorrow and help out if that's all right." Chris sent a warning look to Adelaide and preempted her words with his. "I know I don't have to, but I want to. Tell Everett I said hello.

I think I'll head over to the mercantile to see if my parents will let me take over for them and close out. Y'all enjoy the rest of the evening."

Adelaide returned his parting wave, then took the chair beside her mother. Nervousness seeped into her stomach along with a hefty amount of trepidation. Even so, she couldn't help but nod toward the book. "I'm afraid I'll regret asking this, but now that you've read my books, what do you think of them?"

Rose's smile was soft and genuine. "They're riveting and well written. I've had a hard time putting them down. Don't look so skeptical. I truly mean it. You are very talented."

"Thank you." As much as she'd longed for her mother's approval concerning her writing, she'd never truly believed she'd receive it. She was glad for it. Yet, now that she had it, she found it actually didn't change much. Writing was still something she enjoyed doing. It was something that she'd started doing for Chris and had continued doing for herself. It had become a part of who she was—a part that she'd never been ashamed of despite her mother's request that she keep it quiet. If only Adelaide had the temerity to apply that commitment to other areas of her life— such as her relationship with Chris. Actually, that was exactly what she had been doing. She was under no illusions that her mother approved of their courtship, but that hadn't stopped her from continuing to spend time with him. Perhaps Adelaide was slowly making progress, after all.

"I know it may not seem like it to you, but I've given a lot of thought to what you said back in Houston, about how I tried to make you over into a socialite.

I suppose that is what I did. But I thought I was giving you the best chance at a secure future. I realize now that the future I was trying to arrange for you might have kept you secure but it wouldn't have made you happy. You're happy here in this town, writing these books and spending time with your friends. That is enough for me."

Adelaide searched her mother's eyes, certain this conversation couldn't be headed where she suspected it was going. "Ma, what are you saying?"

Rose reached over to stroke Adelaide's cheek, something she hadn't done since Adelaide was a little girl. "My darling, you will always have a home with me and your pa if that is what you wish. I'm sure he will leave you a sizable inheritance to see to your needs after we're gone. Your future comfort is secure. You needn't marry unless you are certain it would make you more content than you are right now."

"You…you wouldn't mind having a spinster daughter?"

"I wouldn't have a spinster daughter. I'd have a daughter whom I love dearly staying with me. There is nothing wrong with that."

"Does that mean no more matchmaking?"

"No more matchmaking."

"And you approve of my writing?"

Rose nodded. Adelaide couldn't believe it. Her plan had worked. She'd convinced her mother to let her live in peace as a spinster and as an author. She'd dreamed of that life for so long. She couldn't deny it still held a certain appeal for her. It promised her heart a chance at safety, control and seclusion. Yet to choose that life would mean abandoning her chance at an even older, dearer dream.

"This is about Chris, isn't it? You want me to stop seeing him."

Rose smiled. "In a town this small, it would be utterly impossible for you not to run into him, so not seeing him isn't a practical option."

"You know what I mean."

"I do." Rose was quiet for a moment. She continued slowly. "I'll not ask you to end your courtship—mostly because I've seen what little impact that request has had on you in the past. Whatever happens between the two of you is your decision."

Adelaide shook her head. There had to be a catch. There was no way her mother could be leaving this decision up to Adelaide. Then again, it always had been Adelaide's decision, hadn't it? Well, it had been ever since Adelaide had reached the legal age to marry without her mother's consent. Yet, this was the first time Rose had ever acknowledged that. Now that she had, Adelaide found herself leaning forward, seeking her mother's opinion. "But, you still think marrying Chris would be the wrong decision."

"I do, and you know why." Rose tilted her head. "What about you? Do you still think you've made the right decision?"

She had until a few minutes ago. Actually, that wasn't true. She'd been having doubts all along. Adelaide bit her lip as she stared in the direction Chris had gone. "Britta was at the housewarming party today. She spent the whole time flirting with Chris's brothers in an effort to make him jealous."

"Did it work?"

"He said it only made him angry."

Rose lifted one shoulder in a shrug. "Well, anger and jealousy often go hand in hand."

Adelaide sighed. "I know."

"There are other telltale signs. Did he seem distracted by her or was his focus mostly on you?"

Without a doubt, Chris *had* seemed distracted. Though, surely, that was simply because he'd been concerned about protecting his brothers. Adelaide frowned and decided to focus on the other side of the equation. "You know her better than I do. What is her problem? Why can't she respect the fact that he is courting me?"

"From her perspective, you're the one who isn't respecting the fact that he was promised to her."

"He may have been promised to her by his parents, but he made his choice and chose me."

Rose shrugged. "She thinks she can change his mind. I have to admit that I've encouraged her to try."

Adelaide stared at her mother in disbelief. "Why would you do that?"

"If Chris is the kind of man who's easily swayed in that way, wouldn't you rather know it once and for all? Wouldn't it be better to find that out now before you allow your feelings to deepen any more than they already have?"

"I suppose." Adelaide shook her head. "I only wish I had more of a fighting chance. Britta is so pretty. She has a way about her that makes men take notice. I've never been that way. I don't even know how to flirt."

Rose reached over to take Adelaide's hand. "I want you to listen to me, Adelaide, because this is a lesson I had to learn long ago. Love shouldn't be a competition. People's affections can't be stolen. A man has to want to stray for you to lose him. It has nothing to do with you lacking something that she has or vice versa. It all comes down to his lack of commitment to you and your relationship."

"So, you're saying there's nothing I can do?"

"I'm saying that you don't have to change who you are to try to attract him. He knows that you're interested in him. That should be enough."

"And if it isn't?"

"Then maybe it wasn't meant to be."

Adelaide slid her fingers into her hair and let out a sigh. Now she was really confused. She cared for Chris. As Sophia had once said, she probably always would on some level. Yet, she'd be risking so much if she gave him her heart. Her mother was offering her approval of the life Adelaide had thought she wanted—never marrying and finding contentment without the perils of romance.

She couldn't deny the common sense of her mother's words even though her instincts said that she should do everything within her power to fight for Chris. He'd told her she didn't have to. At least, that's what she'd thought he was trying to tell her before he'd suddenly rushed off to find his brother at the party. She wasn't so certain now.

What if the fears and doubts she'd been having were more than simply a culmination of her own insecurities? What if they were a warning?

She shook her head. She didn't want to believe that. Maybe she was being foolish, but she wasn't ready to give up yet. She was already on her guard so there was really nothing more to do besides see how things played out. Eventually she was going to have to make a decision about exactly what kind of future she wanted for herself. She could only hope that when the time came she'd be strong enough to do what was best.

Chapter Fourteen

A knock sounded on Chris's apartment door late that evening. He took one look through the peephole out into the alley and heaved a sigh. Stepping out the door, he locked it behind himself and immediately set off down the stairs. "Come on, Britta. I'll walk you back to the boardinghouse."

An offended huff sounded behind him. He glanced back to find her glaring at him in the moonlight. She lifted her chin as she ever so slowly followed him down the stairs. "In Norway it is customary to greet your visitors and invite them in before escorting them home."

"In Peppin, women do not show up unaccompanied at a bachelor's house at nine o'clock at night." He frowned when laughter filled her eyes. "What is so funny?"

She tilted her head. "You called me a woman."

"So?"

"You try so hard to treat me as a child. Now, suddenly, I am a woman. That *is* funny." She switched to English. "Listen, I'm not here to argue with you. I simply want to talk."

He reached up to catch her arm when she tried to step backward. Warning filled his voice. "Not in my apartment."

She froze and peered down at him. "I honestly can't tell if you're being a fraidy cat or just a stick-in-the-muck."

"The expression is stick-in-the-*mud.*"

"Well, you would know, wouldn't you?"

Chris narrowed his eyes. He'd walked straight into that one and couldn't think of a single response. In fact, it was all he could do not to laugh. Britta seemed to sense it for she offered a self-satisfied smile, then brushed past him down the stairs to the alleyway. Glancing back up at him, she called, "Aren't you coming?"

Chris joined her as she headed in the direction of the boardinghouse. "What do you want to talk about?"

"I wanted to thank you for the lecture I received from your parents this afternoon."

"You're welcome."

She switched to Norwegian. "It was embarrassing. I cannot believe you told them I was flirting with your brothers. You could have come to me, spoken to me first. I would have listened to you. It was not necessary to involve your parents."

"Britta, my parents invited you here. That means you are their responsibility—not mine."

"I am responsible for myself." She glanced away and shook her head before meeting his gaze again. "Your parents are not my parents. I do not need you to pretend to be my father, either. I have one of those back in Norway. You were…you were supposed to be my husband. For that reason, I respect your opinion. I care what you think. However, you have given up your claim to me which means I am free to flirt with whomever I please."

"That may be true. However, if I see you flirting with more than one of my brothers, I am absolutely going to say something to them and my parents because I can't see any honorable interpretation for your actions. I do not let people play games with my family. I protect them. I look out for them. That is who I am. That is what I do. I am not going to apologize for that."

She stared at him for a long moment, then tilted her head. "Have you ever considered the fact that you might be taking all of this a little too seriously? You make it sound as though I was doing something indecent. I was only flirting."

"And why were you flirting?"

"Because…" She trailed a hand down his arm, then frowned when he caught her wrist to still her progress. "Flirting is fun. I could tell your brothers were not taking me seriously, and I wanted to see if it bothered you. Obviously, it did—although not quite in the way I was hoping."

"So you *were* trying to make me jealous."

"Of course I was."

He sighed. As much as she tried to convince him she was a woman, she still behaved and thought very much like an adolescent. "Listen, we talked about this before. We agreed to be friends."

"I want to be more than that. I want what I was promised."

"That isn't something I can give you."

"It's because of Adelaide, isn't it? If it weren't for her…" Tears filled Britta's eyes and she shook her head. "Don't bother walking me home. I know the way."

Chris didn't try to stop her as she dashed off, knowing there was little he could do to make this situation easier for her. To be honest, he wasn't entirely sure why it was so hard for her to understand. Yes, his parents had promised her his hand, but they really hadn't had the authority to do so. He'd been honest with her and she'd seemed to accept that at first. She'd said herself that they barely knew each other. So why was she so dead set on marrying him? Or, at the very least, capturing his attention? He groaned at the realization that she'd managed to do exactly that for most of the day. She had distracted him from what should have been his main focus at the party—courting Adelaide.

Since he'd spoken to his parents and sorted things out with his brothers, Chris resolved that he wouldn't waste another moment worrying about what Britta might do next. He'd much rather spend that time and energy thinking about the best way to go about winning Adelaide's heart.

With that in mind, he was more than happy to begin the next day by heading over to the newspaper office. He arrived just as Everett was setting a ladder against the front of his newly purchased newspaper office. Rose and Adelaide stood on the sidewalk admiring the sign propped against the side of the building. Chris called out a greeting, then nodded toward the sign. "It looks like y'all have some very official business going on here at *The Peppin Herald*."

Adelaide held out her hand to him. "Come and see it. Tell us what you think."

"It looks great." He took her hand and gave it a quick squeeze before glancing to Everett. "The black lettering is fancy, but easy to read. The white background will be a good contrast to the dark teal of the building. It also picks up the white accents of the windows and trim. Altogether, the effect should be eye-catching."

Rose gave him a small but appreciative nod. "Spoken like a true businessman."

"Well, my pa would be glad to know I've learned something over the years." Chris stepped forward to test the weight of the sign with his free hand. "Yep, I figured it would be heavy. Ungainly, too. It's probably going to take both of us to get it up there, Everett. Do you have another ladder? If not, I can grab one from the mercantile."

Everett shaded his eyes as he glanced up at the building's false front. "I have one, but it will probably be too short."

"I'll go get mine, then. Is there anything else I should get for you?"

"No. The sign maker left everything else I'll need. I suppose I could have let him and his assistant put it up like they offered."

Chris shook his head. "Where's the fun in that?"

Everett grinned. "Exactly."

"I'll be right back."

When he didn't release her hand before walking off, Adelaide called over her shoulder to her parents, "Apparently I'm going with him."

"You sure are," Chris said as they fell into step on the sidewalk. "I want to talk you."

Curiosity filled her spring-green eyes. "About what?"

"Well, it seems to me that most of the time we spend together is when we're with our families. As much as I enjoy that, I was thinking it might be nice if we could spend some time with just the two of us."

"Oh." She lifted a brow and tilted her head. "You mean somewhere other than alleyways and coat closets?"

"Hey, there was only one coat closet and I got us out of there pretty quickly."

"I remember." Her gaze turned thoughtful. It seemed to lower to his mouth before meeting his again. "Whatever happened with that Britta situation?"

It took a moment for her words to process because he was too busy thinking about how he'd managed to cheat himself out of a kiss. That truly had been the worst party in the history of parties. He shook his head and forced himself to refocus. "My parents are going to deal with it. I don't want to talk about her, though. I want to talk about you and me spending time together."

"All right. What did you have in mind?"

In his best attempt at being graceful, Chris swept a hand toward the hotel down the street. "Supper in the hotel garden at sunset."

Her eyes widened. "That sounds so romantic."

"Good. I hope it will be. I talked to Mr. Bradley. He'll let us have the garden to ourselves if we go on a day that isn't usually busy. How does Tuesday evening sound?"

"Perfect. Should I dress formally?"

Chris paused beside the mercantile window knowing that his family would want to chat with Adelaide as soon as they entered the store. "We could if you'd like. Otherwise, we don't have to."

"I always hated having to wear an evening gown for society parties. It felt so pretentious. For this, however, I think it might be fun."

"Then that's what we'll do. Now, we'd better get the ladder and go back to your folks before they send a search party after us."

It didn't take long to put the sign in place once Chris returned with the ladder. They all lingered on the sidewalk to admire it for a good while before finally going inside the office. Chris was amazed to see how much progress had been made on the building since Everett had initially shown it to them. What had originally been a dark, dusty and outdated interior was now light, airy and welcoming. New damask wallpaper covered the walls with blue and cream. For the next hour, Chris and Everett had the privilege of arranging and rearranging each and every piece of furniture in the room according to Adelaide and Rose's directions. There were four mahogany desks in a variety of sizes for the office portion of the room. The waiting area near the door consisted of a small cream settee, gold chair, wooden bench and a low-slung table.

Once the women finally deemed the setup acceptable, Rose clasped her hands together. "Now, let's move on to the drapes and the paintings."

Everett waved her off. "That's where I draw the line. You know I can't stomach all this decorating.

It's an office not a parlor. I appreciate your help, but we don't need all of this."

"You are going to spend as much time here as you do at home. It should look nice. Even if you don't want all of this for yourself, think about Adelaide. Don't you want her to be comfortable when she's working here?"

"She has her own writing to do. She'll only be here a few hours a week. I'm sure she'd be fine."

They looked to Adelaide for her reaction. She lifted one shoulder in a shrug. "Drapes are kind of a basic necessity, Pa. Especially if you plan on working late nights here on deadline."

Everett gave a long-suffering sigh. "Fine, but I want to go through those paintings first because I'm not letting you put up any flowery ones."

Rose gave an offended little huff. Chris hid a grin and settled onto the settee to watch them go through the paintings. Shaking her head at her parents, Adelaide joined him. "This may take a while."

"That's all right." He tilted his head. "I didn't know you were going to be working here."

"I'm going to fill in as a reporter until Pa can hire someone else."

Chris frowned. "You know how to..." Remembering how adamant Everett had been about teaching him to be a journalist when he hadn't half the writing talent of Adelaide, Chris shook his head and grinned. "Never mind. Of course you do."

Everett must have overheard them for he said, "I'd love for you to come aboard, too, Chris—with whatever time you can spare from the mercantile. I'm hoping to start you off as a reporter. I'd be happy to teach you whatever you need to know. I need a man like you—someone who has his finger on the pulse of this town. You have connections here that I don't. In news, connections—or as we call them, sources—are everything."

Chris shrugged. "Adelaide is from here. She has connections."

"I've been gone for five years, Chris. So much has changed. I wouldn't be nearly as helpful as you."

He gave into the temptation to capture Adelaide's gaze. "You think I can do this?"

"Absolutely."

The certainty in her voice made his decision a simple one. "Count me in."

Everett grinned. "Welcome to the staff. Your first assignment would be a story on the fire engine you told me so much about. I'll have you interview Sheriff Sean O'Brien and that fellow whose house burned down. His name's Rhett Granger, isn't it? I've heard they're going to make him the volunteer fire chief. I have an interview with Judge Hendricks for another story in a little while, but I think we have time to come up with some questions for your story first. Ladies, I'm sorry. We'll have to finish all of this another day."

Even Chris had to laugh at Everett's obvious attempt to shoo the ladies away. Rose shook her head. "Oh, no. We'll finish this today. Don't worry about that. You and Chris go right ahead with your work. Adelaide and I won't bother y'all a bit."

Adelaide patted Chris's knee and stood. "That's my cue."

While Adelaide and Rose quietly hung curtains, Everett helped Chris came up with a myriad of questions to ask Sean and Rhett. Everett allowed Chris to sit in on his interview with Judge Hendricks to see how an interview should go. Once that was done, Chris visited the smithy to arrange a time to interview Rhett. Sean, on the other hand, didn't bother to set up another meeting. He simply pushed the paperwork he'd been filling out aside and encouraged Chris to ask him whatever he wanted. Chris took down the sheriff's answers, then hurried back to the *Herald* to tell Everett about the unexpected first interview.

Adelaide was the only one in the office. She glanced up from when he entered. Not wanting to break her concentration, he waited until she finished writing to speak. "I just did my first interview."

"Well, that's exciting. Who was it with? How did it go?" She gave the chair beside her desk a push so that it rolled toward him.

He sat in it, then slid back across the floor toward her. "I think it went pretty well. It was with Sean. He wrote down the questions he didn't have answers for and promised to get back to me."

"That's good. We're not in a big rush since Everett hasn't set the date for the first deadline. He's still waiting on the paper and ink to arrive. He's sending a telegram about it now. I'm sure he'll be back soon. In the meantime, I could teach you some of the basics of newswriting if you want. It will be like old times when we studied together."

"I'd like that." He wanted to ask her if she knew how crazy he'd been about her back then. She hadn't given him any indication that she'd returned his romantic feelings until that first fateful kiss. He'd been too afraid to ask to court her until then. That kiss had buoyed him up so completely that he'd gone straight for a marriage proposal.

Once she'd broken off their proposal he'd buried those memories deep out of self-preservation. Now that his bitterness had eased, he could recognize how sweet those times had been. He wanted to dig those memories up and examine them one by one. Most of all, he wanted to build a happy future—a new beginning for them. He could only pray that it wouldn't end in the same old heartbreak.

Embarrassment warmed Adelaide's cheeks as she led her parents down the church aisle and into one of the back pews. They were just as tardy this week as they had been last week and the week before. She'd like to say they'd really tried to be on time but that wouldn't be the least bit true. All three of them had dragged their feet. While she feared her parents did so out of lack of interest, Adelaide couldn't quite explain her reluctance. She shouldn't have any—especially since Chris and Sophia had been so sweet as to pray for her reconnection with God not so long ago. Truth be told, she hadn't really felt much of a difference in her faith since then. That hadn't stopped God from answering the portion of the prayer concerning her hopes to stay in Peppin, so she had to assume she hadn't been doing her part. It was for that reason that she'd finally taken charge and hastened everyone out of the house.

Now that they had arrived, she was struck again by how different this church was from the one they'd attended in Houston. It wasn't just the style of music or the friendliness of the people. It went deeper than that.

The very atmosphere felt richer and more intimate as though God Himself was present and endeavoring to draw them closer—draw *her* closer. It created such a strange feeling inside her, almost as if a battle was raging within her. Part of her wanted to lean into that tug. The other part wanted to escape it.

Pastor Brightly was a dynamic speaker whose style reminded her of the tent revivalist they'd run across when she was a child. Hiram had whipped the horses into a lather in an effort to get past the open field where the service was being held. The preacher's voice had chased them far down the road before it faded into stillness.

There was no silencing the Word of God today as Adelaide dutifully opened her Bible to follow along with the reading of the scripture. "Wherefore seeing we also are compassed about with so great a cloud of witnesses, let us lay aside every weight, and the sin which doth so easily beset us, and let us run with patience the race that is set before us…"

Adelaide was able to remain relatively unmoved until the sermon seemed to be nearing a close. The dark-haired pastor grasped either side of the pulpit while his penetrating yet caring gaze scanned the room. "This verse doesn't say *let us walk*. It doesn't say let us mosey or wander or start and stop or sit on our hands. It says let us *run*. I believe Paul purposefully chose this word because he knew that you can't run if you're constantly looking over your shoulder at your past. That's why he tells us to lay aside the weights and the sins that entangle us."

He closed his Bible and stepped from behind the podium, a sure sign the message was coming to a close.

"Finally, you can't run unless you are committed to the course God has set before you. Commitment…" He paused, and for some reason she had a feeling that what he said next was not entirely planned. Perhaps that was because there was no practiced air to it. Rather, his words were slow and gentle as though they were coming to him one by one in that moment. "That can be such a hard thing to do, especially not knowing what lies ahead. We want to know the answers, minimize risks and protect ourselves. Yet, God often calls us to run our race on a course filled with questions and risks and dangers of one kind or another. That doesn't make it any less worthy of running."

He glanced back at the podium where she'd seen him place his pocket watch. "I'll have to go into that more next week. Right now, there's something else I need to say. When I attended college back east, I ran track and field. I learned that before you can begin your race, you have to prepare yourself. You have to get into position. Do you know what position that is?" He knelt with one leg slightly in front of the other. "It's right here. It's on your knees. That's where some of you need to start your race today—in prayer, committing or recommitting your life to Christ."

He led the congregation in a prayer, but Adelaide couldn't seem to utter a word. Everett didn't seem to have that problem, for he spoke the words with a conviction that made Adelaide smile even as she threaded her fingers together in an effort to control their slight trembling. Once the service was over, she did her best to shake off her disquiet before joining Chris on the drive he'd promised her.

He stopped the buggy deep in the woods and tied

off the horses before escorting her down a winding trail. Just when her curiosity began to get the best of her, the trail opened up to reveal a rolling meadow blanketed in bluebonnets. Losing her breath, Adelaide shook her head in awe. "Chris, this is absolutely stunning."

"And secluded."

Eyebrows lifting, she glanced over her shoulder to meet his dark blue gaze.

"So…"

She stilled as he stepped up behind her to wrap his arms around her waist.

"We won't be interrupted while you tell me what's had you holding back tears this entire trip."

"Oh." She leaned back against his chest and sighed even as tears filled her eyes again. "Chris, we don't have to…"

He silenced her protests with a look as he stepped past her to lay his coat on one of the few sections of the ground not covered in bluebonnets. He patted the coat to indicate she should sit on it. After a second of hesitation, she did so. He settled across from her, close enough that their knees almost touched. He captured her gaze. "Talk to me, sweetheart."

For a moment, she couldn't say a word. And this time, her silence was solely due to the man in front of her. The color of his eyes seemed to envelope her in shades so deep and vibrant that it put the blossoms surrounding them to shame. His complete concentration focused on her only intensified his gaze. Her attention drifted to the rest of his classically handsome features. However, it wasn't only his attractiveness that caught her attention, but the caring and concern she found there.

He lifted a dark-gold eyebrow to prod an answer from her. She forced herself to glance away. Internally chided herself for thinking about Chris instead of staying focused on things of a more spiritual nature, she lifted one shoulder in a shrug. "I feel a little silly about it now, but Pastor Brightly's sermon really got to me."

"That isn't silly at all. What was it specifically that affected you so much?"

"I… I didn't say the prayer."

Chris's confusion lasted only for a moment. "But you wanted to, is that it?"

Adelaide bit her lip in indecision. Remembered what Pastor Brightly had just said about committing to faith, she nodded. "Yes."

Chris smiled. "Would you like to now?"

"I don't know what to say."

"Whatever's in your heart."

Adelaide nodded, then bowed her head. "God, You know this isn't easy for me, but I want to come back to You. I want to be close to You. I want to… I want to be Your daughter again. Be my Lord, my Savior and my Father. In Jesus' name, amen."

"Amen." Chris took her hand and pressed a kiss to her fingers. "Thank you."

"For what?"

"Sharing that moment with me. It means a lot."

Realizing there was more that she hadn't shared, Adelaide put aside her misgivings to do so. "Chris, I had a talk with my mother a while ago, and it got me thinking."

Caution filled his eyes. "About what?"

"The future. She told me I'd always have a home with her and Everett."

"What does that mean?" Chris stood, guiding her to her feet along with him. A hint of indignation crept into his voice. "Was she planning on throwing you out?"

"What? No," she said with a laugh. "She would never have done that... I don't think. I suppose what she meant is that she won't be matchmaking anymore."

"Why would she be matchmaking if you and I are courting?"

"She wasn't. She was simply saying she wouldn't in the future, either." She picked up his jacket and shook off the dried grass that clung to it. "All I'm saying is that she helped me realize that our situations have changed. I'm free to write and stay at home without having to worry about my mother's desperate attempts at matchmaking. You don't have to marry Britta. Your father is doing better. He isn't trying to match you with anyone else, either. We both have what we wanted."

He took hold of the coat she offered him and used it to tug her closer. "That was what we wanted. *Was*. We want something different now. Or, at least, I thought we did. Is this...are you...breaking up with me?"

Her breath caught in her throat. "*No*, Chris."

His jaw tightened. Shaking his head, his knowing gaze captured her. "You mean, *not yet*."

She stiffened. "I didn't say that."

He was a little bit right, though. She knew that. If the distrustful look he gave her was any indication, so did he.

Adelaide covered her face with her hands, then slid her fingers through her hair. This conversation was not going at all as she had hoped it would. She'd only intended to share her troubles. She'd also wanted to get an idea of exactly how serious Chris was about their relationship. Now, she was beginning to wish she'd never brought it up. The tension radiating from Chris told her that he was probably wishing the same thing. Unfortunately, forging on was likely the only way to straighten out the mess she'd unintentionally made. She just wasn't sure how to continue.

Chris didn't wait for her to figure it out before squaring his shoulder. "You know what? No. If you'd wanted to break up, you wouldn't be this indecisive about it. You would have already done it. I know that from last time."

"Hey, that's rude."

"That's a fact. You want this as much as I do, Adelaide." He shook his head and searched her eyes. "Why are you so intent on pushing me away?"

"I'm not…" She bit her lip, realizing he was right. She crossed her arm about her waist. "I don't know. Instinct?"

"Instinct?"

She glanced away, trying to hide the fact that she was every bit as surprised as he was by her response. She had a lot of good reasons for pushing him away. Several of them were women—specifically all the women he'd proposed to other than her. Why couldn't she have picked one of those? Perhaps because deep down inside she knew her reservations went beyond that.

"It's your instinct to push me away?" A light of discovery flickered in his eyes. "Is this what happened with our first engagement?"

"I don't know. I suppose so."

He shook his head. "How did I not notice this before?"

"Perhaps because I didn't notice it, either." She searched her mind to figure out how that could be. "Everything happened so fast the first time we got engaged. I know it probably sounds horrible, but I think I was a little relieved when I was forced to move away right after that. I guess the distance made me feel safe. However, the closer I got to my birthday, the more I began to panic. Then I heard about you and Amy. I was hurt, but it made my decision that much easier."

A maddening hint of a smile curved his lips. "Now, we're getting too close again. It's making you uncomfortable."

She frowned at him. "Well, you don't have to sound so excited about it." She ignored his laugh and the strange mixture of relief and panic it set fluttering in her belly. "I have options now. I don't have to be close. We both have what we wanted. Maybe that should be enough."

"Maybe, but I don't think it is. Not anymore. I suppose it's my job to convince you of that."

She barely held back a sigh. It would be so much easier if he didn't put up a fight. He hadn't last time. What was so different now? Still, it was only fair to let him have a shot at it. It would still be her decision. As wonderful as he was, he was still a risk. Britta was still out there gunning for him. There were those other women, too. She couldn't forget about any of that. Not yet. Nor could she totally ignore the still, small voice that whispered that all of those reasons were simply excuses to pull back and to keep her guard up. However, in a situation like this, what else was a sensible woman to do?

Chapter Fifteen

Despite the illusion of confidence Chris had managed to show Adelaide, he couldn't help feeling shaken by how close she'd been to calling off the courtship. Even so, he couldn't help but be a little proud of himself for how he'd responded. He hadn't given in or surrendered to his doubts. He'd somehow managed to move their relationship back to steadier ground. He only wished he could be certain that he'd be able to keep it from crumbling again.

All of those thoughts were heavy on his mind when he went to the Grangers' house to interview Rhett for the newspaper the following evening. After Chris had all of the information he needed for the news story, he accepted the couple's invitation to stay for coffee. Rhett didn't bother to beat around the bush. He just leaned back in his chair across the table and asked, "How are things going with you and Adelaide?"

"Actually, I could use some advice about that." Chris paused, searching for the right words. "The trouble is, she's holding back. I need her not to. I need to know that she's falling in love with me, or at least that she's willing to marry me."

Alarm filled Isabelle's green eyes. "At least? Chris, you didn't propose to her already."

"No! I mean, technically…that was a long time… Listen, let's focus on the present. All right?"

"All right, but only because I'm very confused right now."

Rhett covered Isabelle's hand with his. "He proposed to her before she left town five years ago. She said yes, but ended the engagement later. You must have missed that when you were eavesdropping the other day. Let's back up for a minute, though. Chris, it sounds to me like you might be getting the buggy in front of the horse. You said you need her to stop holding back and fall in love with you. Do you know why she's holding back?"

"Yes." Chris stretched out the word until it turned into a *no*. "Sorry. I'm just realizing that she didn't actually give me any details."

"There you go." Rhett finished his coffee, then stood to place his cup in the sink. "Figure out what the issue is. That way you can help her deal with and move past it."

Isabelle crossed her arms on the table, then leaned forward, her perceptive eyes searching his. "So you're in love with her, huh?"

"What?"

"You're in love with Adelaide."

"I never said that."

She smiled and he felt as though he'd walked right into her trap. "Yes, I noticed. So here's my question to you, my friend. If you can't admit your feelings for her in your own heart, how is it that you expect her to reveal her feelings to you?"

Speechless, Chris stared at Isabelle until Rhett came up behind her and leaned down to kiss her cheek. "Man, my wife is smart."

Isabelle tilted her head back to smile at Rhett. He rewarded her with a quick kiss. Chris glanced away to gather his thoughts. "Listen, I know it might seem unfair, but this is something I can't budge on, given my history with her. I don't want to be invested more heavily in this than she is. Couldn't I marry her first and then figure out that other stuff?"

"Quinn would say yes. I say it's hard enough to convince a gal to marry you without leaving out the most important stuff."

Chris was fully aware of that, having botched several proposals himself without ever using the L word. In fact, that was precisely why Isabelle had turned him down. She'd told him that he should marry for love. Now that it was within his grasp, he couldn't even manage to say the word.

Rhett frowned. "Besides, you know that isn't how courtships work. Now, I don't claim to be an expert on the subject—"

"You got the girl. That makes you more knowledgeable than me."

"Right. Well, if you want to get anywhere…" Rhett held out a hand to Isabelle, guided her from her seat, then twirled her under his arm. "She needs to be able follow your lead. It's up to you to get her on the floor and dance. You know that."

Chris did. He simply hadn't wanted to take the chance and give Adelaide the opportunity to reject him. He sighed as he watched the couple dance across the kitchen. Isabelle sure seemed content to take her cues from Rhett. They made it look easy. Chris was pretty sure that when it came to him and Adelaide, it wouldn't be. He had to start somewhere, though. Apparently, *somewhere* was admitting his feelings for Adelaide to himself, if not to her. If he planned to do that, it wasn't going to happen in Rhett and Isabelle's kitchen. He thanked them for their help and saw himself out a few minutes later.

Maybe Adelaide was right. Maybe this was a good time to call it quits. Adelaide seemed to think if they did so now, they would somehow be able to avoid being seriously hurt by the separation. That's what bothered him the most about all of this. He couldn't believe, after all they'd been through and all they'd meant to each other, that there was any way to end this without pain. She may not have realized it yet, but he did. That's why it was so hard to call his feelings what they were. It seemed to him that doing so would only give them more power over him—make the eventual hurt all the worse. That meant he had a decision to make. He either had to be all in or completely out.

He kicked at a twig on the sidewalk and buried his hands in his pockets. A quick look around told him no one was in hearing distance so he lowered his head and mumbled, "All right, God, I admit it. I love her. I love her something awful. I'm going to do everything I can to convince her it's safe to love me, too. I'm going to need some help, though, because I have no idea how to go about this. I lost her once. I don't want to lose her again. Like I said, *please* help me."

He hadn't meant it to be a prayer but that's what

it was so he finished with an "Amen." Of course, his fool heart couldn't be satisfied with that. It had to go and lead him right to Adelaide's porch. He knocked on the door. Everett opened it and greeted him with surprise in his voice. "Hello, Chris. Come in. I didn't know Adelaide was expecting you."

Chris shook his head. "She isn't. Thank you, but I'll stay out here. I'd like to talk to Adelaide for a minute if she's available."

Everett tilted his head and narrowed his eyes to survey Chris. Then, letting the front door close behind him, the man stepped onto the porch and crossed his arms. "Maybe you ought to run it by me first."

"Oh. I don't think—"

Everett placed a heavy hand on Chris's shoulder. "Son, you look like you're going to burst any second. Now, you don't seem angry so I'm guessing you're love struck. Is that right?"

"How did you know?"

"You look how I felt with Rose a time or two—all eager and busting with the need to tell her how you feel. Trust me. That isn't the way to go about this. Let's take a walk. I'll see if I can't teach you a thing or two about how to handle these ladies."

Chris stayed put as Everett walked down the front steps. His gaze trailed from Adelaide's stepfather back to the front door. He was so close. Yet Everett was right. This wasn't the right way to tell Adelaide how he felt—with no warning and no romance. That didn't mean he had to like it. Frowning, Chris joined Everett on the path in the yard. "Why did you stop me?"

"Because you were about to mess things up for good."

"By telling her how I felt?"

"Absolutely."

"I need her to know."

"By all means show her, but if you get into an all-fired hurry to tell her and make things official, you're going to send her running for the hills."

Judging by Adelaide's previous behavior, Everett's assessment sounded frighteningly accurate. Still, Everett wasn't privy to that information. "How can you be so certain of that?"

Everett sighed. "Adelaide and Rose are more alike than you might think—especially when it comes to their perception of men. The only way I was able to win Rose over was by steady, patient persistence. Adelaide will be the same way. Only you might have it even harder than I did, considering how you look."

"What's wrong with how I look?"

"Nothing, according to Adelaide—and that's bad."

Chris shook his head. "You've lost me."

Everett stopped walking to cross his arms. "How much do you know about Hiram?"

"Who?"

"Hiram Harper was Adelaide's father, Rose's first husband. Has Adelaide told you anything at all about him?"

"I know that he was gone a lot when they lived here because he was a traveling salesman. He died when she was fifteen. They buried him in town." Chris frowned and tried to think. "That's about it."

"She's been holding back on you, then." Everett waited until a buggy passed before he crossed Main Street. "Hiram Harper was a no-good, philandering snake in the grass—God rest his soul. All that being said, I believe the man truly loved his daughter. Adelaide was his darling. She, like most little girls, thought her father was a shining knight, a paragon—until she stumbled on him kissing a woman who wasn't her ma. She was only six at the time."

"That's awful."

"He convinced her not to say a word about it to Rose. He told her it would only upset her ma, and since he promised to never do it again, there was no need. Of course, he did do it again pretty often. Occasionally, he'd slip up and Adelaide would find out. Each time, Adelaide would beg him to stop, threaten to tell her mother and eventually agree to keep quiet to protect Rose. She didn't know that Rose had known since not long after their marriage. It was a nice little arrangement for Hiram because, with them both trying to protect each other from the knowledge of his transgressions, his actions were never addressed. He could control them by playing them against each other. As far as I know, that lasted until he died."

Chris shook his head. "Adelaide didn't tell me any of that."

"Well, don't feel bad. She didn't tell me, either. I only know about all of this through what Rose managed to figure out over the years." Everett's brow wrinkled into well-worn lines of concern. "Adelaide hasn't said a word about any of it to anyone as far as I know. She needs to, though. She needs to talk to you. Whatever she's keeping inside is going to affect the two of you. In fact, it already has."

"You think this has something to do with why she broke our engagement?"

"I won't presume to know all of the details surrounding that decision. However, I suspect that it might have had some influence on her." Everett stopped outside the closed mercantile. "I'm telling you all of this because I love my daughter. I think you do, too. Show her that, but be patient with her. You've done a good job of that so far."

"That's only because I was too afraid to move any faster." Chris frowned. "I don't want to be afraid anymore."

Everett shrugged. "Then don't be. There are many ways to be brave in your love for her. Just make sure you're being wise, as well."

"I can do that." At least, he hoped he could. He had to admit the history of his interactions with women didn't exactly inspire much self-confidence. He seemed to have a habit of being...well, impetuous. Seeing as that hadn't worked out too well for him, perhaps it was time to try a more patient and deliberate approach.

"Good." Everett scanned the street, then stepped a bit closer. "Listen, there's one more thing. I wanted to tell you earlier, but I didn't have a chance. I received a threatening letter about the newspaper today. It wasn't like the ones that were routinely sent to my office in Houston. It seemed more personal and specifically directed at Adelaide."

"What are you going to do?"

"I've talked to Rose and we decided that we can't keep running. We're going to stay in Peppin. I've already notified the authorities. They're actively trying to find this person. Meanwhile, I'd appreciate it if you could help me by watching out for Adelaide. I'm planning to tell her tonight. I think it's best that she's aware of what's happening so that she can be on her guard."

"I agree, and I'd be happy to help in whatever way I can."

"Thank you, Chris."

"You're more than welcome. Thank *you*, by the way, for your advice. I want you to know that I'm going to take it to heart."

Everett gave an approving nod. "Good man. I'd better get back to the house now. I don't want the ladies to worry. You have a good evening, Chris."

"You, too." Chris climbed the stairs to enter his apartment and sat for a while, deep in thought. Now that Chris knew more about Adelaide's past, he understood why she found remaining unmarried an appealing option. However, their marriage would be nothing like her parents' had been. He had to find a way of convincing her of that. He also needed to find out why she was pushing him away, and why she had such a fear of being close to him.

It might have something to do with Hiram, but he wouldn't know for sure unless he was able to get her to confide in him. That wouldn't be easy since she seemed unable or unwilling to be that vulnerable with anyone.

Yes, he definitely had his work cut out for him, but he was eager to do it. He'd admitted his love for her to God, himself and Adelaide's father. He'd committed to this—to Adelaide. He was going to see it through every single solitary terrifying second to the end. He could only pray that end didn't include facing yet another rejection from Adelaide.

After Everett informed them about the renewed threats to the newspaper and their family, Adelaide was more than content to spend Monday at home, writing.

He'd softened the news by giving Adelaide and Rose each a pearl-handled Remington derringer. At least it had softened the news for Adelaide. Rose had seemed a little intimidated by the firearm. Adelaide wasn't, but that was probably because she'd convinced Everett to let her learn to shoot with his Colt .45 years ago for research purposes.

Adelaide kept her gun on the desk beside her as she worked. Seeing it there helped her to refocus on the Wild West adventure she was writing any time her mind started to wander toward Chris, which happened disturbingly frequently. Even so, the day flew by until her growling stomach told her it was past time to help her mother start dinner. She set her typewriter aside and tucked the Remington into her pocket before going downstairs.

She found Rose sitting on the gold settee in the parlor surrounded by moving boxes. It seemed they never could get finished unpacking all of them. It didn't help that, despite Rose's valiant efforts otherwise, their frantic packing had degenerated into unorganized chaos those last few days in Houston. Adelaide's energy for sorting things out had long since waned, even though she was still missing a few essentials. Realizing Rose hadn't responded to her first query about supper, Adelaide asked, "Mother, did you hear me?"

"Adelaide, what is this?"

Adelaide stepped forward to take the paper Rose handed to her. Glancing down at it, Adelaide swallowed hard. "Oh. I see you found one of my boxes."

"What I found is your marriage certificate. Adelaide, how it is possible that you and Chris have been married for five years? When were you going to tell me?"

"I wasn't going to at all because we *haven't* been married, not really. I mean, we filled out the paperwork, got the license, had a secret ceremony with Reverend Sparks and signed the certificate, but we aren't actually married. You told me so yourself."

"I…" Rose shook her head. Pure confusion filled her voice. "What? When?"

"Right before we left Peppin for Houston. Everything happened so fast. Chris and I kissed for the first time. He proposed. I said yes. We knew you wouldn't approve of the engagement so we thought we might as well get married right away and break the news to you afterward. It was silly, I know, but I was so caught up in the moment that it made perfect sense at the time. Anyway, I came right home after the ceremony to tell you the truth. I was going to ease you into it. Remember? I said, 'Ma, Chris asked me to marry him.' Before I could say anything else, you laughed. Then you told me—"

"I told you that you were underage and couldn't legally marry without my consent."

"Right. You said I'd have to wait until I was eighteen. That's when I realized that someone at the courthouse must have made a mistake. I couldn't possibly be legally married to Chris. Nor was I likely to be, since you weren't going to consent—especially after I'd gone behind your back. There wasn't much that I could do besides leave Chris a note asking him to figure it out. He was supposed to come for me if we were actually married, but we weren't. You were right. I was too young. The county clerk shouldn't have given us a marriage certificate to begin with, so the marriage wasn't valid. We resolved to get married again when

I turned eighteen. Only that never happened. I suppose I should have thrown the certificate away. I just never could manage to do it."

"Oh, Adelaide." Rose's fingers came to rest at her temple. "I'm afraid I've gotten you into a mess."

Adelaide frowned. "What? How?"

Rose caught her hand and guided her to sit on the settee beside her. "Sweetheart, you were eighteen when you got married."

"No. I was seventeen."

"I was already expecting you when I married your father. In fact, that's why I married him. Hiram and I left the town where we lived to have the baby. Once my father got sick, we moved back home so I could nurse him. You were so small for your age. People just assumed you were younger than you were. That helped me keep my respectability so I let them. No, I more than let them. I ran with it. After my father died, Hiram and I started traveling again. I didn't want you to know the truth about what we'd done, so we kept up the ruse that you were a year younger than you actually are. You were eighteen when you got married. You can talk to Judge Hendricks to make sure, but if everything else was done according to the proper procedures, then most likely… I'm afraid… Adelaide, you're still married to Chris."

Chapter Sixteen

Stunned, Adelaide stared at her mother. "What? No. I—" Shaking her head, she grasped on to the only part of any of this that made sense. "You…you lied to me."

"Adelaide, please—"

She shied away from her mother's touch, standing so quickly that she stumbled over the boxes. "How could you do that?"

Rose stood, but didn't try to close the distance between them. "I was ashamed. I was just another one of your father's conquests, but my father tracked him down once he realized I was expecting you. I literally had a shotgun wedding. I didn't want you to know that. Please, you must understand."

"I do. Truly. What I don't understand is how you could use it against me."

"Use it against you? I didn't—"

"Yes, you did. You *knew* that I was eighteen—fully capable of making my own legal decision about marriage. You lied when you told me I needed your consent. You used my trust in you to control me just like Papa always did."

"That is not the same thing. I was trying to protect you."

"You were protecting yourself. The fact that it kept me away from Chris was simply an added bonus."

Rose was quiet for a long moment. Finally, she gave a shallow nod. "Maybe so, but I still think I did the right thing. You were too young. He had too much of a hold on you. You were willing to marry him after one kiss. What else would you have been willing to do if he'd asked? I was trying to keep you from making the same mistakes I did." Rose tilted her head, her eyes narrowing. "What about Chris? What was he doing in all of this? He thought you were seventeen. Didn't he know that you were too young and the marriage would be invalid? Maybe that's why he rushed you into it in the first place."

Adelaide couldn't think. She could hardly breathe. She didn't know what to feel. She startled when the front door opened. Everett stepped inside. The tension in the room must have been palpable for he stopped in his tracks to glance back and forth between them. He spoke slowly, his words filled with caution and concern. "What did I miss?"

Adelaide shook her head. "I have to go."

He tried to catch her arms as she rushed past. She managed to avoid his grasp. She was out the door and out the front gate before he could even call her name in protest. Instead of his voice, she heard only an echo of the past.

"Hey, A-dumb-laide! Come back here."

Not even sparing a glance behind her, Adelaide took off running away from the mean schoolboys who'd been making fun of her all week. Their taunts

*faded as she darted across the street, then into a back
alley. A few more turns and she was certain she'd lost
them. Relieved, she stopped to place her hands on her
knees and pull in some gasping breaths. She glanced
around and realized that she had no idea where she
was or how to get home. Fear and panic coursed
through her until a distant, familiar laugh caught her
ear. She raced toward it, only to stop yards away from
its source in disappointment. It wasn't her pa, after
all. It was some man kissing a woman. Gross. She grimaced and looked away. Maybe once they stopped,
she could ask—*

"Adelaide?"

*"Pa?" She glanced up at his shocked face, then ran
toward him. "It is you."*

*He caught her in his arms. "My darling girl, what
are you doing here?"*

*She wrapped her arms around his neck and held
on tight. "I got lost."*

*She'd almost forgotten about the woman until
she spoke up. "I'll say. Hiram, you didn't mention a
daughter."*

"I'll explain later. Adelaide, let's get you home."

*Adelaide waited until they were out on the main
street to ask. "Who was that lady? Why were you kissing her? Where's Ma?"*

*Setting her down outside the flow of traffic, he knelt
so that he was eye level with her. "That lady was just
an old friend. I was kissing her goodbye. She's leaving soon to go far away."*

*Adelaide lifted her chin. "I don't care. You shouldn't
have done that. Ma wouldn't like it."*

"You know, now that I think of it, you're probably

*right. That's why I won't do it ever again. I promise.
All right?" He waited until she gave a reluctant nod.
"Will you do something for me? Don't say anything to
your ma. We don't want to upset her, do we?"*

Reaching the courthouse, Adelaide pulled at the
doors only to find that they were locked. Everyone
had already left for the day. Her shoulders slumped
as turned to walk down the courthouse steps. She'd
been hoping to find out for sure if the marriage was
valid. Without that goal as a distraction, there was little else to do but sink to one of the courtyard benches
and allow the past to consume her.

How many times had she repeated Hiram's words
to herself over the years? "Don't say anything to your
ma. We don't want to upset her." It had all been so
pointless. Of course, it had taken her years to figure
that out.

*"I'm leaving. Are you going to walk me to the train
station, my darling girl?"*

*Even all grown up at fourteen years old, Adelaide
couldn't help but smile in response to Hiram's grin
and his familiar term of endearment. Both were so
genuine and affectionate that she wanted to freeze
this moment and hold on to it. The loud snap of his
suitcase closing stole it from her. "Of course. Did you
say goodbye to Ma yet?"*

*The light in his pale green eyes dimmed slightly.
"No, I couldn't find her."*

*"Well, it helps to look," she said with a bit of teas-
ing. "She's out back doing the laundry."*

*"All right, then." He ran his fingers through his
chocolate-brown hair that had only recently become
tinged with a distinguished gray. She stepped aside*

*so he could move past her and place his suitcase by
the front door. "I'll be back in a minute."*

*She checked around the bedroom to make sure
he hadn't forgotten anything, which he routinely did.
Spotting a piece of paper on the floor at the end of
the bed, she bent to pick it up muttering, "What are
you leaving this time, Pa?"*

*She gave a passing glance at its contents. Feeling
the blood draining from her face, she grasped the bed
post for support. She shouldn't be surprise. She really
shouldn't, but—*

"Adelaide, let's go."

*She tucked the letter into her dress pocket and fol-
lowed him out the door. They were almost to the train
station before she found her voice. "You're getting
sloppy, you know that?"*

"What?"

*She pulled the letter from her pocket, then took his
hand and slapped it into his palm. "It was lying on the
floor. Ma could have found it."*

*Concern filled his voice as he caught her arm to
pull her to a secluded corner. "Adelaide, I can explain."*

*"I'm done listening to your explanations. I thought
things were getting better. I thought this arrangement
of us staying in Peppin while you travel for work had
enabled you to settle down. Instead, you have some
woman stashed away in another town. And you let her
write to you here." She held up her hands and shook
her head. "I can't stay silent anymore. I'm going to
tell Ma everything. You can't stop me."*

"Don't bother. She already knows."

"What? She knows?"

"She's always known. She only kept quiet about it for your sake. She didn't want to spoil your 'illusions of my grand character' as she's said a thousand times. I figured I'd take a peaceful household for as long as I could have it."

"Peaceful? That's what you care about? Not Mother or me or what you're doing to our family, but peace." Suddenly all the pieces of the puzzle shifted into place. *"That's why she cries after you leave. Not because she misses you, but because she knows you're off philandering."*

He froze as seemingly genuine regret filled his pale green eyes. *"She cries?"*

She scoffed at his concern. *"Oh, don't act like you care."*

"I do care about you and your mother."

"You have a despicable way of showing it," she said over the distant train whistle.

"I don't have time for this. I have to go." For a moment, he hesitated, as though hoping she might say something else. Was he waiting for her to ask him to stay, forget about the trip and whoever might be waiting for him elsewhere? She wanted to—desperately. Yet, she had no confidence that he could do so. He'd never kept his promises in the past. She shook her head. *"Why? Why must you always do this?"*

"There's so much out there in the world, Adelaide."

"So many women."

"They go along with the places and the experiences. Something inside me cannot rest until I've tried it all. How can I be satisfied with what I have when there is so much more out there to...to chase?"

His words made her feel sick to her stomach. She

couldn't stop her lip from curling in disgust. "There is no hope for you, then. I see that. You've surrendered to your base desires and have no will to fight them. Fine, then. If the chase is all you want, you are welcome to it but nothing else."

"What does that mean?"

"It means that I'm not your 'darling girl' anymore. I'm done forgiving you. I'm done letting you play games with me and my mother. I'm done caring about your exploits. I'm done with everything about you. I don't even want to be near you."

His face drained of color. "Adelaide, please. You don't mean that."

"I've never meant anything more. Go on. Catch your train. If there's any decency left in you, do us all a favor. Don't come back."

The touch of Everett's hand on her shoulder startled Adelaide back to the present. She shook her head in a desperate attempt to free her mind from the hold of memories long buried, then met his gaze. "I told you not to follow me."

"I didn't want to worry you, but I got another threatening letter about the newspaper today. I couldn't let you run off like that by yourself. You might not be safe." He took the seat beside her. "Now, why don't you tell me what this is all about?"

She took a deep breath, then told him everything her mother had said. Once she finished, he stroked a hand over his beard. "Well now, that sure does put an interesting spin on things. Seems to me we shouldn't jump to conclusions, though. First things first, we should talk to Judge Hendricks and see what he has to say about the marriage's validity. Then we can arrange for you and Chris to sit down and talk things out."

"Do you think Ma was right about Chris trying to take advantage of me?"

"It sounds like neither of y'all were doing much thinking when y'all got married, but if that's something that's worrying you, you should talk to him about it." He stood. "Let's go find the judge."

"Now?"

"No time like the present."

She glanced at the hand he offered her, reminded of her and Chris's discussion about being close to people. It was strange that she hadn't thought to mention her relationship with Everett. Perhaps that was because she and Everett didn't often talk about the deeper things in life. Even so, he'd been the most reliable, steady and supportive presence in her life since he'd entered it. She accepted his assistance to stand, then gave him a quick hug, as well. "Thank you."

He smiled and patted her back. "Come on. It's time to find out if you're Mrs. Adelaide Johansen."

That old familiar feeling seeped through Chris's bones. It was the same one he'd gotten just before every proposal—a dreadful excitement that made his stomach a pool of nerves. It didn't matter. He wouldn't let himself so much as think about proposing. Instead, he was going to put Everett's advice into practice. At least, that's what he kept telling himself.

It didn't help his resolve to find that the hotel staff had completely outdone themselves in setting up for the sunset supper in the garden. A candlelit table for two was tucked into a curve of the garden path and shaded by the cradling branches of a tall oak tree. Shafts of golden light shifted through the garden as the sun began its surrender to an inevitable night. The atmosphere made him long for his violin so he could add to its beauty, but he hadn't thought to bring it. The soft patter of the nearby fountain would have to do because there wasn't enough time to retrieve it.

Adelaide should be arriving at any moment.

He'd planned on picking her up from her house in a buggy. However, Everett had dropped by the mercantile to tell Chris that Adelaide had some other business to attend to first. Everett would drop her off as soon as they finished. Chris had asked for more details but Everett hadn't given any. Now Chris was beginning to fear that she'd decided not to show at all. Before he could check his pocket watch again, Adelaide stepped out onto the hotel porch.

Everything Chris had told himself about slowing down and not being impetuous seemed to fade away like a long lost memory as he met her at the base of the porch steps. He picked her up, twirled her in a circle and kissed her cheek before setting her down beside the fountain. She tilted her head back to look up at him with wide green eyes. His gaze strayed to the bemused smile on her lips as she asked, "What was that for?"

"Adelaide, I…" He stopped, realizing that saying those next two small words begging to fall off his lips would open him up to a whole world of pain if Adelaide couldn't say them in return. He swallowed them. "I'm glad you're here. I was afraid you wouldn't be able to make it. Everett said you had some business to take care of first."

"Yes, I did." Like a cloud passing over the sun,

her smile faded and was replaced by wariness. She stepped back to wrap her arms around her waist. "Chris…I'm not sure how to tell you this."

Panic stole over him. Somehow in admitting his feelings for her to himself, he'd forgotten just how close she'd come to breaking things off with him during their last conversation. He'd hope to romance her tonight, convince her that she'd made the right decision by sticking with him. He needed that chance. He took her arm and led her toward the table where the waiter was placing their food. "Then don't. Our food is here. Let's eat."

She bit her lip, but gave in with a nod. Her tension remained as the last of the sunlight faded to twilight. Somewhere between their entrée and the dessert Chris realized that he was only delaying the inevitable. If Adelaide had made up her mind to stop courting, then he needed to respect her decision even if he absolutely abhorred it. First, he had to try one last time even if it meant going against Everett's advice.

As soon as the waiter cleared away their plates, Chris took Adelaide's hand and led her back over to the fountain. Sinking to one knee was the hardest thing he'd ever done. Adelaide didn't make it any easier by staring down at him in confusion and alarm. "Chris, are you all right? Are you sick? You're in pain, aren't you? I'm going get Doc Williams."

He nearly fell over in his attempt to keep her from running off. "I don't need Doc."

She frowned. "You're sure? Then what are you—? Oh." Her gaze swept over him and her eyes widened. "*Oh*. Chris, you aren't propos—"

His heavy sigh was so loud that it cut her off. He

couldn't help it. How was it that even in a setting such as this, he couldn't manage a romantic proposal? His jaw clenched. The frustration in his voice didn't exactly lend a courteous tone to his question. "Adelaide Harper, will you marry me?"

She didn't laugh. That was something. Instead, her mouth opened and closed without uttering a word. She bit the corner of her mouth. Narrowing her eyes, she tilted her head, then sat on the edge of the fountain. She patted the spot beside her. "Come and sit."

History had taught him to be cautious around women to whom he'd recently proposed. He jutted out his chin. "Why? Are you going to push me in the fountain?"

"Chris, I would never do that! Actually, under other circumstances, it might be fun. But truly, right now, all I want to do is talk to you."

He stood and placed his hands in his pockets. Only then did he realize that he hadn't even had a ring to give her if she'd said yes. Of course, he'd never proposed with a ring in hand, so that was nothing new. He shrugged. "Well, if it's all the same to you, I'll stand here. Say what you need to say."

He wondered what approach she would take to refuse. Most of the other women had taken the whole *we're friends and we should stay friends* tactic. Adelaide couldn't use that one because they'd been more than friends for a long time. She couldn't use Amy's *I'm in love with someone else* speech. No, Adelaide's would probably be more along the lines of *I'd rather be alone for the rest of my life than spend it with you*.

She braced her hands on either side of her and leaned back slightly to look up at him. "You proposed

to me once before. Do you remember what I said to
you then?"

"You said yes."

"And then we got married."

Chris frowned. She sound awfully depressed about
it. Not that it mattered, because...

"We didn't actually get married. You know that.
You were too young."

Her green eyes turned inscrutable. "Did you know
that I was too young?"

"Of course not. I'd heard of other people marrying
at our ages. It never occurred to me they'd needed their
parents' permission. We kissed for the first time, then
that proposal went flying out my mouth. I couldn't believe it when you accepted. I thought for sure you'd
change your mind or your mother would change it for
you. I didn't want to wait for that to happen."

He paused, realizing that was exactly what had
happened. She'd eventually changed her mind about
marrying him. All of that rushing had accomplished
nothing. Before he could say as much, Adelaide picked
up the story where he'd left off.

"It was raining, remember? The county clerk had
left his windows open at home so he rushed us through
the paperwork. Reverend Sparks didn't want to agree
to the secret ceremony, but his wife convinced him
it was romantic. He gave in, and we said our vows."

"Then you ran off to tell your ma. That was the
last I saw of you until you walked into the mercantile a few weeks ago." Chris shook his head. "Listen,
there's no use in reminiscing about all of this. It isn't
going to change anything."

She leaned forward. "Chris, the story might not have changed, but the facts did."

He frowned. "What does that mean?"

"The only thing that made our marriage invalid back then was the fact that I was seventeen."

"So?"

"So I was actually eighteen. I just didn't know it because my mother let me think I was a year younger than I actually am."

Chris gaped at her for a minute, unable to process the implications of what she was saying. Finally, he managed to say, "Why would she do that?"

"She didn't want me to know that she had a shotgun marriage to my father because they were expecting me."

He shook his head. "Man, your father was a real piece of work, wasn't he?"

"How did you—? You've been talking to Everett. Haven't you?" She held up a hand and shook her head. "You know what? That isn't important. Chris, do you understand what I'm telling you?"

"You were eighteen when we got married."

She gave a firm nod. "Right."

Cautious hope filled his chest. "What does that mean for us?"

"It means the marriage was valid."

"Really?" He managed to keep all but a hint of relief from his voice. He tensed again. "Are you sure?"

She nodded. "Judge Hendricks is the ultimate authority on this kind of thing in Peppin. He says if I was of age, gave my consent and followed all of the other proper procedures—"

"Which we did."

"Then the marriage is legal and binding."

His eyebrows rose along with his heart rate. He wanted to shout for joy but the serious expression on Adelaide's face reminded him she might not feel the same way. He needed to be cautious, find out all the details and make sure he was hearing things right before he let it all sink in. He cautiously took the seat she'd offered earlier. "Legal and binding? That sounds…permanent."

"There is another option." She angled toward him and searched his gaze as she spoke. "Judge Hendricks said that we're the first couple he's run across who had sufficient grounds for annulment. He's had requests before, but only gave out the paperwork in the hope that it would shock the couple to their senses or give him a chance to sit down with them and convince them otherwise. However, since I left town right after the ceremony and stayed gone for five years, he's willing to file the annulment without giving us any trouble about it."

Her words put a damper on the joy he'd been feeling and prompted a frown. "An annulment would say our…marriage…never existed. Right?" At her nod, he slowly shook his head. "I don't think that would be true. Adelaide, I meant those vows. You did, too. We both thought you were of age, and you were. When you went home that day to find your mother packing your bags—if she hadn't mentioned you were under the age of consent, would you have gone to Houston with her or would you have stayed with me?"

She was silent for a long moment, then the truth rang out in a whisper. "As nervous as I was… I still would have stayed. I know that without a doubt."

"We would have been married all these years."

"We *were* married all of these years." She straightened, her eyes widening. "It's a good thing you didn't give in and marry Britta."

"Yeah, having two wives at once is a little Old Testament—not to mention illegal." Glad to see a hint of a smile on her face again, he gently bumped her with his shoulder. "Speaking of which, I guess it's a good thing you didn't marry that other fellow who proposed to you. What was his name?"

"Bertrand. There were several before him, though." She eyed him thoughtfully. "You're being awfully calm about all of this. I almost hyperventilated or swooned or something."

"I'm not all that calm on the inside, I assure you. It's just that… Well, I guess I've just always felt that we belonged to each other. That made this come as more of a confirmation of what I already knew deep down rather than a huge shock."

"That's really sweet and I'm glad that you're taking it well, but I'm still a little…" She waved her hands in uneven circles until one of them came to rest on her forehead. "We're married! What are we going to do?"

Chris searched her face. Unable to discern her feeling about the matter beyond her obvious confusion, he offered the most logical answer. "Be married?"

She gave him a disbelieving look. "Chris, I was having trouble with our courtship. Now I'm supposed to be fine with our marriage? That isn't going to happen. I'm not even close to being ready for this."

"You were ready five years ago. What's so different now?"

"*I'm* different. I grew up. So did you."

He frowned and glanced away. "Yeah, that's what you said in your letter—that we'd 'outgrown each other and we're no longer suited.' I thought that was just an excuse."

"It was, back then."

"And it isn't now?"

"Why would it be?"

He stood. "Because it's the same thing with you over and over. You let me get close to you. You let me marry you. Then you push me away for any and every trumped-up reason you can find."

"These are not trumped-up reasons, Chris. The fact that you can't see that is concerning."

Chris could see his future playing out before his eyes. It wasn't at all as he'd hoped or imagined it. Marriage was supposed to mean safety, be a resting place that would bring healing to his broken heart. Instead, it promised the opposite. A lifetime of courting a woman who would constantly reject him, pushing him away any time he got too close for her liking, breaking his heart a little more each year. That didn't change the fact that he felt honor-bound and determined to honor his marriage vows. It only meant there was nothing he could do about it.

Chapter Seventeen

Adelaide jumped when the sound of the hotel's screen door slapping shut cut through the silence. Chris turned to greet Mr. Bradley. The man gave them a regretful smile. "I'm sorry to interrupt. Y'all are welcome to stay for a while longer. I just wanted to let y'all know that I'm going to have to open up the garden to the hotel guests now. So if you see other people wandering through, that's why."

Chris offered the man a handshake. "We were just about to head out. Thank you for arranging all of this for us. Your staff did a wonderful job."

"You're most welcome. I'll tell them you said so." Mr. Bradley turned to her. "Miss Harper, I hope you enjoyed the evening."

"I did. Everything was perfect." At least, it had been until the last few minutes. She might not have been able to shake the tension that had been coursing through her body since her mother's revelation, but Chris had been so engaging during dinner that she'd managed to forget her troubles for a little while. She slid a glance toward him, but he was busy staring at the concrete tiles that made up the hotel's patio.

Mr. Bradley nodded. "I'm glad to hear it. Well, you two have a good rest of the night."

She gave him a little wave as he walked away. Suddenly realizing how tired the day had made her, she released a weary sigh. "I'd like to go home now, Chris."

"I'll take you." He swept a hand toward the hotel. She followed him out to the buggy. They had a lot to talk about and work through, but the ride was a quiet one until they passed the newspaper office. Even then, Chris only spoke to comment on the lamplight seeping through the curtains. "Should we go in and turn it off? The last thing this town needs is another fire."

"No. It's probably Everett. He often stays at the office late. He must have gone back in to work on something after he dropped me off at the hotel."

Chris turned into her neighborhood. "Look, I know we need to talk and figure out this marriage business. We'll probably be more clearheaded once we've slept on it. I'll call on you in a day or so. We'll talk about it then."

She didn't tell him she'd already slept on it. Otherwise, she wouldn't have been nearly as calm. It was only fair that he have time to think about it, too.

Ever the gentleman despite their disagreement, Chris walked Adelaide to the door. Everett opened it for them, looking every bit as worried as he had when he'd dropped Adelaide off. "How did it go?"

"It was..." Adelaide began, then paused. "Wait. I thought you were at the *Herald* office."

"Why?"

"When we drove by, there was a lamp on inside,"

Chris said. "I can turn it off for you when I return my buggy to the livery. You've got to be careful about that, though. The town's been wary of fires since that last one."

"I haven't been in there this evening, and I certainly wouldn't have left a lamp on around all the paper that recently arrived. You saw it just now?" At their nods, he stepped inside and grabbed his boots. "Someone is in there who shouldn't be. Chris, can you take the buggy to notify the sheriff or the deputy? I'll meet y'all at the *Herald*."

"Wait!" Adelaide said in time to keep both men from rushing in different directions. "What do I do?"

In tandem, they both said. "Stay here."

Everett added, "Lock the door. Keep your gun handy."

Chris gave him a disbelieving look. "You gave her a gun?"

"I know how to shoot it," she said while Everett grabbed the rifle from over the interior threshold. "I should come with y'all."

Everett shook his head. "We don't have time to waste arguing. Do as I say."

She followed them down the path. "What if it's a plot to lure y'all away from the house so that they can snatch me again?"

The men exchanged a look. Chris frowned. "You know she's only saying that to come along."

"Yes, but she's right that it's a possibility. Take her with you. I'll get Rose."

Adelaide rushed ahead of Chris so that she was waiting in the buggy when he hopped in and set it in motion. He shook his head at her. "Adelaide, you know this isn't one of your stories, don't you?"

"I know. I could be in real danger. That's why I have a real gun." She pulled it from her boot to show him.

"That's been there the whole time? You could have shot off your foot."

"It isn't loaded...yet." She emptied the bullets from her pockets and loaded the derringer while Chris muttered beneath his breath. She caught the words "trigger happy" but ignored the rest. By the time they convened outside the newspaper office with the sheriff, the interior appeared to be totally dark. Sean went inside to check it out first. The lamp flickered to life again. Sean appeared at the door a little while later to wave them in. "I'm afraid whoever did this is long gone."

"What did they do?" Everett asked.

The second they stepped inside they saw the answer. The place had been trashed. The furniture had been turned over. Much of the upholstery had been slashed. Some of the stuffing had been taken out and scattered across the floor, seemingly along with every piece of paper and book in the office. Through the dark relief of shadows, Adelaide saw a dripping red line on the back wall. She hesitantly stepped closer to it. "What is that?"

Sean moved the pale lamplight closer to illuminate the line, which became part of a letter, then a word. Finally, it revealed the full message that dripped down the wall in rivulets of red. Rose whispered, "'Leave or she dies.'"

Adelaide shuddered. *"She?"*

"Adelaide," Everett said gravely. "The threats specifically target you."

She swallowed down the bitter taste of fear. "Right. Of course they do. That's only a little terrifying. We—"

Chris's hand gave her arm a comforting stroke. She turned to bury her face in his chest. His arms slid around her. "We aren't going to let anyone harm you. Everett, our wives don't need to see this. Let's take them home. We can decide what to do there."

The ease with which Chris had slipped into the role of husband was unsettling. Still, it somehow gave her the strength to push away from his chest and face the wall once more. She stole one last glance at it before Sean set the lantern on a far table, casting the wall back into shadows.

Everett agreed with Chris's assessment and led the procession out of the building. They all gathered at the Holdens' house minutes later. Adelaide took the opportunity to slip upstairs to her room. She leaned back against the door, closed her eyes and tried to calm her racing heart. How was it possible that this was so much scarier than being chloroformed and blindfolded in that closed carriage? Perhaps because this time she was fully aware, fully awake. Besides, this was Peppin— she was supposed to be safe here.

She gave her head a quick shake and straightened her shoulders. She hadn't given herself over to fear the first time. She wouldn't do it now. She'd change out of her evening gown into something more practical. After that, she'd go downstairs to contribute to the discussion.

She turned to do just that, but froze at the sight of her bed. The quilt had been pulled back to reveal sheets and pillows drenched in what appeared to be blood. It pooled from the knife that had been plunged into her mattress. Her gasp turned into a scream as she stumbled backward to scramble from the room. The sheriff reached her first. He assessed her with a glance. "Is there an intruder in the house?"

"I don't know."

He stepped past her into the bedroom with his gun at the ready.

Chris caught her arms, looking her over for injuries. "Are you hurt?"

"No. Just scared."

Everett placed a hand on her back. "What happened?"

Sean appeared at the door. "The intruder must have doubled back here while we were inspecting the newspaper office. This room is clear. I'm going to check the rest of the house. Stay in this area until I'm done."

Chris released her and stepped inside her room with Everett on his heels. Adelaide swayed a little without their support until Rose put an arm around her waist. "Take a deep breath, Adelaide."

After obeying her mother, she rubbed her hand against her temple. "I'm sorry. I shouldn't have screamed like that."

Everett stepped into the hallway. "Yes, you should have. Rose…" Everett tipped his head toward the room to tell her to take a look. Despite his protests, Adelaide entered the room, as well. Chris turned from studying the scene and she walked into his arms as naturally as he opened them to her. It was only then that she realized she'd reentered the room expressly for this purpose. Keeping hold of her hands, he stepped back to meet her gaze with determination filling his. "You aren't safe here. I'm taking you home with me."

She pulled away from him and crossed the room to peer out the window into the darkness. She couldn't do it. She couldn't go with him. She knew that if she did, she wouldn't be returning to her family's house. In her fear and vulnerability, she'd let him convince her that her place was with him as his wife in the apartment he'd prepared for her. Eventually, she'd let him into her heart completely. Her love for him would consume her. Then, one day, he'd betray her just as her father had with his women and the way her mother had by concealing the truth.

Sean's reflection strode across the window's glass as he stepped into the room. "I've been through the entire house and the yard. Nothing else seems disturbed, but I'd like y'all to make sure of that by walking through yourselves. I can't find a point of entry. Does anyone remember leaving a door unlocked?"

"I locked the front door on my way out," Rose said. "Everything else should have been locked, as well."

"Then the intruder must have had a key."

Adelaide sank down to sit on the window bench as Chris, her parents and the sheriff discussed how that might be possible. She couldn't quite get herself to focus on the conversation until it turned to what they were going to do about the situation. It was then that Adelaide realized Chris had taken her silence for acquiescence to returning to his apartment with him. Rose must have realized the same thing because she sent Adelaide an alarmed look before saying, "Hold on, Chris. I don't believe Adelaide's agreed to that plan yet."

Catching his inquiring gaze, Adelaide lifted her chin. "I haven't. I know your apartment is probably the safest place for me, but I still don't think it's a good idea. It wouldn't look right. No one in town knows we're married besides the sheriff, whom I reckon is pretty confused by all of this."

They all glanced at Sean, who held up his hands to say he wanted no part of this discussion, before she continued. "Not even your family knows."

"So we'll tell the town and my family in the morning."

"I agree with Adelaide." Rose came to stand beside her. "It would be better to have the societal credibility of a public wedding—one your families can actually attend."

Chris rubbed his forehead. "Fine. Adelaide can stay with my family tonight. We'll have the wedding tomorrow."

Rose shook her head. "We can't possibly pull a wedding together by tomorrow. We need at least a week."

Everett placed a hand on Chris's shoulder and answered for him. "Rose, Adelaide's safety is far more important than the trappings of a fancy wedding. They're already married. You can't change that by delaying another wedding. Besides, I have a feeling that the Johansens can pull together a wedding faster than you'd think."

Rose turned to Adelaide as though seeking direction. Realizing that the men both had solid arguments, Adelaide glanced past them to the ruined bed. Perhaps she was getting a little ahead of herself in worrying about her marriage to Chris. The first, most important step toward figuring out her future was living to see it. There was nothing left to do but give in.

Chris had no illusions that this wedding was for anything but show. The clandestine ceremony he and Adelaide had shared five years ago would always be the one he considered their real wedding. Yet Chris couldn't deny that this was special in its own way. Not when seeing Adelaide walk down the makeshift aisle on Everett's arm in his parents' parlor made the rest of the world fade away.

A wreath of orange blossoms adorned her hair. The cream dress she wore had an understated elegance befitting the occasion. Only when Adelaide drew closer was Chris reminded that this was not a love match on her part. The look in her eyes was one of resignation. Her smile, though beautiful, was subdued. Nevertheless, she faced Pastor Brightly with a resolute lift of her chin as Chris received her hand from Everett.

Pastor Brightly soon pronounced them husband and wife and entreated Chris to kiss the bride. Chris glanced down at Adelaide's mouth, wondering if he wouldn't do better to simply aim for her cheek, instead. She must have been impatient to get it all over with, for she rose on her tiptoes and stepped closer to press her lips against his. Ignoring the cautionary voice in his head, he caught her waist and deepened the kiss. An ember of hope flared to life when she responded.

Catcalls and whoops filled the air. To Chris's surprise, they only intensified once the kiss ended. Chris glanced at his friends and family in confusion even as he grinned at their exuberance. He let out a yell of his own as a couple of his burly friends swept him off his feet and carried him around the room before depositing him in a chair across the room from Adelaide. Quinn sank to his knees beside the chair, strumming his banjo incessantly and intently. Rhett appeared on Chris's other side, swaying back and forth while warbling on his harmonica. Meanwhile, Lawson came up behind him to pat his shoulder and yell what Chris could only assume were congratulations.

Sean offered Chris a hand, then urged him out of the chair with a tug. The sheriff had to lean close to be heard. "I told everyone that there would be no shivaree later due to safety concerns. I'm guessing this is their response. Do you want me to shut this down?"

Chris laughed. "No. Let them have their fun. I've played a hand in a few shivarees myself, so it's only fair. They'll wear themselves out soon enough."

"Well, congratulations to you and the bride on *both* of your weddings. I'll keep you up-to-date on anything I find concerning that intruder, but y'all try to enjoy yourselves and don't let one person's cruelty ruin this for you."

Chris only had time to nod in appreciation before bracing for a bear hug from his three younger brothers as they congratulated him. Once they released him, he mussed eight-year-old Hans's hair before patting August on the back, then clasping Viktor on the shoulder. "I wanted to thank y'all for spreading the word about the wedding to my friends. I have no idea how y'all managed to rustle up a houseful of people in such a short time."

Viktor waved a finger between himself and August. "We've got to confess. We only personally invited about a third of these people. The rest of them showed up on their own."

Hans patted Chris's leg to get his attention. "Sophia told me Adelaide is my sister now, too. Is that true?"

"It sure is."

Hans let out a whoop, then pulled out his flute to join the cacophony with the older men.

Chris turned at the sound of his father calling his name. Olan placed his hands on Chris's shoulders and gave him an affectionate shake. "My son! Married! I thought I'd never see the day. Little did I know I already had. I'm proud of you for settling down and honoring your commitment to Adelaide. I know I gave y'all a hard time, but I want you to know I think you made a good choice in her."

Chris grinned but couldn't resist lifting a brow. "Even though she isn't Norwegian?"

"She's the woman you love. What more could I ask for in a daughter-in-law?"

"Thank you, Pa. Would you mind telling her that? I think it would mean a lot."

"*Ja*, of course I will." Olan gave Chris's shoulder one last pat before heading across the room toward Adelaide.

Chris turned to see Wes run into the parlor. The man stopped and glanced around. His face was clouded over with worry. "I ran here from work. Am I too late? Are they already married?"

"It's all right," Adelaide called. "You're still in time for the reception."

"And the shivaree apparently." Stepping forward,

Chris extended his hand to welcome the man. Wes's fist flashed toward him. Pain shot through Chris jaw. He stumbled backward over a chair and landed on the floor. Gasps rent the air. Stunned, Chris stared up at Wes who was being held back by Rhett.

"Chris!" Adelaide slid to her knees beside him. She gently touched his jaw, then settled her hand on his chest before turning to look up at Wes. Accusation filled her voice. "What is wrong with you?"

"He's a low-down cheating skunk. That's what's wrong with me."

Chris was close enough to hear Adelaide's breath catch. Her green eyes met his. In their depths, he saw a tumult of hurt and betrayal. He reached for her hand as it left his chest, but she shied from his touch. "Adelaide, it isn't true. I don't know what he's talking about."

"I'm talking about Britta," Wes spat out. "You've been carrying on with her since Rhett and Isabelle's housewarming party."

"That's a lie."

"I saw you walking her back to the boardinghouse after my shift late one night. Y'all were standing close and flirting. You held her hands."

Before he could say he'd only been trying to keep them off of him, Adelaide turned to him with tears filling her eyes. "Chris, please just tell the truth."

His aching jaw fell open. She truly didn't believe him. Or, didn't *want* to believe him. Everything Everett had said about her father flashed through his mind. How could she honestly believe that Chris would do to her what her father had done to Rose? Didn't she know him at all? Catching her arms, he helped her stand with him. "Adelaide, you have to believe me. I *am* telling the truth. I've never carried on with Britta or given her the slightest reason to believe I was interested in her."

"You weren't out walking with her late at night?"

He hated to disappoint the hope in her voice, but he knew he had to be honest. "She showed up at my apartment uninvited. I was taking her home. That's all there was to it."

She seemed to waver for an instant, but then her delicate jaw set with resolve. She stepped out of his grasp and shook her head. "I've been ignoring all of the signs, but I can't any longer."

"What signs?"

"Your relationship with Amy. All of those women you wooed and proposed to."

"Amy and I courted after you and I had broken up. I've told you that before. You've just chosen not to believe me. Two of the women I supposedly wooed are here—Ellie and Isabelle. Ask them whatever you want to know. As for Britta..." He scanned the crowd for her. She stood near the kitchen door as though half entranced by what was happening and half prepared to flee it. He walked over and caught her arm to lead her to the center of the room. "Britta, please. Adelaide and I are married. You won't gain anything by lying about this. Tell everyone I wasn't carrying on with you."

Britta's gaze rested briefly on Adelaide before meeting his. "The truth is you have broken my heart. You made me promises you have not kept. Through it all, I have loved you. I still do, but I cannot keep secret that you have wooed me all these weeks." She turned to Adelaide. "Chris and I have met often. Always at night. I tried to hide it as he wished, but I am not so good at sneaking. Wes has caught me several times."

"Last night was the final straw. I was going to confront you in private today, Chris, but then I heard about the wedding—"

"Wait. Last night?" Relief filled him. He turned to see that Adelaide had stilled. Her face remained inscrutable, but that didn't keep the triumph from his voice. "Last night I was with Adelaide, her family and the sheriff."

Wes frowned. "Until nine-thirty?"

"Let me think." He glanced around the room until he found Adelaide's parents. Everett was glaring at Wes. Rose seemed to be cautiously taking it all in. "We brought Adelaide here around ten, didn't we?"

The sheriff was quick to answer. "Yes, and you were still here when I left at eleven."

Everett's firm voice added, "You escorted Rose and I back home at midnight. You left our house a little after that."

"Britta dear," Rose said, pinning the girl with her suspicion-filled gaze. "If you weren't with Chris, what *were* you doing?"

Gabe crossed his arms and leaned back onto a nearby wall. "She wasn't at the saloon. What? I go there from time to time to sketch folks. I've seen her there hanging around with one of our old boarders in the evenings. They seemed pretty close."

Wes shot him a look. "You could have told me that."

"How was I to know what lies she was telling you? Anyway, you could have not jumped to conclusions and punched a man on his wedding day."

The sheriff held up a hand. "Everyone just hold on

for a second. Miss Solberg, would you please tell me where you were and what you were doing last night?"

Britta pulled free of Chris's grasp and rubbed her arm even though he hadn't been holding her tight enough to hurt her. "That is no one's business but mine."

"Miss Solberg, someone in this town sent letters to Mr. Holden that threatened his livelihood and his daughter. They followed that up by breaking into his place of business where they caused extensive damage through vandalism. They then entered the Holdens' home to deface Adelaide Johansen's bedroom. On top of all of that, they have made repeated, escalated threats against her life. I will find this person. When I do, they will face criminal charges for all they've done. Now, I could bring you into my office to question you about all of this. Or you could save yourself a lot of trouble by simply and truthfully answering my question now."

"Criminal charges?" Britta's face went pale. Her wide gray eyes were filled with panic. "Does that mean you will put me in jail? But you can't. I did not hurt anyone. They were just supposed to get scared and leave town. Then Chris would have married me."

Adelaide finally spoke again. "So you made all of it up? Everything about you and Chris…it was a lie?"

He wanted to yell that of course it was. However, he held his tongue, realizing those words would be most convincing coming from Britta. He could only pray she'd finally tell the truth. Lightning seemed to flash in the thunderclouds of Britta's gray eyes. For the first time since she'd arrived, she spoke to Adelaide. "What else could I do? This man…" She turned to Chris again and shook her head in disdain. "He is as cold as a fjord in the winter. No warmth. No love. No heart. He has the passion of a…a stone."

Chris glanced past Britta to meet Adelaide's contemplative gaze just before it lowered to his mouth. Was she remembering all of their kisses? He certainly was. The hint of a blush spilling across her cheeks said she was, too.

Britta's voiced droned on in the background as Chris waited. "I thought that I could change him, but he would never let me near enough to try."

There it was. Realization stole over Adelaide's features, clearing it of doubt and suspicion. Relief followed. Her gaze shot to his, filled with remorse so intense that everything and everyone else seemed to fade away.

It was only then—when he saw how guilty she felt over how completely she'd believed in his transgression—that he felt pain penetrate through the shock that had been shielding his heart. The sting of tears threatening his eyes forced him to lower his head. He swallowed hard. Refocusing on Britta's voice enabled him to wrangle his emotions into a more manageable state.

"He was my betrothed and you had no right to him, but I think you deserve him. You will discover how unfeeling he is soon enough, and then you will be miserable."

There was no "then" about it. They were both plenty miserable right now. There was only one way to keep them from staying that way. Chris was resolved to do it even though he knew without a shadow of a doubt that it would break his carefully protected heart.

Chapter Eighteen

Shame settled like a rock in Adelaide's stomach as she realized what she'd done. She'd been so afraid of being betrayed by Chris that she'd betrayed him in front of his family and closest friends. There was no other way to describe it. Her accusation against his character hung in the air, weighing on her shoulders in the wake of Britta's confessions.

Glancing around at the folks gathered together, she realized that most had satisfied or even triumphant looks on their faces. It seemed as if they'd known all along that Chris was innocent and had only been waiting for the truth to come to light. How was it that they had known and she hadn't?

She'd like to blame her history with her father and the more recent betrayal by her mother, but this went deeper than that. Wasn't that what Chris was always telling her? That she kept searching for reasons to push him away? Well, she'd been given one—a significant one—and she hadn't hesitated to latch on to it. An apology rose to her lips, but Wes beat her to it.

"Chris, I am *truly* sorry. Gabe's right. I shouldn't

have jumped to conclusions. I apologize especially for hitting you. I hope I didn't do too much damage."

Chris tested his jaw by working it back and forth. "It's fine. You didn't hit me hard. I was just stunned more than anything. I wouldn't have gone down if I hadn't stumbled over the chair. As for jumping to conclusions... Britta had been lying to you for weeks and you don't know me well enough to know better. I understand why you were concerned."

"Well, since I started all this, I guess it's only right I finish it." Wes swept a protesting Britta over his shoulder and headed for the door. "I'm making a citizen's arrest. C'mon, sheriff."

Sean grabbed his hat and rushed out after them calling, "Wes, put her down. That isn't how a citizen's arrest works."

Quinn strummed a chord on his banjo to gain everyone's attention. "Look, I don't know about y'all, but I thought this was a celebration."

Helen called out a song request while Lawson began to clear some room for a dance floor. Adelaide appreciated their friends' attempt to cover any lingering awkwardness in the aftermath of what had just happened. However, there was no covering up what she'd done. Nor could she take back the words she'd said. She took a step toward Chris, but he turned on his heel and disappeared into the kitchen. She hesitated for an instant, then followed him.

Seeing him standing in front of the ice box, chopping a piece of ice off the block, she dampened a cloth with cool water and handed it to him. He covered the ice with it, then pressed it against his jaw before meeting her gaze. She barely held back a wince as the hurt she saw there reverberated through her own heart. "I'm sorry, Chris. I'm sorry for believing her. I should have given you a chance to explain."

"I held Britta's hands to keep them off me. I called on Ellie once with a bouquet of flowers. She refused my offer of courtship and that was that. I was a little more successful with Isabelle. I managed to get her to dance with me once. I also drove her home from Quinn's house so that I could propose to her. I've already told you all there is to know about Maddie and Amy. Other than my relationship with you, that is the extent of my history with women. You may not believe any of that, but it's the truth. I've never lied to you about any of it."

"I know that, Chris. I think I always have. I just didn't want to believe it. I knew if I did, there would be no reason to…no way to…"

"Keep your distance?" He sighed and lowered his head. "Maybe it's time I let you."

Her heart sank in her chest. "Chris, no."

"Yes, but let's get one thing straight first." He set the ice aside. He lifted her chin to cradle her face in his hands. Tilting his head closer, he arrested her gaze. "I love you, Adelaide Johansen. I would never stray from you. You are *everything* I have ever wanted. No one else in the world holds a candle to you. If I thought that there was some way I could prove that to you, I would spend the rest of my life trying. But I can't convince you when you don't want to believe. And that has nothing to do with me. It's about you and… I don't know what. Maybe your father? Your mother? Whatever it is that's keeping us apart isn't something I can fix. I have to stop trying."

He released her, and took a step back. "You're safe now. Britta won't be causing any more trouble. There's no reason for you to move into my apartment. I won't agree to annul our marriage, but I will give you the life you wanted. Stay with your parents or move to your own place. Write to your heart's content. You won't have to marry. As your husband, I'll support you if you have any financial needs. I'm sure there's more to figure out, but we can do that later. Right now, I'm… I'm going to leave."

Suddenly she felt as though she was back at that train station watching her father walk away. She'd never told anyone about how she'd all but demanded that he leave and stay gone. She'd never said a word about how much she'd wished he'd turned around at the last minute, agreed to come home and promised to make them a family again. Only her mother knew that when he'd finally returned to make his peace and, in those few final moments, begged for forgiveness, Adelaide had denied him hers.

She hadn't allowed herself to love anyone fully since that day. Now it was happening all over again. Only this time, she was the one who'd done the betraying. She was the one in need of forgiveness. And she was the one who wouldn't receive it. That became clear the moment the back door closed behind Chris. Adelaide had never felt more alone than she did in that moment.

This was what she'd wanted, wasn't it? To be safe. To not have to open herself up to love and all of its uncertainties. It wasn't at all what she'd imagined it would be.

She had a choice. She could continue to live insulated, afraid, detached and uncommitted. Or she could let in love, in spite of her fears.

That's when she felt it. A stirring in her soul, a warmth with no explanation—God's love. She'd invited it inside. Now it wanted out of the little box she'd placed it in. It wanted to spread out, to consume her fears, to make room for other kinds of love. Tears filling her eyes, she yielded just a little. It swelled in her chest and dropped her to her knees right there in the middle of the Johansen's kitchen where someone could walk in on her at any second. She didn't care.

She closed her eyes and prayed. *God, I'm so sorry for resisting Your love and the love of all those You've placed in my life. It wasn't fair to them. Nor was it fair to me. Open my heart again. Let me love like You do. Take away my fears and help me to be brave— brave enough to run the race You set out for me with no holding back.*

The kitchen door swung open. Adelaide glanced up to meet her mother's gaze. Rose's eyes filled with tears. "Oh, sweetheart, I'm so sorry. This is all my fault. From the very beginning I insisted Chris was like Hiram. If I hadn't—"

"Ma, stop." Adelaide stood and took Rose's hand. "I should have known it wasn't true. I was so desperately afraid to love anyone again that I put up every wall I could construct. I need to tear them down. I need you to help me."

"What can I do?"

"Come with me."

Realization filled Rose's gray eyes. "To the graveyard?"

"No, to the railroad station."

Rose tilted her head. "We're not leaving town again, are we?"

Adelaide smiled. "No. I just need to do something there."

Rose didn't ask any more questions until they arrived at the alleyway near the station. Even then, she only sent an inquiring glance. Adelaide pulled in a deep breath. "This is where I lost Papa. Not when he died, but right here, where we had our last fight. I told him to leave and never come back. He did once and only once."

"I know. He wrote to me and told me."

"I wish… I wish that he had stayed." She pulled in a trembling breath. "I loved him so much."

"Adelaide, he loved you, too. He just wasn't the staying kind of man. He tried from time to time, but it never stuck. There was a restlessness inside of him that couldn't be tamed. He kept searching for something he couldn't find. In the end, he realized that was because he'd been running from it all his life."

She shook her head in confusion. "What was he running from?"

"God."

"God?" In her mind, she saw a younger version of herself hanging on to the side of the wagon as Hiram sped away from the resounding voice of a tent preacher. "You mean he became a Christian? Why didn't you tell me?"

"You didn't want to talk about him after he died. Neither did I. Before that, I wasn't ready to believe he'd changed until he returned." She smiled. "He credited you for setting him back on the right path. He said what you did that day at the station awakened his conscience. The next time he heard a minister preaching about forgiveness, he didn't run. He listened and started trying to turn his life around. He was already on his way back here when he got sick. That's why he was so intent on asking forgiveness."

"I should have forgiven him. It's just that after all he'd done, I couldn't. I never understood how you managed it, either."

"I didn't." Rose gave a helpless shrug at Adelaide's confused look. "I said the words he wanted to hear. I didn't mean them."

"Well, maybe it's time we both said them and meant them. What do you say?"

Rose was thoughtful for a long, quiet moment, then nodded. "If you don't mind, I'll take a little walk and do it in private."

Adelaide understood the desire for privacy. She wanted some, too. She waited until Rose had claimed a bench beside the station to set about the task that needed to be done. "All right, Papa. I know you can't hear me, but I need to say this out loud and maybe God will pass along the message. I forgive you. I know you weren't perfect, but neither am I. Lord, I'm sorry for holding on to that for so long."

Something made her glance over to where her mother sat. Knowing what she had to do next, she gave an internal groan. Why was this harder to do? Perhaps because the cut was so fresh. She waited until Rose glanced up before walking over to meet her by the bench. "Ma, I want you to know. I forgive you, too."

Tears spilled onto Rose's cheeks. "I was just about to tell again you how sorry I am."

"Well, you don't need to." Adelaide paused then,

remembering how she'd prayed about having more love toward others. Finally, she said, "But I would like a hug."

Rose didn't hesitate to give her one. "We should do this more often."

"I think so, too." Adelaide sat on the bench and patted the seat next to her. "There's something I've wanted to ask you for a long time, but haven't had the gumption."

"Uh-oh."

Ignoring the cautious look on Rose's face, Adelaide asked, "How is it that you and Everett ended up with such a healthy marriage after what happened with Pa?"

Rose smiled. "It's Everett. Since the day we met, he has never stopped fighting for me. What could I do in return but the same? Now, turnabout is fair play. What happened with you and Chris?" Rose listened as Adelaide explained the arrangement Chris had suggested, then asked, "And how do you feel about that?"

"Miserable. I love him. I want to live with him and be his wife."

"Let me show you something, then." Rose pulled a piece of paper from the pocket of her dress. "I'm not supposed to have this. I found it in Chris's room while we were staying at his apartment. Have you ever heard of the Bachelor List?"

"I've heard folks mention it in passing. Why? Is that it?"

"It certainly is. Town lore says the couples matched on this list belong together." Rose handed her the list. "Take a look at who Chris's match is."

Adelaide ran her finger down the paper until she

reached his name. "He's matched with me. But why? I wasn't even in town when Ellie created it."

"I asked Ellie about it. She said she spent several weeks trying to figure out who Chris's match was. Then she realized the reason she couldn't figure it out was because his match didn't live in town—she lived in Houston. As for town lore… Well, I think you already know you belong together. You just need to convince Chris of that."

Adelaide shook her head. "That will not be as easy as you make it sound."

"No, but will it be worth it? Is your husband worth fighting for?"

"Absolutely."

Rose grinned. "Then we have work to do."

After all of his worrying about Adelaide breaking his heart, he'd done it to himself by walking away from her and the promise of a life together. Yet Chris knew it was far better for it to have happened once, at his own hand in his own time, than repeatedly at her instigation for the rest of his life. He'd done himself a favor. He knew that. It just didn't feel that way.

It had been unexpectedly hard to untangle his life from Adelaide's in the week since their wedding. It hadn't helped that she'd convinced him to let her move into the apartment above the mercantile. He'd moved out the same day and had started looking for a new place. That search would probably go a lot faster if Chris could find any motivation to look. For now, he was staying in his old room at his parents' house.

Sophia hadn't been willing to give up having a sister, so Adelaide came over for dinner more often than not. She said there wasn't much use in going through all of the trouble to cook for one. When she did, she'd bring down the leftovers into the mercantile for him and whoever else might be working at the time.

He also ran into her at the newspaper office relatively often. He'd thought about quitting, but it wouldn't have been right to renege on his promise to Everett, especially since he'd been in the middle of working on an important story. Besides, living in the same town with her meant they would have to learn to coexist. She didn't seem to be having a problem with it, which he found downright maddening since it was pure torture for him.

Hearing her voice in the kitchen with Sophia, he slipped out the front door and hurried to work. Olan lifted an eyebrow when Chris joined him behind the front counter. "You're early again. Can I assume that means Adelaide is at our house?"

"I see her so often we might as well be married."

"You *are* married."

He sent his amused father an unappreciative look. "You know what I mean."

"She left something for you on the desk in the store office."

Chris sighed. "Of course she did."

Olan shook his head. "How long are you going to be angry at her, son?"

"About as long as it takes to get her out of my heart and off of my mind."

"Man doesn't live that long." In an obvious reference to his heart flutters, Olan patted his chest. "Take it from me. You can't just let any old thing steep in your heart. Anger and resentment are nothing to hold on to, especially when it comes to your wife."

Chris couldn't agree with that. Not when he knew his wife was far more dangerous to his heart than a little bit of anger and frustration. "I know what I'm doing, Pa."

"That's debatable." Olan sent a glance heavenward and walked off muttering in Norwegian about stubborn children and young love.

Chris heaved a heavy sigh, then gave in to the temptation to peek inside his office at what Adelaide had left for him. It was a manuscript. Was it the latest Joe Flanagan novel? The one she'd been working on? No. Confusingly enough, the title page listed Adelaide Harper as the author. What was that supposed to mean? Had she discarded her pseudonym? If so, why not use her married name?

The dedication page revealed the answer. They hadn't been married when she'd written this. Well, at least, they hadn't known they were married. She'd written it for *Chris Johansen—my champion, best friend and beloved fiancé.* He reluctantly pulled his gaze from the first few intriguing lines of prose on the next page to glance at the clock. He'd have to wait to read it until after work.

His anticipation grew until he was finally able to lock up the store and head back to the office where he'd left the story.

He read until the light waned, then he lit a lamp and read some more. Once he finished it, he leaned back in his chair a little too hard, which caused it to wobble. He grasped for the desk to steady himself and sent a few books tumbling to the floor in the process. He was kneeling to pick them up when the door swung open. Adelaide eased into view with her gun drawn. He froze so as not to startle her and kept his voice calm. "Adelaide, it's Chris. Put the gun down."

"Oh." She sagged against the door frame in relief and laid her free hand over her heart. "Chris, I thought you'd left hours ago, then I heard a noise down here…" She shook her head. Placing the gun on the desk, she sat beside it and wrapped her arms around her waist. "Living alone is scarier than I thought it would be. Every little noise sets me on edge."

He placed the books on the desk near the gun. "You could always move back in with your parents."

Silence greeted his remark. He made the mistake of looking at her. Her pale green eyes held a world of longing. The shadows beneath them revealed that this week had not been as easy on her as she had managed to make it seem. Something inside him softened. It was all he could do not to reach out to trace the lamp-light's glow across her cheek and down to her chin.

He forced himself to look away and caught sight of her gun. Grateful for the reminder of their topic of conversation, he said, "You shouldn't have come down here if you thought there was an intruder. If you find yourself in that situation again, stay in the apartment with the doors locked and your gun loaded. Or take your gun and get out of here entirely. Come find me."

"I will."

Stepping behind the desk, he collected his hat and keys from one of the drawers. "I should go."

She slid off the desk. Instead of heading for the door, she came around to stand on the side of the desk, effectively blocking his escape. She glanced down at the manuscript, then up at him. "I see you found my present for you. Is that why you're here so late? Were you reading the manuscript?"

"I finished it."

"You did?" She searched his gaze, seemingly unaware of the vulnerability in hers. "What did you think of it? It was the first book I ever wrote so I know it's a little rough around the edges."

He found himself stepping closer. "No, it wasn't. I thought it was excellent. I could see the beginning of several themes that carried over in your other works. There was so much adventure in it and..." He forced himself to stop rambling and allowed his perplexity to enter his voice. "You made me the hero. Why?"

She smiled and lifted one shoulder in a shrug. "There were many reasons. For one, I'd always intended to give it to you as a present. You'd talked so much about dime novels that I thought it would be fun for you to read about yourself living in one. Looking back, I think there was more to it than that." Her voice softened. "You were the first man to enter my life and be a hero to me. You have always treated me with the utmost respect and caring."

Fearing he'd weaken under the weight of her words and the pure appreciation on her face, he glanced away and tightened his jaw.

"Even now, when you can hardly stand to be in the same room with me, you're still looking out for my safety. I guess that I was without someone like you in my life for so long that when you came into it I didn't know what to do about it. I ran away and I pushed you away and I'm..."

She tentatively touched his arm and he glanced

down to find her eyes sparkling with unshed tears. "I'm *so* sorry for that. I would give anything to change the way I behaved, but I can't. I can only change the choices I make from here on out. That's what I'm trying to do. I've forgiven my father. I've decided I'm not going to let the bad things in my past decide my future. I'm moving on. I want to move on with you."

He shook his head. "Adelaide, I'm not going to do this anymore. I'm not going to let you pull me closer only to push me away again. We have a plan. Separate lives. Separate houses. You can make things easier for both of us by sticking to it."

"Chris, if you weren't angry with me right now, what would you do?"

Before he could even fully process the question his gaze dropped to her lips. It lingered there as a hint of a smile curved them.

"That's what I thought." She moved toward him.

He took a step back and sent her a warning look. "Adelaide."

Her finger landed on his chest. "You are the pot calling the kettle black, Chris Johansen. I'm not pushing you away. I'm doing everything I possibly can to pull you in. I'm living in your house, for crying out loud, and I know you still have a key. You can come home to me any time you want. Instead, you're using the anger you feel to shield you from your feelings for me. I know, because that's what I did with my doubts about you. Well, one day that anger is going to fade away just like my doubts did. You know what you're going to be left with? Love."

Everything within him stilled, waiting. "What do you mean? Are you—are you saying—?"

"I love you."

He felt the conviction in her words down to his soul. His heart longed to answer her words in kind but fear held him back. He'd said them once and somehow been able to walk away. He couldn't chance it twice.

"I will *always* love you." She splayed her left hand over his heart. "You see this ring? It means I'm yours." She picked up his left hand in her right and placed it on her cheek. "This one means you're mine. We belong together. God did not go to the trouble of reuniting us so that we could live separate lives. You know that. Now, please forgive me. And, when you're ready, come home. I'll be waiting."

Leaning forward, she rose on her tiptoes to give him a gentle, parting kiss before she left.

He stood there, too caught up in her to move. The memory of her words swept through his mind like a gentle wave lapping at his defenses, eroding them bit by bit. If he was being truthful, he had to admit she was right about his anger. It had been the quickest, most convenient barrier he could erect between them. Any time that fire began to burn out, he'd found some way to fan the flames. The process was utterly exhausting.

It was only a matter of time before the separate lives he'd insisted they lead drove him mad. The only reason he'd manage to last this long was because he saw her every day. And, what did he do every night? He went over every interaction, every glance and every word they'd shared that day, so much so that she filled his dreams when he finally went to sleep.

He sunk into the chair as his defenses began to crumble. Who was he fooling? He loved Adelaide with all of his heart. There was no him without her. There was only misery.

Then what was holding him back? Why hadn't he returned the words of love she already knew he felt? She couldn't break his heart more than he already had. In fact, she was probably the only one who could mend it.

Wait. No. That wasn't right.

God was the one who mended broken hearts. So where was God in any of this? Certainly not in Chris's anger or refusal to forgive.

That's when Chris realized he'd done it again. He'd slowly but surely booted God out of his life in favor of his own plans, understanding and desires. He'd been trying so hard to control his own destiny that he was right on his way to missing it completely. His destiny wasn't wrapped up in a mail-order bride or Adelaide or the mercantile or the newspaper. It was in his relationship with God and how he allowed that relationship to define his interactions, behavior and ultimately his purpose.

No wonder he was miserable. He'd been neglecting his Heavenly Love even worse than his earthly one. All because he was too afraid to surrender his will to the One who loved him and wanted the best for him. Well, no more.

Chris sank to his knees beside the desk. The fear was still there, but Chris had learned that the only thing scarier than surrendering to God was living a life under his own control, so he didn't let it stop him. He bowed his head. "Lord, I surrender my life to You. I surrender my need to control it. I choose to trust You with it instead. I choose to seek Your will and yield to it. Right now, I give you all of my anger and all of my fears. I place my thoughts, my actions and my relationship under Your authority. God, I pray not my will but Yours be done in my life from this day forward."

As he said "Amen," he felt a weight lift from his chest and shoulders. A new sense of freedom filled him and prompted his first genuine smile in at least a week. On its heels came certainty and purpose.

Seeing that Adelaide had left her gun behind, he locked it in his desk for safekeeping, then grabbed his keys. He went back to his parents' house, packed his bags and returned to the darkened mercantile. Light shone out of the second story windows promising that Adelaide was still awake. He climbed the stairs to the apartment landing and pulled out his key. There would be no going back after this. If he unlocked this door, he would be declaring himself completely committed to his marriage and totally surrendered to God.

He slid the key inside the lock, making plenty of noise to alert Adelaide to his presence. He gave it a quick twist to unlock it. Pushing the door open, he stepped inside. Adelaide stood frozen by the stove in the kitchen where she seemed to have been starting a late supper. Her face shone with hope. He leaned back on the door to close it behind him.

"I'm going to spend the rest of my life loving you, Adelaide Johansen," he announced. "I promise to stay with you, be true to you and give you my whole heart each and every day. I will not for one more moment take for granted the love or trust you have placed in me. This is my vow to you. Nothing in this world can stop me from keeping it."

With a tremulous smile on her lips, Adelaide

crossed the room to take the suitcase from his hand and set it aside. She wrapped her arms around his shoulders. Then, cradling his head with one hand, she kissed his cheek. Then his lips. Her gaze traced his face reverently. "You were right at our wedding. No one knows you better than me. I know how hard this week must have been for you. My arms are open to you, Chris, now and forever. Your heart is safe with me."

"I know, sweetheart. Even if it wasn't, I'd still want you to have it. You were right earlier, too. It belongs to you."

A tear rolled down her cheek. She brushed it away, then caught his hand and gave it a little tug. "It's been a hard week. Come and rest. I'll make you supper, then you can unpack…"

She chattered on about all of the things they could do together while he followed her to the kitchen. He leaned against the counter not saying much. It was enough to be with her as husband and wife in the home he'd made for her. He could see the future stretching out before him—them reading books together by the fire on chilly winter nights, spending lazy Sunday afternoons with their families, having long talks about the Lord in bluebonnet fields. The view from here was pretty perfect, all right.

Then suddenly it wasn't.

Reaching around Adelaide, he turned the burner off on the stove. She spun to offer a confused protest, which he cut off with a sound kiss. When he pulled back, her lashes slowly lifted to reveal green eyes that started to sparkle. She caught the collar of his shirt and guided him down for another one. He could hardly do it properly since he was too busy grinning.

Yeah. This was much better. What a way to start the future.

* * * * *

Dear Reader,

I am blessed to have the most amazing readers a writer could ever ask for. Over the course of my writing career I have received so many inspiring messages from you. I can't tell you how valuable they are to me. God has used them to minister to me in many different ways. Sometimes it's to encourage me when I feel as if my writing is lacking. Other times it's to make me smile when I'm having a bad day. Most often it's to remind me of why I do what I do.

It isn't to see my name of the cover of a book, though I have to admit that is pretty awesome. It's to spread God's love and truth. I pray He uses this story to break down the barriers we so often and sometimes unknowingly erect around our hearts to keep out people and His presence. I pray He heals any broken hearts that might be reading this. Finally, I pray that He gives us all the strength to forgive and keep on forgiving others and ourselves.

I hope you enjoyed this visit to Peppin. If you'd like to share your thoughts about the story, you can email me directly at author@noellemarchand.com. You also can check out my website at NoelleMarchand.com for updates and a list of my backlist books. Or connect with me on Facebook, Goodreads, Twitter or Pinterest. I'd love to hear from you!

May God bless and keep you,

Noelle Marchand

THE COWBOY'S READY-MADE FAMILY
Montana Cowboys
by Linda Ford

Susanne Collins has her hands full raising her brother's four orphaned children and running the farm. When cowboy Tanner Harding offers his help in exchange for use of her corrals, will he prove to be the strong, solid man she's been hoping for?

PONY EXPRESS COURTSHIP
Saddles and Spurs
by Rhonda Gibson

When Seth Armstrong arrived at recently widowed Rebecca Young's farm to teach her seven adopted sons how to become pony express riders, neither expected they'd soon wish for more than a business arrangement.

THE MARRIAGE BARGAIN
by Angel Moore

Town blacksmith Edward Stone needs a mother figure for his orphaned niece, so when hat shop owner Lily Warren's reputation is compromised, he proposes the perfect solution to both of their problems—a marriage of convenience.

A HOME OF HER OWN
by Keli Gwyn

Falsely accused of arson, Becky Martin flees to the West and takes a job caring for James O'Brien's ailing mother. With her past hanging over her head, can she open her heart and learn to love this intriguing man?

LIHCNM0216

REQUEST YOUR FREE BOOKS!

2 FREE INSPIRATIONAL NOVELS
PLUS 2 *FREE* MYSTERY GIFTS

Love Inspired® HISTORICAL

SPECIAL EXCERPT FROM

Love Inspired HISTORICAL

Susanne Collins has her hands full raising her brother's four orphaned children and running the farm. When cowboy Tanner Harding offers his help in exchange for use of her corrals, will he prove to be the strong, solid man she's been hoping for?

Read on for a sneak peek of
THE COWBOY'S READY-MADE FAMILY
by **Linda Ford,**
available March 2016 from Love Inspired Historical.

Tanner rode past the farm, then stopped to look again at the corrals behind him. They were sturdy enough to hold wild horses…and he desperately needed such a corral.

He shifted his gaze past the corrals to the overgrown garden and beyond to the field, where a crop had been harvested last fall and stood waiting to be reseeded. He thought of the disorderly tack room. His gaze rested on the idle plow.

This family needed help. He needed corrals. Was it really that simple?

Only one way to find out. He rode back to the farm and dismounted to face a startled Miss Susanne. "Ma'am, I know you don't want to accept help…"

Her lips pursed.

"But you have something I need so maybe we can help each other."

Her eyes narrowed. She crossed her arms across her chest. "I don't see how."

He half smiled at the challenging tone of her voice. "Let me explain. I have wild horses to train and no place to train them. But you have a set of corrals that are ideal."

"I fail to see how that would help me."

"Let me suggest a deal. If you let me bring my horses here to work with them, in return I will plow your field and plant your crop."

"I have no desire to have a bunch of wild horses here. Someone is likely to get hurt."

"You got another way of getting that crop in?" He gave her a second to contemplate that, then added softly, "How will you feed the livestock and provide for the children if you don't?"

She turned away so he couldn't see her face, but he didn't need to in order to understand that she fought a war between her stubborn pride and her necessity.

Her shoulders sagged and she bowed her head. Slowly she came about to face him. "I agree to your plan." Her eyes flashed a warning. "With a few conditions."

Pick up
THE COWBOY'S READY-MADE FAMILY
by Linda Ford,
available March 2016 wherever
Love Inspired® Historical books and ebooks are sold.

www.LoveInspired.com

LIHEXP0216

SPECIAL EXCERPT FROM

Love Inspired®

When a woman's old love returns to town,
will she be able to resist his charms?

Read on for a sneak preview of
THE RANCHER'S FIRST LOVE
The next book in the series
MARTIN'S CROSSING

"What are you doing here?" she asked as she stretched. When she straightened, he was leaning against the side of his truck, watching her.

"I would have gone running with you if you'd called," he said.

She lifted one shoulder. "I like to run alone."

That was what had changed about her in the years since she'd been sent away. She'd gotten used to being alone.

"Of course." He sat on the tailgate of his truck. "I was driving through town and I saw you running. I didn't like the idea of leaving you here alone."

"I'm a big girl. No one needs to protect me or rescue me."

The words slipped out and she wished she'd kept quiet. Not that he would understand what she meant. He wouldn't guess that she'd waited for him to rescue her from her aunt Mavis, believing he'd show up and take her away.

But he hadn't rescued her. There hadn't been a letter or a phone call. Not once in all of those years had she ever heard from him.

LIEXP0216

"Sam?" The quiet, husky voice broke into her thoughts.

She faced the man who had broken her fifteen-year-old heart.

"Remington, I don't want to do this. I don't want to talk about what happened. I don't want to figure out the past. I'm building a future for myself. I have a job I love. I have a home, my family and a life I'm reclaiming. Don't make this about what happened before, because I don't want to go back."

He held up his hands in surrender. "I know. I promise, I'm here to talk about the future. Sit down, please."

"I don't want to sit."

"Stubborn as always." He grinned as he said it.

"Not stubborn. I just don't want to sit down."

"I'm sorry they sent you away," he said quietly. In the distance a train whistle echoed in the night. His words were soft, shifting things inside her that she didn't want shifted. Like the walls she'd built up around her.

"Me, too." She rubbed her hands down her arms. "I wasn't prepared to see you today."

She opened her mouth to tell him more but she couldn't. Not yet. Not tonight.

Don't miss
THE RANCHER'S FIRST LOVE by Brenda Minton
available March 2016 wherever
Love Inspired® books and ebooks are sold.

www.LoveInspired.com